Transferred Malice
Steven Wright

Cover design and formatting by John Amy
www.ebookdesigner.co.uk

Contents

Chapter One	5
Chapter Two	13
Chapter Three	21
Chapter Four	29
Chapter Five	38
Chapter Six	46
Chapter Seven	52
Chapter Eight	60
Chapter Nine	67
Chapter Ten	76
Chapter Eleven	84
Chapter Twelve	93
Chapter Thirteen	100
Chapter Fourteen	108
Chapter Fifteen	113
Chapter Sixteen	124
Chapter Seventeen	132
Chapter Eighteen	138
Chapter Nineteen	147
Chapter Twenty	158
Chapter Twenty-One	167
Chapter Twenty-Two	171
Chapter Twenty-Three	176
Chapter Twenty-Four	180
Chapter Twenty-Five	185
Chapter Twenty-Six	191
Chapter Twenty-Seven	198
Chapter Twenty-Eight	206
Chapter Twenty-Nine	212
Chapter Thirty	220
Chapter Thirty-One	225
Chapter Thirty-Two	232
Chapter Thirty-Three	238
Chapter Thirty-Four	250
Chapter Thirty-Five	257
Chapter Thirty-Six	263

Chapter One

There was a horrible squealing, like a small animal in terror, as the tyres of the big black car gripped the road.

The detective slammed his brake pedal to the floor and wrenched the steering wheel sideways to avoid the screeching vehicle in front of him. His car lurched to the left and skidded to a stop, its bonnet buried in the hedge running alongside the quiet country lane.

He clung to the wheel and stared in disbelief at the black car which had stopped ten yards ahead, its engine idling in a strangely menacing manner.

"What the hell was he playing at?" he muttered.

Nothing moved. The seconds ticked by. Then the driver's door of the black car flew open. A man emerged and turned to face the detective.

He immediately saw two things, and they sent a chill through his whole body.

The man's face was covered by a black balaclava with slits for eyeholes. And in his right hand he was holding a weapon. A lethal weapon. The detective did not need his twenty-odd years as a policeman to tell him it was a sawn-off shotgun.

Slowly and deliberately, the man raised the gun and pointed it at the detective, frozen in fear behind the wheel. He motioned with his free hand, indicating he was to get out of the car.

The detective remained where he was. His heart was thumping in sheer terror. He was unable to move.

His body was numb, but gradually the fog that shrouded

his brain started to lift. He began to think – maybe he could restart the car and reverse away from the danger?

Freeing his body from its paralysis, he frantically turned the key in the ignition. Nothing. He tried again, yanking desperately at the key and pumping the accelerator furiously. Still nothing.

He raised his head and looked at the masked man. He was still pointing the gun at him. Then he took a pace forward and gesticulated angrily with his left hand. For the first time he spoke. One word.

"Out!"

The voice seemed vaguely familiar.

Fearing to alarm the gunman by any sudden movement, the detective reached for the handle and gently pushed open the driver's door. The gunman's eyes narrowed, but his weapon arm remained rock steady.

The detective slid out of his seat. Slowly, he raised himself to his full six-foot height and stepped away from the car. He kept his hands clear of his body, the palms outstretched – like a Wild West gunfighter preparing to draw. But he was unarmed, and he wanted the gunman to see that.

"Stop!" the gunman ordered. Again, the faint recognition.

The detective stood silently and waited. He gazed at the barrel of the shotgun, barely ten feet away and aimed at his chest. Without moving his head, he raised his eyes and met those behind the mask, narrow slits peering out from the eyeholes.

Suddenly he knew who they belonged to, and the whole terrifying episode made sense.

And he knew he was about to die. A certainty about the end of his own mortality, right here and now, hit him – as surely as the vicious pellets of the shotgun would at any moment. And he was afraid. Terribly and painfully afraid.

The gunman saw his fear, felt it, breathed it, like a lion with his doomed prey in front of him the moment before he pounces.

His eyes glinted and from within the mask came a laugh – long, deep and grating. And mirthless.

The gunman raised his left hand and, in a swift, deft movement, whipped the balaclava from his head, revealing his identity.

He laughed again. Gloating. Then he stopped and smiled. A cold smile. The smirk of an executioner.

He spoke for the last time, and now there was nothing vague about his voice.

"So, Haydn Daniel. Prepare to die."

The detective saw the gunman's hand grip the gun tighter, his finger on the trigger.

"No, no, NOOOH!"

****

Haydn Daniel sat up in bed and stared ahead wildly as the echoes of his screams bounced off the walls and faded to an uneasy silence. Panting for breath, he clutched the pillows, soaked in his sweat, and held on to them until he was sure they were real and the gunman was just another bad dream.

He laid back his head and gazed at the familiar white-washed, oak-beamed ceiling of his bedroom while his breathing slowly returned to normal.

Finally reassured, he threw back the bed covers and swung his muscular legs to the carpeted floor. He glanced at the bedside alarm clock and saw that it was half past six. Shafts of pale light were filtering into the room, another day was dawning.

Running his hand through his tousled, reddish fair hair, he

strode to the en suite bathroom and took a long and luxurious shower. He needed to wash himself clean of the horrible nightmare, one that he had kept having since quitting the police force and taking early retirement nine months ago. It was always the same and though he dreamed it less often now, it still terrified him.

Haydn stood in front of the bathroom mirror to shave. He gazed thoughtfully at his reflection. Looking back at him was a not unattractive man in his mid-forties with twinkling blue eyes, strong bony features and a full head of short wavy hair. He had laughter lines either side of his oval-shaped mouth, but his skin was good and he felt he was wearing well.

His face did not reflect the traumas he had suffered in recent years – his wife's affair and the breakup of his marriage; the death of his parents in a terrible accident; and the alarming threats of a vengeful gangster.

But he was a survivor and his life was now taking a different, upward path. The future looked brighter, except for that awful nightmare.

Dressing himself in jeans and a thick checked shirt, he pushed the memory of the bad dream aside and, pulling open the bedroom curtains to let in the faint light, he embraced the day.

The bells of the village church chimed out seven o'clock. A weak sun peeped over the low stone wall surrounding the small but neat garden behind his farmhouse cottage. Its tender rays reached tentatively out towards the skinny, frost-lined branches of the little group of apple trees guarding the wall, which in turn stretched encouragingly up to greet them. A thick, white coat of dew coated the lawn and glistened on the water of the little pond at the centre of it.

It was a typical late February morning, crisp and cold but inviting. Winter was fading and the sweet march of spring was gathering pace.

Haydn made his way to the traditional stone-floored kitchen and was met with excitement by Timmy, his three-year-old rescue greyhound. The jet black dog jumped up from his cosy cushion, next to the warming stove, and skittered Bambi-like across the floor, tail wagging furiously. He curled himself around the legs of his beloved owner and peered up expectantly at him.

"All right, Timmy! I'm ready now," said Haydn, affectionately patting the long, lean dog.

He grabbed Timmy's leather collar and chain lead from its hook on the back door and attached it to the eager hound. Then he took his thick Barbour coat from its peg, fastened it round himself, pulled on his boots and prepared to open the solid wooden stable door to the back garden.

He whistled softly to his black and white cats, Cedric and Cecil, curled up contentedly in their basket on the opposite side of the stove from Timmy's cushion. The brothers stretched and yawned.

"Come on, you guys. Time to go out."

The cats reluctantly got to their feet, ambled across the stone floor – Cedric in front as always – sidled round the door and disappeared off together.

Haydn took hold of Timmy's lead. The dog stood obediently as his master locked the stable door behind them. They marched together down the path to the green-painted, slatted garden gate and set out along the stony track to the little wood and the fields beyond.

As they reached the belt of trees, Haydn slipped off Timmy's lead and the hound bounded away, sniffing in the undergrowth and pattering along happily.

Haydn strolled after him, his hands thrust into the warmth of the deep Barbour pockets. He loved these early morning walks. He enjoyed the dog's company and was at ease with the natural surroundings. He felt safe. Nothing here was going to hurt him. Unlike his old life.

The walks gave him the chance to think, calmly and clearly and without the pressure that had clouded his mind for so many years. Now his thoughts were positive, and he had plans to go with them.

The last few months had seen a remarkable transformation in his life. He had turned his back on the police force after nearly thirty years in the job – and not a moment too soon. How it had changed.

He remembered when he started out as a fresh-faced, enthusiastic eighteen-year-old officer, determined to help those in need; the victims of crime, accidents and terrible tragedies. And he had done, many times over.

But policing was very different now.

Increasingly it was about numbers and not people. You had to balance the books and tick the correct boxes. Victims had to take their place, which was not why he had become a policeman.

He became disillusioned with the spending cuts and the lack of resources, which meant you couldn't serve the public as well as you wanted to, and with the justice system that somehow seemed more in favour of the criminal than the victim.

He had been a detective for the last twenty-three years of his career, solving crimes and putting people behind bars for the protection of the public.

And yet, more and more he had felt he was doing the job with one hand tied behind his back. Never enough time or manpower to do all the enquiries he would have liked; bouncing from one job to the next without being able to take a step back and think things through; and always the Crown

Prosecution Service lawyers telling him there wasn't "enough evidence for a realistic prospect of a conviction." It was all about success rates. Ticking the boxes. Never about taking on a tough case and going hell for leather to put the bastard away for as long as possible.

And when you took the villains to court, the law didn't back you up. You had to put up with the prosecution accepting guilty pleas to lesser charges to get a conviction; the sentencing guidelines from Parliament that tied the hands of judges; the third off the sentence for pleading guilty – even when the evidence gave the criminal no room to escape justice.

If you got the killers, gangsters and burglars banged up in prison, they would serve less than half their sentence and then be out on licence. What kind of licence? The licence to kill, beat and steal again.

Suddenly frustrated, he swung his boot violently at a wild mushroom, severing it from its stem and propelling it into a clutter of tangled branches, scattering a pair of wood pigeons.

He watched the birds flap to the top of the tall beech tree and nestle in the highest branches, and he felt tranquillity return to him.

What could humble Haydn Daniel do about it? Nothing. He couldn't then and he certainly couldn't now. He had been a small cog in a big machine. Now he wasn't a part of the machine at all. How glad he felt about that.

He called out to Timmy who came running up, tail going ten to the dozen.

Haydn patted the adoring dog, who he adored equally in return.

"Time for breakfast," he said.

As they crunched their way back through the leafy bed of the wood, Haydn's thoughts turned to another love of his life.

He had known Paddy for just four months, but he was head

over heels about him. Who would have thought a horse would have such an impact on him?

It was fair to say that Haydn was an animal lover. Always had been. Now his marriage was over and he was on his own he took pleasure and comfort from them even more. He had felt drawn to horses all his life. But he never thought he would ride one, let alone own one. Now he did both.

Haydn was stopped in his tracks by his own meandering reflections. He stood and shook his head in wonder.

Gazing ahead, he said, to no-one in particular: "Funny, what cards life deals you."

He felt a nudge to his leg. Timmy was looking up at him, eyes bright, tail inevitably wagging.

Haydn's laughter lines curled as a great smile spread across his face.

He affectionately pulled the dog's ears. "Yes, you were definitely an ace."

Chapter Two

"Right then, Weston. Make sure you've got everything. Today's the day."

Kane Weston glanced up from the single bed in his cell and cast a cocky smirk at the prison officer. "You're gonna miss me."

The warder fixed him with a steely stare. "Like a hole in the head," he growled back.

Weston's grin broadened, crinkling his thin features and making him look older than his thirty-six years. "It can be arranged … at a price!"

The convict laughed. "I do special offers for them on the wrong side of the law – like you."

"Yeah, yeah," the officer responded. "I'll be back in half an hour to take you to sign your release papers. Then you can piss off back to where you belong."

He slammed the iron cell door shut behind him, the clang echoing around the walls and merging with the laughter of the inmate.

Weston lay back on the hard bed and gazed up at the dingy grey ceiling. It had become a familiar sight during his five years of imprisonment. Like so many times before, into his mind came the clear features of the obsessive detective who had put him there, looking down at him – in the same arrogant way he had looked across the courtroom to the secure dock as Weston was given his ten-year jail sentence.

As the custody officers snapped the cuffs around his wrists, Weston had stared defiantly at the detective in the public gallery and shouted across the court: "I won't forget you, Daniel. Think of me when I get out. I'll make you pay for this, I promise you."

And he had not forgotten about Haydn Daniel. The memory of what he had done to him remained at the forefront of his mind as each day, each week, each month and each year of his long and tedious incarceration dragged by, helping him through it. Now, on the threshold of freedom, the image of the loathsome cop was still vivid.

Weston had coped well with prison. He was held in a tough category A Yorkshire jail, built out of granite to hold serious criminals – murderers, rapists and gangsters. But he was a tough category A prisoner and most inmates knew better than to try to mess with him. On the inside, he was able to pull the strings just as he had on the outside. He had his loyal lieutenants, eager to do what was asked of them to gain their own kudos and protection, and he enjoyed the little luxuries to which someone of his criminal importance was entitled, like the black market gifts of aftershave, cigars, and porn movies.

Then there was the coke. It was easy to get drugs in prison, almost as easy as it had been before he was jailed. Of course, his well-earned reputation as a drugs mastermind stood him in good stead behind the prison walls. No matter that he had finally been caught. The fact that he had helped to run such a lucrative national and international narcotics empire meant he merely had to click his fingers and a free delivery of cocaine would find its way to its secret place in the prison kitchen where he worked.

Weston knew the game well enough to keep his nose clean in other respects. He was a model prisoner, working hard in the kitchen, studying for NVQs in English, maths and computers and even attending drug rehabilitation courses. He mused at the irony of a convicted drug conspirator getting lessons in how to kick the habit.

But it was all designed to get him out at the first opportunity – five and a half years for good behaviour in his case. That day had now arrived.

He heard the heavy key turn in the lock. His cell door swung open. The same warder, Barker, stood framed in the doorway. He jerked his head towards the landing. "Come on."

Weston followed him out of the small and bare room he had called home. He did not look back. A second warder slipped into position behind him and the three of them clanged along the metal floors and steel steps of the grim, labyrinthine jail.

As they went, respectful voices could be heard from within cells, with relieved farewells. "Good luck Mr Weston," and "Look after yourself, Boss."

Weston ignored them and strode purposefully towards the exit. They stopped at the office, where the gangster signed the relevant paperwork and picked up his bulging sports bag of belongings.

A senior probation officer stepped forward and handed over a brown envelope containing Weston's licence details, which he would have to adhere to for the next five years. He stuffed it nonchalantly into a side pocket of the sports bag.

"Your first appointment with us is on Tuesday at Mallard House. Your probation officer will be David Parsons, details are in your probation pack."

The officer visibly flinched as the criminal fixed him with a malevolent glare. "Look forward to it," said Weston, suddenly grinning. But his eyes were cold.

The formalities were almost over. The Deputy Governor stepped forward and proffered his hand. "Keep up the good work, Kane. The rest of your life starts here."

Weston nodded. "Yeah, there's a lot I want to achieve."

He stepped through the huge metal entrance gates and

heard them slam to behind him. It was a cold day but fine. Fastening his overcoat, Kane Weston took his first deep breath of freedom and walked to a waiting car.

★★★★★★★★★★

Weston stretched out his legs in the back of the black Range Rover and idly observed pedestrians and vehicles as they passed by. The windows of the car were tinted, so the gangster could look out but he could not be seen.

The driver, a ferret-faced young man in his early twenties, concentrated on the road ahead. He was silent. He knew better than to chit chat. If Mr Weston wanted a conversation he would begin one.

But the criminal was in no mood to talk. He wanted to think. Think about how it felt to be free once more. About what had been happening while he was away. And about what his plans were now.

Weston took freedom in his stride, rather as he had his time in prison. His self-confidence and influence on others meant it mattered little where he was. He could always get what he wanted. He had been able to do so from a young age.

He had bunked off school at fifteen. He hadn't seen the point of going, so he didn't. Instead he would meet up with a gang of mates, a year or two older than him, and chill out in the local park drinking strong lager, smoking weed and chatting up the girls.

His dad, Tommy, wasn't around, serving yet another prison sentence for housebreaking, and his mum, Michelle, had enough on her hands with the four younger siblings to do anything about his non-attendance at school. But Kane always went home to lend a hand with his brother and three sisters, making sure they cleared up after tea and went to bed when their mother told them to. "I don't know what I'd do without you," Michelle would say.

By the time he was seventeen he was following in Tommy's footsteps, breaking into people's homes, stealing their valuables and flogging them off in the pub to help his mum put food on the table.

He teamed up with his old school pal, Billy Naughton. Kane would do the homework, checking out the most vulnerable properties, seeing when the householders and their neighbours went out, working out the best entry point and when to strike. Then he would send in Billy to do the breaking and entering while Kane kept a discreet watch. They would disappear into the shadows with their stolen goods and make their escape in Billy's battered old Ford Fiesta that they had parked on a quiet corner nearby.

Word got around among local villains on their estate about the teenage duo's burglary exploits.

One Sunday lunchtime, the pair were playing pool in the back room of the Black Swan when a muscular, clean-shaven man of about twenty-five walked in. He stood with his back to the bar, sipping a half of lager and watching the teenagers. The man was casually dressed in jeans and an open-necked shirt, but Kane recognised that he had a presence and authority about him.

Kane cleared up the last few balls to win the game and turned to speak to the stranger. But he was gone.

Kane shrugged. "Another pint, Billy?"

"Why not."

Kelly, the barmaid, plonked two pints of lager down on the counter and Kane fished for a fiver in his pocket.

"It's paid for," Kelly said. Kane raised his eyebrows inquiringly. "The guy who was stood at the bar," Kelly explained. "And he left you this." She handed over a plain white envelope folded in half.

He slipped it in his pocket. Something told him to open it in private. When he got home he went upstairs to his room, took out the envelope and tore the seal. Inside was a single sheet of lined paper. In black biro was written the name Raymond and a mobile phone number. Nothing more.

Kane did not ring the number for a week. Keep them waiting, he thought. That will get them wondering. When he did call, the phone was answered but nobody spoke. There was silence for several seconds. Then a smooth voice on the end of the line said simply: "Kane."

"Yes."

"So glad you called. I have a proposition for you. Meet me at the snooker club on East Street, tomorrow at 8pm."

There was a click as the call was ended. A wave of excitement washed over Kane. He did not know what this was, but he recognised it was an opportunity.

The large and gloomy club was quiet when he arrived, just a handful of snooker tables were in use. Wreaths of cigarette smoke circled them. The pungent smell of cannabis pierced the air, making Kane feel at ease.

The man from the pub was sitting at a small table in a dingy corner away from the bar. In front of him was a large glass of neat whisky. He signalled to Kane to sit opposite him. As he did so, the barman placed a second tumbler of whisky in front of him. He nodded his thanks to the man across the table, who was staring intently at him. Kane forced himself to return his gaze.

Their eyes locked for almost a minute. Then Raymond smiled thinly and spoke. "We've heard a lot about you, Kane. You are getting a reputation."

"Who is we?"

Raymond leaned forward, his hands clasped on the table.

"When you have earned our respect, then you can ask questions."

He sat back and smiled again. But this time there was warmth in it. "We have a job for you, if you want it."

Kane was about to ask what the job was but instead he said: "I want it."

Now Raymond grinned. "You're a quick learner. That's good.

"The job will make use of your ability to get into places where you shouldn't be. You will be part of a small but select team. It won't be easy, but the rewards will be worth it."

"I'm up for it," Kane replied, trying to keep the excitement out of his voice.

"Good. We are just finalising the details. I will call you when we are ready to have a final meet. I will tell you then what you will be paid."

And so it was that at eighteen, Kane Weston became a member of the Collins gang and played his part in a smash and grab raid on a bank ATM machine. He was only a foot soldier, but those feet were on the first rung of the ladder and he was determined to climb it.

Kane Weston smiled at the memory and reflected with pride on how far he had climbed since. Almost to the top.

The Range Rover pulled into the large car park of the Stanley Arms. The driver opened the nearside rear passenger door and Kane got out. "Wait in the car," he ordered.

He glanced towards the entrance of the big, stone-built pub, nestling in front of fields on the edge of a council estate, and saw his trusted lieutenant, Jim Lee, standing in the doorway. Lee saluted with mock gravity. Weston nodded at his deputy. He approved of his sense of humour, it went well with his deference and loyalty. Soon Kane would know everything about what had taken place in his personal and professional world while he had been locked up. He knew most of it already, but Lee would fill in any gaps.

Only then could he properly consider what path his life would follow next. There was one thing he knew for sure – Haydn Daniel would be on the same path.

Chapter Three

The impressive electronic gates of Wickham Court Equestrian Centre swung silently open. Haydn Daniel guided his Land Rover Freelander through them and glanced back in his mirror to see them close automatically behind him. He was still getting used to the state of the art facilities and, even more so, that he was the part-owner of them.

Haydn drove slowly along the entrance road as it made its way between neat and flat paddocks. The pips on the car radio told him it was eight o'clock but already he could see horses dotted around, grazing happily in the fields beneath the gentle early morning sun. Ahead of him, staff were leading out more. It was their first job of the day and they didn't hang about. Haydn had always been amazed at their efficiency and professionalism. Now he was used to it.

He waved at Jenny and Alison as they marched past, each leading two horses. They called out a cheery good morning.

The driveway curved round towards the stables, and Haydn turned into the car park, swinging into a space and switching off the engine.

He got out and gazed across at the outdoor arenas on the other side of the drive. There were four of them. They were all large and had wonderful, expensive surfaces. Haydn could see one of the livery customers in the nearest arena, a smart-looking lady on a big warm blood horse.

He watched for a few moments as they cantered elegantly round, and then opened the rear of the car. Timmy was perched expectantly in the back. Haydn clipped on his lead and the dog jumped out, shaking his lean body from side to side and then standing to wait while Haydn locked up.

He allowed the dog to have a pee on a patch of grass and then strode across to the office, opened the door and walked in.

"Morning Scott," he said to a good-looking young man, who was sitting behind a big oak desk and poring intently over a large diary.

The young man grunted in reply and continued to earnestly study the ledger.

"Problem?"

Scott looked up. His brow remained furrowed. "Nar. Frannie Dutton wants to switch her horse camp from May to June, but we've already got two other camps, two dressage competitions and a one-day event that month. I'll work it out."

His face brightened as he caught sight of Timmy.

"Ah! My favourite pooch!"

He called to the dog, who jumped up at him, tail wagging furiously, and planted a huge lick on his cheek. Scott laughed and grabbed the hound in a playful embrace.

Haydn smiled. It was a happy scene. He felt a great warmth towards the younger man. They were business partners, but they also had a close personal bond.

Scott Stevens was thirty-two years old and had been an international showjumper before he broke his leg in three places in a horrible fall. He had not been able to ride for six months and although he had fought his way back to fitness, he now only competed locally.

He had channelled all his energy into running Wickham Court, and giving riding lessons. That was how Haydn had got to know him.

"All well with the livery customers?" the older man asked.

"Fine," said Scott, grasping a piece of paper from the desk.

"Fiona Castleton asked for her mare to be kept in because she is going to a showjumping competition this afternoon. I've told Daisy. That's all."

"Good. I'll get cracking. I want to fix that broken top rail at Stroller Paddock and check the rest of the fencing today."

Haydn left the office and walked into the adjoining barn, where twenty horses were stabled, including his own. There were three stable blocks at the centre, which was home to sixty horses. They belonged to the livery customers, except for Haydn's horse, Paddy; Scott's two showjumpers, Lady Diva and Lord Percy; and a thoroughbred gelding called Des, who was owned by the yard's head girl Daisy Langridge.

The stable blocks had been converted from old barns and they were modern, light, airy and spotlessly clean. The stables were lined up in rows of ten, facing each other across large aisles. The beds of dust-free wood shavings were generous and each barn had its own feed room and hay store.

Haydn unbolted the door to Paddy's stable. It was empty, the horse having already been taken out to his field with his friends. Haydn had been quick to learn that routine was important to the happiness of any horse–and crucial to the smooth running of a busy livery yard.

Everyone knew the daily routine at Wickham. The horses were turned out at 7.30am. In the winter they were brought in at lunchtime. When spring arrived they were out all day. That time was rapidly approaching.

Once the horses were out, the staff would muck out the stables, fill the haynets and sweep the yard until it was pristine. It was hard work and they were glad of their extended lunch break and the chance to relax or to ride.

Haydn took off Timmy's lead and ushered him into Paddy's stable. The dog also knew the routine and soon nestled down in a cosy corner and rested his head on his paws. He looked with big soulful eyes at his master.

"See you in a little while."

Haydn headed to the workshop, behind the barn, and filled a felt bag with tools. He put it on the passenger seat of the Mule, an open-sided mini jeep ideal for scooting around the fields, placed a pile of wooden posts and rails in the back and set off for Stroller Paddock.

It made things easier to have names for the fields when allocating them to the horses. Scott had named them after famous showjumping horses. So there was also Boomerang Pasture and Milton Meadow.

Haydn revved the Mule and sped off, past the outdoor arenas, and up the immaculately fenced track running between the meadows, until he reached Stroller. He prided himself on the upkeep of Wickham. It was his responsibility to maintain the stables, the arenas, the fencing, the cross-country course – everything that the customers and their horses used – and he took that responsibility very seriously. He had noted a couple of days ago that a small section of rail in Stroller was broken and had put it at the top of his 'to do' list.

Parking up the Mule, he unloaded the wood and the bag of tools, then stopped to take in the view across the fields. Horses swished their tails contentedly and roamed around in their quest for the tastiest grass. In the distance he could see the barns and arenas.

The views, and the equestrian centre, were still a novelty to him, and a complete contrast to the urban life he had led before. But he had embraced the rural world, and its freedoms, with open arms.

For decades, as a policeman and a husband, he had lived in suburbia bringing up his family in a semi-detached house in north Leeds. It had been a comfortable home, but he had felt hemmed in by the rows of identical houses on Yew Tree Close, and the warren of similar streets surrounding it. Mostly, he had been too busy to worry about it. He worked round the clock. When he wasn't at work, he happily threw himself into his role of family man.

His job and his home meant everything. They represented a familiar and rather cosseted existence.

That stability had been shattered just under a year ago when he found out about his wife's affair. The foundations of his life came tumbling down and he was cast adrift on a rolling sea of emotional turmoil.

He moved out of the family home and spent three months in a bachelor pad on the city's waterfront. It was clean and smart, but without class or character.

Six months ago he bought his two hundred year-old, two-bedroomed, stone-built cottage, tucked away in a corner of a quiet village north of Leeds, and he felt he was once more standing on solid ground. He was now part of a rural community and it felt entirely natural.

He had loved trips out to the countryside with his parents when he was a child, exploring the hills and woods and fields, and being close to the animals, great and small. That affection for the country had never left him.

The cottage was his sanctuary, a place where he could relax, admire the views, and just enjoy life with his pets and his simple possessions.

Haydn hammered the last piece of rail to the solid wooden post and stepped back to survey his work. He shook the fence. It was secure. Satisfied, he got back in the Mule and began skirting the field, making sure the rest of the fencing was in good order. Maintaining nearly five hundred acres of land and facilities was hard, physical work. But he had never been afraid of that. To be able to do it in the great outdoors was a bonus.

A hundred yards ahead, he could see Scott on foot in the

centre of one of the arenas. A woman was trotting round the school on a big grey horse, and Scott was clearly giving her a lesson.

Haydn reflected on how quickly he had clicked with the showjumper.

They had met at the right time for both of them.

Haydn had just moved into his cottage. He had been having lessons at a small, informal riding school in Leeds. It had given him something to focus on as he adjusted to life as a single man for the first time since his teens. It was also a chance to indulge himself. Horse riding was something he had wanted to try as a youngster, but he'd never had the opportunity.

The lessons had gone well. He soon grasped the basics and found that riding came naturally to him. When he moved to the village, he looked for somewhere nearer for his tuition. It was a 'horsey' area and he was spoiled for choice.

One day he was talking on the phone to his daughter, Emily. She was now twenty and at university, but as a horse mad teenager she had ridden regularly and still had many equestrian friends.

"Why don't you try Scott Stevens, Dad? Everyone says he's the best teacher. He won't be cheap, but you can afford the best now."

Haydn's rich parents had been killed in a car crash and his inheritance had recently come through. It was substantial and, although he had spent a proportion of it on the cottage, there was plenty left. Enough for a half share in an equestrian centre as it turned out.

He had called Scott straight away and two days later he was driving through the electronic gates at Wickham Court for his first lesson.

"Have you got a horse?" Scott had asked on the phone.

"No."

"We'll see how you get on with mine," he replied. It was a gesture of good faith and trust that instantly established their friendship.

Haydn could not fail to be impressed by his new tutor. Scott obviously knew everything there was to know about horses. But there was a warmth and humility about him that Haydn liked. No airs and graces. Just a quiet confidence, and a ready, genuine smile.

For his part, Scott was struck by the older man's honesty and determination to succeed. And he was not a little impressed by his riding skills.

After half a dozen sessions under Scott's expert eye, Haydn's riding had improved no end. Lord Percy was by far the best horse he had ridden, but he was a good natured animal and there were no alarms.

"You're a natural. You deserve to have your own horse," said Scott.

"I wouldn't know where to start looking," Haydn replied.

"Don't worry. I'll find you one."

Six weeks later, Paddy arrived.

Scott's equestrian contacts spread far and wide and he had an 'eye' for a horse. One phone call, to Eamonn O'Shea in Ireland, was enough to find what he was looking for.

"He'll be just right," said Eamonn. "He's well bred and has a super temperament, good as gold. And he'll jump."

"All Irish horses can jump," Scott declared.

And so Paddy made the journey across the Irish Sea to Liverpool, where he was met by Scott and his gleaming, huge four-horse wagon. Haydn perched nervously in the passenger seat, clutching his cheque book and wondering if he was having a mid-life crisis.

Paddy was five years old, a magnificent-looking grey gelding, who was a part-thoroughbred Irish sports horse. He was sixteen and a half hands high and looked tall and powerful. His father had hunted and jumped big fences in team chasing and eventing, while his thoroughbred mother had enjoyed minor success in a handful of hurdle races.

Haydn wrote out a cheque for £4,000, which included the cost of transport, handed it over to Eamonn, and watched in awe and trepidation as Paddy was loaded into the wagon. The horse walked straight in, without looking to either side, and immediately began to tug contentedly at the chunky haynet which Scott had tied up for him.

Haydn stood at the bottom of the wagon's ramp and gazed up at the fit-looking horse. Paddy cast him a nonchalant sidelong glance and continued to munch.

"He looks friendly enough," Haydn proffered.

"He's got a kind eye. He'll suit you very well," Scott replied.

That was four months ago, and Scott had been proved right. Haydn and Paddy had quickly formed a bond. They understood each other and the youth of the horse and the inexperience of the rider had not been a barrier. They had talent and with Scott there to help, their partnership was literally coming on in leaps and bounds. After a couple of months of hacking out and schooling, Haydn and Paddy started to jump. Poles on the ground at first. Then tiny little showjumps. Now they were happily jumping two-foot-high fences and Haydn felt nearly ready to begin competing.

He drove the Mule back on to the yard, parked up and switched off the engine. The woman on the grey horse had left the arena, her lesson at an end.

Scott called across to his friend. "Your turn. Go fetch your horse. If you both behave, you can jump a course today."

He winked. Haydn grinned back. "About time!"

On the outside he was relaxed. But inside he was a flutter. He would soon know how ready they were.

Chapter Four

Haydn brushed his horse with firm, downward strokes removing as much of the caked on mud as he could in a hurry. The problem with grey horses was that every speck of dirt stood out against their light colour. Paddy had clearly been having fun in the field. He was a darker, dappled grey but he still looked filthy.

"I'm sure you do it on purpose. Every time we have a lesson, you come in looking like you've spent all day having a mud bath!" Haydn complained. He smiled at the horse, who snorted in response.

He didn't mind really, grooming Paddy was always a soothing experience. Haydn had soon realised how rewarding it was to be around horses. To brush them, talk to them, or simply watch them eat. He might have had the cares of the world on his shoulders but they would be swept away by a few minutes in the company of the four-legged creatures. He was surprised by how close he had become to Paddy, just by spending time with him. And the horse seemed equally at ease in his company.

Haydn knew how much their relaxed and trusting attitude towards each other had helped in developing a partnership when they rode together. It was especially important when they began jumping.

He had followed Scott's sensible advice not to rush his riding. It was a risky business and horses could be unpredictable, particularly young ones. Accidents happened and serious injury often lurked around the corner, ready to pounce on the unwary. Haydn had taken a couple of minor tumbles trotting round at the old riding school, but nothing to stop him getting straight back on. His nerve had not yet been seriously tested.

Paddy was young, but he was good natured and had been brought up sensibly. He had been backed at three years old. He had then been left to grow and get stronger. At four he was ridden down the roads and in a school. Before being sold to Haydn he had been jumped over small cross poles in an arena, and was happy to do so. He still had a lot to learn, but he was willing and nothing seemed to faze him.

Haydn had a couple of wobbly moments when they started jumping together, but with Scott's guidance he learned to go forward with the horse when he took off and then get back into the saddle as he landed.

But going over a single jump, or even two in a row, was a lot different to negotiating a whole course which he would have to do if he was to take part in showjumping competitions. That had to be practised at home and today was the day.

Satisfied that Paddy was presentable, Haydn put away the grooming tools and tacked him up. The black leather saddle and bridle contrasted well with the horse's coat, he looked smart.

Haydn put on a pair of short black riding boots with matching leather chaps around his lower legs, and swapped his thick Barbour coat for a lighter riding jacket. He led Paddy to the stone mounting block and got on.

Giving the horse a gentle pat down the neck, he said: "Right then, bloke! Time to put on our serious heads."

Paddy briefly shook his head from side to side, swished his tail, and sprang forward into a positive walk. They clip-clopped noisily out of the stable yard, Paddy's metal shoes clanging on the hard surface, and marched briskly into one of the outdoor schools, where Scott was waiting for them.

The showjumper gazed critically at the horse and liked what he saw. Paddy looked fit and well. His coat gleamed with vitality, he appeared to be the perfect weight, and his eye was bright with enthusiasm. Scott noticed there was a look of steely determination on Haydn's face. The pair looked like they meant business.

They walked around the arena, at first circling left and then changing on to the right rein, allowing Paddy to gently stretch himself.

When Scott was happy the horse had warmed up, he called out: "Give me a trot."

Haydn squeezed Paddy with his lower legs and said: "Trot on." The horse instantly moved up to the quicker pace. Scott nodded approvingly at Paddy's perfect rhythm and his rider's balance. They were a team.

Scott had them changing the rein and making smaller circles within the school. The rhythm and balance remained. Then he asked them to quicken into a canter and still the team was together.

"Back straight, shoulders back," he shouted, seeking perfection. Haydn obliged.

"All right, come to the pink and white cross pole. Sit back, look ahead. And go!"

Paddy was up and over the two-foot-high obstacle, Haydn with him all the way.

"Good, Haydn. Just slip your reins a little more, so as not to pull him in the mouth."

They came round and jumped the pink and white poles again. This time Haydn let the reins run through his fingers slightly as they descended, allowing the horse to stretch his neck and look at what he was doing with his feet.

"Better. And again."

Paddy was more energetic the third time, enjoying the jumping, and standing further off the little fence to leap bigger. Haydn was almost taken by surprise but put his weight forward in the nick of time, quickly sliding back into the saddle as they landed on a steeper angle.

"All right, relax for a minute or two and then we'll look at something different."

Haydn walked Paddy round on a longer rein as Scott built a new fence in the middle of the arena. This one had two straight poles, one above the other. He then added two more, positioned beyond the first two and making the obstacle wider. Haydn had jumped such a fence, known as a spread, but not one quite as wide as this.

"Okay," said Scott. "Approach the fence just the same as the other one. Don't look down!"

Paddy cantered to the fence. He put his head down, measuring the jump, and then skipped easily over it.

Haydn whooped with delight. He had hardly noticed the extra width they had cleared. They jumped the fence twice more, with equal alacrity.

"Okay. Let's give you something else to think about," said Scott. "This is the sort of thing you will see a lot of when you start competing."

He dragged two oblong wooden planks into position underneath the poles. The 'fillers' did what their name suggested – filled the gaps beneath the fence. They gave the jumps a very different appearance and could shock an inexperienced or nervous horse. They could be decorated in different colours and patterns and Scott's selection was deliberately scary. His fillers had vivid yellow and black bees painted on them.

Haydn eyed the new fence warily. It stood out, and not in

an encouraging way.

"Remember, Paddy won't have seen anything like this before," said Scott. "Just ride him positively, keep him moving forward and don't look down. If you look at it, so will he."

Haydn nodded.

"My guess is, he won't worry about it. But ride him as if he will."

Haydn trotted Paddy in a wide arc around the scary fence. His heart was beating faster. But Paddy felt calm.

He asked for a canter and got it at once. Then he turned to face the fence. Paddy moved forward. Haydn sat up straight and squeezed the horse on with his leg. The jump loomed up. Three strides out. Two. The approach seemed perfect. Haydn prepared to move his body weight forward as Paddy hit the take off stride.

Then he was moving at speed through the air. But Paddy wasn't with him.

Haydn was out of the saddle and out of control. The wooden outside wing of the fence suddenly filled his vision. A fraction of a second later he crashed into it, slamming it over with his shoulder. He bounced to the ground with a thud and lay on his side in a daze.

He heard an urgent voice. "Stay there, Haydn. Don't move." He recognised Scott.

Haydn was panting. His breath came in short, sharp, difficult gasps. There was a pain in his abdomen.

His head was spinning but Scott's voice pierced the fog. "Breathe deep and slow. Try and relax."

A hand rested gently on his left shoulder. Then he heard another voice, that of a woman. "You're all right. We're here for you."

As he lay on the sandy surface, the pain in his stomach slowly eased and his mind began to clear. He realised his eyes had been closed, so he opened them.

He looked up into the anxious, hazel eyes of head girl Daisy Langridge. She was knelt beside him, with a troubled expression. It was her hand on his shoulder.

Crouched over him was Scott, who now unfastened Haydn's riding hat. "Can you sit up?" he asked.

Haydn contemplated the question. His breathing was easier, but there was a dull ache in his right shoulder and hip. He shifted himself on to his back and gazed up at the sky. "I think so."

He bent his knees and, with the help of Scott and Daisy, raised himself into a sitting position, his head between his knees.

"How does that feel?" asked Scott.

"Better."

"Can you move your arms and legs okay?"

Haydn stretched and unstretched his legs and gently circled his arms. "Yes."

"Any pain in your back?"

Haydn reflected. "No," after a few moments.

Now Daisy cupped his cheek in her hand and gently turned his face towards her. "Let's look in your eyes," she said.

He gazed back. Daisy had beautiful, big oval eyes. They normally danced with fun and vitality. Now they were etched with concern.

She suddenly smiled. "They are clear. Nothing going on there."

Again she touched his cheek. "But you have cut your face." She fished out a dainty little handkerchief and dabbed the blood away.

She thrust the handkerchief in his hand. "Keep it," she said softly.

Scott spoke again. "You were winded, Haydn. It's pretty

painful at the time, but you'll be fine now, apart from a few juicy bruises. You'll ache tomorrow."

"What happened?" asked Haydn, at last thinking clearly again.

"Paddy took a fright when he clocked the painted bees. He slammed on the brakes and ducked out to the left, sending you flying off to the right. You had no chance."

"I'm sorry," added the showjumper. "I asked a bit much of the two of you."

"No, you didn't. We've got to learn."

"You were doing fantastic until then," Daisy chipped in.

"I didn't even know you were there," said Haydn.

"I was on my lunch break. I stopped by to watch you."

Haydn was pleased she had taken the time to do that, though he wasn't sure why he felt that way. Then a sudden thought struck him.

"Where's Paddy? Is he all right?"

"He's absolutely fine," assured Scott. "He just had a scare."

"Help me up, please."

Haydn got to his feet and walked over to Paddy, who was stood quietly a few yards away. He patted the horse and put his arms round his neck. "Sorry, lad. That was a bit frightening. It's all right now."

There was an anxious look in Paddy's eye and a tenseness in his neck, but the young horse relaxed as Haydn stroked him soothingly.

Scott strode up. "I'll get on him and jump the fence. We mustn't let it fester in his mind."

Haydn saw the logic. But he knew he needed to get back on, or he too could lose his confidence.

Scott read his mind. "We don't want two of you getting anxious together. Once he's jumped it a couple of times with me, you can take over. Give me a leg up."

He swung nimbly into the saddle and rode around the arena. Paddy was now relaxed. Scott popped him over a couple of small jumps and then asked Daisy and Haydn to move the bee fillers out of the way.

"We'll jump the fence without them first to give him confidence."

There was no hesitation as Paddy cantered round and jumped the fence. Scott stroked his neck. "Good boy."

They jumped it twice more and Scott ordered the fillers to be put back in place. He walked Paddy up to the scary bees and stopped. Haydn watched his horse closely. Paddy sniffed the bees carefully. He seemed to be more chilled about them. Scott walked him round the fence and back to the bees, but kept him walking past them. Paddy glanced sideways at them, but not in alarm.

"Right. Let's do it!" said Scott.

The pair cantered into the fence. Haydn saw Paddy's ears twitch back and forth attentively as Scott encouraged: "Go on!" The horse stretched his neck to look at the obstacle, but he was moving forward, and then he was soaring over and the scary bees were safely behind him.

Daisy and Haydn applauded. "Well done, Paddy!"

"Now it's my turn," Haydn declared.

"Not to jump that," Scott answered.

"I have to jump it now, or I may never do it."

Scott knew his prodigy was right. It was a good decision, though a brave one. He could not have blamed Haydn if he had made the wrong one.

The riders swapped places. Haydn felt sore and his nerves were jangling. But he was determined.

He was soon cantering Paddy around the school. He stroked the horse and whispered to him: "We can do this together, lad." Paddy's big ears twitched again.

"Pop the little cross pole first," Scott instructed.

But Haydn's mind was made up. It was all or nothing. He would jump the big bee fence, or fall on his sword. To hell with it!

They cantered in. Paddy was locked on to the jump. Haydn realised that his equine pal was looking after him. He was going to take him over it. The fence was in front of them and this time Paddy was leaping. Instinctively, Haydn shut his eyes. He had never done that before. He opened them again as they landed on the other side. An overwhelming feeling of relief welled up inside him and exploded in a shout of joy. He punched the air. "We did it!"

He pulled up the horse and patted him gratefully. "Thanks Paddy."

Daisy rushed up happily, her face wreathed in smiles. "Well done, both of you."

Scott looked on with a wry grin. "You old bugger! There's no point giving you lessons if you're just going to ignore what I say! Well ridden, mate."

"I think we better leave the course for another day," Haydn said.

"You're right about that. Get yourself home and soak in a bath."

"Thanks both of you. See you later."

Haydn collected Timmy and strolled gingerly to the car. It had been an eventful day. There was lots for him to think about. Not least Daisy Langridge.

Chapter Five

Haydn relaxed in the steaming bath and felt the heat of the soapy water soothe his aching body. Dark bruises were already emerging. He knew he would be stiff by the morning but a long soak now would kick start the healing process.

He laid his head back against the enamel and idly looked up at the ceiling, letting his mind roam free.

Despite his tumble, he felt satisfied. He knew that falling off came with the territory, if you rode a horse you had to accept the likelihood of that happening, particularly if you wanted to jump.

What pleased him was that he had got back on and jumped the fence. He and Paddy had faced the challenge together and come through it together. It was a big stride forward in their developing partnership.

The water started to cool, so Haydn got out, dried himself and slipped into his dressing gown.

He stepped into the living room. Timmy was stretched out cosily on the sheepskin rug in front of the stove. The logs of wood Haydn had lit before running his bath were now blazing merrily, golden flames dancing behind the big glass door. The cottage had the modern comforts of central heating and double glazing. But Haydn had wanted the natural attraction of wood-burning stoves in the living room and kitchen. They gave the cottage character and helped to make it a 'proper' home.

He put two more logs on the fire. Timmy lifted his head to watch his master and wagged his tail. Haydn reached down and stroked him, poured a glass of whisky, then laid down on the comfortable, deep sofa and placed his head and back against the large racehorse-patterned cushions. He gazed contentedly at the flames and felt their warmth reaching across the room to his secure resting place.

An air of serenity flowed over him and he now allowed himself to think about Daisy Langridge.

Daisy was thirty years old. She had dark, shoulder-length hair, which she wore in a ponytail at the yard, and was slim but strong. She had been Scott's head girl for three years and he relied heavily on her. Daisy was trustworthy, hard-working and had a natural empathy with the horses.

She had been riding since she was six years old and was an accomplished horsewoman, taking her dark bay thoroughbred Des to local and regional showjumping competitions and one-day events.

In recent weeks she had helped Haydn by giving him flatwork lessons, to run alongside his jumping tuition with Scott, and the novice rider found her to be perceptive and encouraging.

She was a very attractive woman, though Haydn had never permitted himself to think of her in that way. Until now.

Daisy's kindness and obvious concern as Haydn lay winded on the ground had suddenly changed his way of thinking. It was as though someone had forcefully nudged him in the ribs and made him sit up and take notice. The anxiety in her eyes seemed to run deeper than he could have imagined.

He fished out Daisy's pretty pink handkerchief, stained with his blood, and recalled her gentle touch and worried expression.

Haydn had not had a relationship since the break up of his marriage to Claire. The experience had been far too painful to contemplate seeing another woman.

Claire had been his childhood sweetheart.

He often saw her playing on the street with her friends when they were kids. Even then he was struck by her vibrant approach to life.

His parents had sent him to be educated at a private boy's school in his home city of Sheffield. But it was not far from the local girl's school which Claire attended, and their paths inevitably crossed as they made their way home.

Claire was two years younger but they got on well and when Haydn was sixteen they began dating, in an innocent, old-fashioned type of way. Haydn was thrilled. He wooed her with flowers and chocolates, bought with his earnings from his part-time job in a clothes shop. They went to the cinema and, when he could afford it, he paid for them to eat at a cosy restaurant.

The couple were close and had a similar outlook on life. Haydn joined the police at eighteen. Two years later, Claire followed suit. They rented a flat and it was only then that they started sleeping together. They were in love and had regularly kissed and cuddled, but had not had sex. But their physical attraction to each other was strong and they soon made up for lost time. Claire proved to have a healthy sexual appetite.

When Haydn's career was established the sweethearts married. He was twenty-four, his bride was twenty-two. Their daughter, Emily, was soon born and, two years later their son, William.

The couple were earning decent money, enough to buy their own house, and they had everything they wanted.

It seemed to be a match made in heaven, and it was for many years. Haydn could not have been happier. He had a beautiful wife, two lovely children, a nice home and a successful and well paid career. What could possibly go wrong?

It all changed when Claire began to climb the police ranks. She was promoted to sergeant and then to inspector, leading a neighbourhood policing team at a busy station on the east side of Leeds. By then, Haydn was working as a detective sergeant for the specialist Crime Division based in central Leeds. He worked long and unsocial hours as part of a crack squad, tackling organised criminals and gangs. The kids were growing up and Haydn and Claire didn't see so much of each other. They had hectic and responsible jobs. Their marriage began to take second place.

It never entered Haydn's head that his loving and loyal wife might be having an affair, even when she kept getting stuck late at work. It was the nature of the job. Haydn was doing plenty of overtime. Secret police observations and full on door-kicking-in operations could happen at any time of day and night and run from one day to the next. It wasn't unusual for Haydn to get back home in the middle of the night.

Claire's police role was rather different. She was in charge of a team of officers getting out into the communities and dealing with incidents, such as road accidents, break ins and assaults, as they occurred. And though her time was often spent at the police station, liaising with control room staff or organising her team from her office, it was to be expected that her shift could drag on well beyond her finishing time. And the extra overtime she volunteered for helped to pay the bills.

It was an old pal in CID who warned Haydn that something was wrong.

He had been on all day observations outside a drug baron's expensive house, taking surreptitious photos and copious notes of the comings and goings there. He knocked off at eight o'clock in the evening and called in at his station to safely store away his notebook and check for messages.

As he shut down his computer, Detective Sergeant Andy Watson appeared at the office door.

"Fancy a drink?"

Haydn straightened up from his desk and considered his friend. They had started out in the force at the same time and had spent most of their careers together, working from the same CID office for years until Haydn's move to Crime Division. Andy was probably his best mate in the police and was a trusted confidante.

Haydn smiled warmly. "Why not? But it will have to be a quick one. I'll get my coat."

The friends propped up a quiet corner of the bar at The City of Mabgate. They raised their pint glasses and briefly clinked them together.

"Cheers."

Haydn looked across at his pal, who was staring intently at his drink.

"What is it?"

Andy glanced away and did not reply.

"Tell me." Something was clearly wrong. But what?

"Haydn. I'm sorry, mate. It's Claire. She's seeing someone."

"Seeing someone? What do you mean?" The reality had not registered.

Andy took a gulp of his beer. Then: "She's cheating on you… with another bloke."

Haydn stared at his friend, trying to understand, trying to make sense of the words which made no sense at all.

"An affair?"

"Yes."

Haydn's brain processed the words until they finally produced a meaning. Now he had the meaning, but he still did not understand.

"Who? Why?"

"I don't know why, Haydn. But it's a sergeant she works with, Dave Barton."

"I know him, I've worked with him. How could he, how

could they?"

They both now stared in silence into their beers.

After a couple of minutes, Haydn took a swig of his ale and declared: "It can't be right. You must be mistaken, Andy."

"I've seen them together. In a wine bar."

"That doesn't mean anything."

"They were snogging in an alcove."

"Are you sure?"

"Yes."

Haydn stared back at his beer. Five minutes passed. Then he lifted his head.

"How long have you known?"

"A couple of weeks. I heard rumours. People were talking. I didn't believe it. Then I saw them. I'm sorry, Haydn."

Claire was already in bed when he got home. He crawled in beside her, not knowing what else to do, and laid with his back to her. Half asleep, she rolled towards him and placed her hand on his shoulder. The touch made him shudder. He inched away and the hand slid down to the bed.

For two weeks he said nothing. He did not know what to say. He threw himself even more into his work, asking for extra overtime, trying to put the terrible knowledge to the back of his mind.

He felt as if all his work colleagues knew what his wife was up to and were sniggering at him behind his back. There was no escape, at work or at home.

Then, one evening, Claire said she had to go to Newcastle on a two-day training course. She would be staying there overnight.

Haydn could not help himself. "Is Dave Barton on the course, then?"

For a moment, Claire's mouth fell open. Then she recovered herself. "What do you mean?"

But her reaction had confirmed her guilty secret. There was no going back now. "I know about your affair, there's no point denying it."

Her eyes pleaded with him. "It's not what you think."

But it was, and they both knew it. Their marriage was over. Irretrievably.

It had taken Haydn many months to even begin to come to terms with Claire's cheating. The pain and hurt he felt was heightened by the embarrassment of being a cuckold.

Gradually he had allowed himself to go out to the pub with friends and feel more comfortable in female company. But the wound of betrayal had cut deep and he was scared to get close to any woman.

Haydn got up from the sofa, went to the table and refilled his glass from the whisky bottle. As he did so, his mobile phone rang.

He picked it up and saw the name Daisy flashing on the console. Before he could stop it, his heart had skipped a beat.

"Hello," he answered, slightly breathlessly.

"Hi! It's me. I just wanted to check up on you. How are you feeling?"

Her voice instantly lifted his spirits.

"I'm fine. I'm sat in front of a roaring fire with a glass of whisky in my hand. What more could a man want?"

"A companion?"

"I've got Timmy," he replied, and immediately regretted his response.

"It all sounds very cosy. Well, I'm glad you're feeling better. I'll see you tomorrow."

"Yes. Thanks for ringing, Daisy. It means … I appreciate it."

"No problem."

He placed the phone back on the side table. Then he took

Daisy's little pink handkerchief. He put it to his nose and breathed in deeply, her fragrance enveloping him in a powerful embrace.

Chapter Six

Kane Weston leaned back nonchalantly in his chair and stared across the table into the eyes of his probation officer, who quickly dropped his gaze to the file in front of him.

"It seems you were a model prisoner, Mr Weston," said David Parsons, flicking nervously through the pages.

"My name's Kane. There's no need for formalities, David."

Parsons glanced up and was met again by Weston's hard, cold stare, a look that unnerved him and sent a chill down his spine. He had spent nearly twenty years in the probation service, but rarely had he encountered a criminal who made him feel so anxious and vulnerable. Weston had an air about him that reeked of danger.

"Of course," Parsons replied, trying to sound calm. But inside his stomach was churning.

"How do you think it went, Kane? Do you think you have changed?"

Again the stare. "Well, David. I'm five years older."

"And where do you see yourself in five years from now?"

Kane allowed himself a thin smile. It was a very good question. He did not yet know the answer. Did he want to go straight and become a rich and successful legitimate businessman? Or did he want to continue to build his criminal empire? Maybe he could do both.

His deputy, Jim Lee, had done a good job in his absence – following his instructions to the letter and making the right decisions when he had to. The trade in drugs had naturally come to a halt when the cops uncovered the conspiracy which sent Kane to prison. But Lee had worked bloody hard to promote what had been back up earners. Prostitution, protection and insurance scams had come to the fore, making sure that Kane's family and his associates continued to be well provided for. And any rival gangs, fancying their chances of taking a bit of their territory, had soon seen that Weston's hired muscle remained strong.

Lee had told him the foot soldiers were happy and there had been no hint of mutiny or defection. Even with Kane behind bars, they would not have dared.

Kane knew that his contacts, influence and power meant he could easily get the drugs business up and running again. That was where the big money was to be had.

On the other hand, owning the snooker club had proved to be a profitable enterprise. He had bought the club in East Street – the one where he had first met Raymond – six years ago at a knockdown price, using proceeds from his lucrative drugs business for the purchase and to carry out renovations. He had spent £20,000 turning the dingy, pokey old hall into a light and bright quality snooker centre, with decent food and waitress service. He had turfed out the old down and outs and targeted a better quality of customer with money in their pockets.

He upped his prices sensibly and in no time at all he had recouped his outlay and was starting to make good money. Lee had continued to run it at a profit in his absence.

Of course, there were sidelines, like the occasional all-night poker school gambling dens (with a £100 entry fee per player), and the discreet and carefully organised trade in cannabis and cocaine for selected customers.

But the snooker hall was basically legit and Kane had plans to open an upmarket wine bar and bistro in a nearby town centre.

"I will be richer, happier and more successful than I am today," Kane replied to the probation officer's question.

"Well, Kane. Always remember we are here to help you. We have to work   together to achieve your goals, and ours."

"I am sure I will achieve my goals, David."

Parsons shifted uncomfortably. He needed to ask Weston something more personal and he wasn't looking forward to it.

"If we are to work together we need to know where to contact you at all times. How is your home life?"

Parsons busied himself with the file, avoiding the malevolent glare he knew would follow the question. Long prison sentences were never good for marriages.

Kane let his mind focus on his wife, Keeley. When he got home, after his meeting in the pub with Jim Lee, Keeley was waiting. She had sent the kids to stay with her sister and when he walked into the living room he found her draped over the couch, wearing nothing but a tiny black negligee. Her ironed blonde hair tumbled over her ample cleavage, which strained to be released from the flimsy lace garment. He could see her her hard nipples thrusting against the see-through material. Her mouth pouted voluptuously as her hungry eyes undressed him.

Kane carried her upstairs to the main bedroom and tossed her slender body onto the king-size bed. Then he pushed her face into the pillows and fucked her hard from behind, as she squirmed and moaned in pain and ecstasy.

He knew her liking for rough sex, and it suited him on this occasion. It had been a long time – and anyway she deserved to be manhandled. When he was jailed, Keeley vowed she would wait for him. But Kane knew she hadn't and Jim Lee confirmed she had been shagging Judd Ward, a handsome young housebreaker on his payroll who was ten years her junior. They thought they could keep the fling under wraps, but nothing escaped Lee's watchful eye.

Ward was at the top of Kane's list of things to sort. "I want you to deal with it, personally," Kane told Lee. "But not yet. Keep him onside. Let him worry about what he has done for a while. I'll give you the word when I'm ready."

Keeley could also wait. It came as no surprise that she had cheated on him. She had always been a dirty little slut, but that was what had attracted him.

Kane was twenty, and already rising up the ranks with the Collins gang, when he encountered Keeley. Gang leader Danny Collins – impressed by Kane's ambition, confidence and loyalty – promoted him from foot soldier to be one of the brains of the outfit. He was soon in charge of the phone and collect street drug dealing operation and not long after he was invited to become part of the robbery planning team.

One of the gang was Billy Dransfield. Billy was twenty-two, dependable and loyal, but not very bright. He was never going to climb the ladder. He had been going out with Keeley for six months. She was still only sixteen but she already knew what she wanted when it came to boys.

Kane clocked her with him in the pub one day and instantly knew he had to have her. She was wearing the shortest of skirts and her hands were all over Dransfield. A half of lager was in front of her.

Kane joined them uninvited at their table and plonked another pint of lager in front of Billy. He placed a large bacardi and coke before Keeley. Fixing her with his deep, black eyes, he announced: "You're better than a half of lager girl." She giggled seductively in reply.

Three days later he was banging her in the back of his car. A week after that he told Dransfield: "Keeley has decided she will now be going out with me." Billy began to protest but Kane cut him short and gave him his most penetrating stare. "Just accept it, Billy." Something told Billy to do just that.

Keeley had not left his side since. It did not take her long to realise that staying with him could only be good for her. He was clearly going places and she could see a life of relative luxury beckoning her. All she had to do was obey his demands for her to stay true and support him.

Of course, her fidelity had no bearing on his behaviour. As his influence grew in the criminal world and the local community, he found that women threw themselves at him. It would have been rude not to have taken advantage. Keeley turned a blind eye. She had too much to lose to make a fuss.

They were soon married. He was then twenty-two and she was eighteen. She was something of a trophy wife to Kane. But he loved her in his own selfish way. He insisted she used contraception, not wanting her glamorous image spoiled by pregnancy.

But by the age of twenty-eight he was ready for her to bear him children. By then he had broken away from the Collins mob and had set up on his own. The split was fairly amicable. The gang had gone weak. Some of the members had been locked up or drifted away, and Danny Collins had health issues. He had lost interest in crime and wanted to get out and spend more time with his family.

Kane took Collins' best henchmen with him. They included Jim Lee. Kane was soon making crime pay and building a fearsome reputation as a villain not to be crossed. He structured his operation so there was distance between him and the crimes being committed, with Lee as the final buffer. Kane deliberately made himself into a Mafia-style don.

He was already planning for the future, when he would be able to take a back seat, hand over the reins and enjoy the fruits of his criminal labours. So he was delighted when Keeley produced two boys, who he proudly named Al and John, after the famous Mafia gangsters Capone and Gotti.

Kane became aware that the probation officer was looking at him anxiously, wondering if he was going to get an answer to his last question. Kane had been lost in his thoughts.

Now he smiled, and for once it had warmth behind it as he reflected again on his wife's naked body. "My home life could not be better."

"So we can contact you at Sicily House, Long Causeway Road ..."

"Any time," Kane interrupted. "And if I am not there, my wife will always be happy to help you."

"You must not live or stay at any other address without notifying us," Parsons reminded him.

"Now why would I want to be anywhere else?"

Parsons stood up, signalling the end of the appointment. "Mr ... er, Kane. Thank you for being so helpful today. I'll see you here at the same time next Tuesday. Perhaps we can talk then about your plans for work. If you have any problems, or anything you want to ask me, just pick up the phone."

"I'll do that, David. Look forward to next week's instalment!"

Kane marched briskly from the office. "Yes, David," he thought to himself. "There is something you could help with, where is that bastard Haydn Daniel? But I guess that's something I'll have to find out for myself."

Chapter Seven

Haydn studied his reflection in the long mirror in the living area of Daisy's horse wagon, and asked himself what he saw. Looking back at him, it seemed, was a showjumper – albeit clearly a nervous one – in all his finery. He wore black boots, beige breeches, a thin buttoned up black showjumping jacket, smart white shirt, a blue and white spotted stock knotted neatly at the neck and a fox head stock pin with ruby red eyes. All that remained was for him to put on his velvet peaked riding hat. What would my old detective pals make of me dressed like this, he mused.

Haydn had not expected to feel so at home in his showjumping attire. Although his parents had been relatively well-off and as a child he had lacked for nothing, his upbringing had been down-to-earth and he carried no airs and graces with him into independent adult life. He was a Yorkshireman. Plain and simple was his motto. Much as he loved horses, he had not seen himself mixing with the riding set.

Yet here he was doing just that, and about to take part in his first showjumping competition.

He was pleasantly surprised to find that most people at the show were like him – ordinary folk with a passion for horses. There was hardly a toff to be heard among the gruff Yorkshire voices. And the horseboxes and trailers parked up for the event were in the main mature and sturdy vehicles built to do the job, rather than expensive or flashy status symbols.

Daisy's compact four and a half tonne wagon, which had

brought Paddy to the event at the smart but rustic Yorkshire Dales Equestrian Centre, was one such old dependable.

Haydn was delighted when Daisy said she would take him to the competition – and not just because he had no horse transport of his own. She had made sure she was not working so she could act as his chauffeur and groom. He could think of no-one better to be at his side.

The fall from Paddy had left him battered and bruised. His body took on violent shades of black, blue and purple, and he had the aches and pains to match. But the ugly dark blotches paled to a yellower hue, and his discomfort faded in tandem with the change of his skin colour. As his body healed, Haydn was able to file away the dramatic fall in a compartment of his brain marked 'painful memory' and he began to eagerly anticipate the challenge of his first jumping event.

He found it more difficult to put to one side his thoughts about Daisy.

He had noticed her at once when he started having riding lessons with Scott. She always seemed to be there – hard at work, busily organising everything that needed doing, and very much at the heart of the efficient running of Wickham Court.

"She's the one that makes this place tick," Scott told him. And Haydn could see why.

Now he realised he had more than just a professional interest in her.

During their thirty-minute journey from Wickham Court to the event venue, he chatted beside her in the cab of the lorry and felt very much at ease. For the first time he asked her about herself, and allowed her to quiz him.

Daisy knew that Haydn was divorced but she was not aware of the circumstances, and she did not have the impertinence to inquire now. But she was more confident to ask about other aspects of his life.

"What would your parents have thought about you going showjumping? I bet they would have been proud," she said, turning the wagon onto the main A-road which would take them most of the way to their destination.

"I guess they were proud of most things that I did," answered Haydn. "Being the eldest, I suppose I got a lot of attention. They weren't horsey types, but I think they would have been pleased for me."

"Tell me about them, and your brother and sister," said Daisy eagerly.

Family had always been important to Haydn, and he needed no encouragement to talk about them.

He told Daisy about the high-flying legal careers of his parents, Gordon and Fiona; how they had studied for years to become lawyers and then worked all hours to progress along their chosen paths; how they qualified as barristers and were made Queens Counsel. While Fiona was happy to continue as a barrister – after a break to have the family – Gordon chose to move to the other side of the bench, dispensing justice for many years as a Circuit Judge, latterly based at Oxford Crown Court. He was 70 when he finally hung up his wig and was able to look back with satisfaction on a long and rewarding professional life. Fiona, who was two years older than her husband, had been working part-time for a number of years and she now also ended her career.

The couple hoped to enjoy a long and happy retirement, knowing they had earned the luxury of having no financial worries to spoil it. But it was cruelly cut short after five years by the terrible car crash which claimed both their lives. Gordon had been driving them home from a Law Society social event in Oxfordshire. It had been raining for days and that evening there had been a particularly heavy downpour. Their Mercedes aquaplaned on a big puddle, barely visible on the dark country lane, and smashed into a roadside tree. They were killed instantly.

"That must have been hard for you," said Daisy.

"It was. You expect your parents to die of old age, not be torn from you in such a sudden and violent way. But you just have to get on with it."

That was eighteen months ago. Haydn had come to terms with his loss but he still missed his parents terribly. They had always been there for him and in a crisis he had been able to pick up the phone and ask for advice, which was readily given and invariably made sense. He would have loved to have had their input when his marriage broke down, but he'd had to deal with that on his own. Haydn liked to think they would have approved of the decisions he had made since.

"Do you see much of your brother and sister?" asked Daisy as the horsebox trundled smoothly along.

"Not a lot. We all have busy lives. We meet up at Christmas, and visit each other occasionally, and we speak on the phone."

"What do they do? Are they younger than you?"

"I'm the eldest. Felicity is two years younger than me. She's a barrister and lives in London, so I don't see a lot of her. Oliver is the youngest by two years. He's a criminal solicitor in Sheffield. We meet up more often. But we all get on, we were always a close family."

"That must be nice."

Haydn glanced at Daisy, who had turned the horsebox off the main road and was now negotiating a narrower country lane to the equestrian centre. "Do you not get on with your family?"

"We get on all right, but I wouldn't say we are close like you are with yours. I can take them or leave them, I suppose. There's just my mum and dad and my sister, Beth. She's five years older than me, so we always moved in different circles."

Daisy was now expertly guiding the horse wagon along the

entrance drive to the venue. It was single track with the occasional passing place, but she had been there many times before and knew what to expect.

"You just have to watch out for vehicles coming the other way. There isn't much room for manoeuvre when that happens. Sorry, what were you asking?"

Haydn swallowed hard. He did not know if he could repeat the question, which had rushed from his brain to his mouth on a sudden and uncontrollable impulse. It was harder to get the words out a second time.

"I was just, er … I was just wondering if you were close with any, well, friends."

Daisy shot him a quick look of inquisitiveness and amusement. She smiled back at him. "You're asking if I've got a love life."

Haydn kept his eyes focused on the road ahead and tried to stop a blush from burning his cheeks. "Well, I'm not sure I meant to put it quite like that."

Daisy began to swing the wagon into a tight parking spot. She laughed: "No time to discuss whether I'm going out with anyone. You need to watch that trailer on our left for me."

"Will do," replied Haydn, relieved.

Daisy lined up the horsebox perfectly, brought it to a halt and switched off the engine. She opened the driver's door and prepared to leap out. For a moment she paused and looked across at Haydn. "Anyway, the answer is no."

Haydn trotted his horse around the warm up area. In a few minutes they would be heading to the main arena for their competitive debut. They would be jumping the 60 centimetres course, or two-foot in old money. Paddy felt calm beneath him, much more laid back than his rider whose stomach was turning somersaults.

Haydn heard Daisy call out from the sidelines. "Pop him over the practice fence a couple of times. It will get his eye in, and relax you."

He asked Paddy to canter and they came in and cleared the obstacle. The horse was foot perfect.

"And again, Haydn."

The pair circled and once more jumped the fence in fine style. Haydn was starting to feel more determined, taking strength from the confidence of his horse.

"Number seven, make your way up to the start, please," shouted out one of the officials.

"That's us," thought Haydn, with a sudden pang of anxiety. But Daisy was instantly at his side, reassuring him and patting the horse.

"Just go in and enjoy yourself, Haydn. That's all that matters."

And then they were walking into the arena. Haydn looked around at the course. He had walked it on foot earlier, trying to make sure he knew the order in which they would have to jump the fences. Get it wrong and they would be eliminated. It had seemed straightforward, but now it resembled a maze, with brightly-coloured showjumps everywhere he looked.

The public address system crackled into life. "Next to jump is number seven, Haydn Daniel riding Paddy." The announcement was followed by the loud, buzzy sound of a bell signalling that they could start their round.

Haydn found the yellow and white first fence, and moving Paddy into canter they turned to face it. They jumped it well and then locked on to the second fence, pink and white, and cleared that. Now he was riding the course, Haydn knew exactly where he was going. He was focused, and Paddy was jumping round like a veteran, calm and precise. Their round seemed to be over in the blink of an eye. As they went through the finish, Haydn gave Paddy a big pat on the neck and allowed himself a smile of joy and relief. They had gone clear.

Daisy greeted them as they left the arena. She was all smiles. "Well done, you did it!"

Haydn dismounted and Daisy took hold of the horse. "I can't believe it. It couldn't have gone better. Paddy seemed to be quite quick," he said.

"He was, maybe fast enough to get you a place."

Haydn hadn't even thought about that. Just getting round was something to celebrate. But their efforts earned them third place and they were called back into the arena to be presented with a bright yellow rosette, before cantering round the ring as celebratory music was played and the audience clapped their appreciation.

"This isn't real. It happens to other people," said Haydn.

Now he had to decide whether to have a crack at the 70 centimetres class. It sounded to him like a challenge.

But Daisy was positive. "You should always finish on a good note, then you and the horse go away with confidence for next time. But on what I have seen today, there's no reason why you shouldn't do well in the next class. Anyway, I'm enjoying the day too much for it to end yet."

Haydn had similar thoughts. The more time he spent with Daisy, the more he liked it. "All right, let's go for it."

They finished out of the rosettes after Paddy didn't get high enough at the first jump and knocked off the top pole with his front legs. But he was otherwise immaculate and Haydn felt proud of his horse as they loaded him back in the wagon.

"He's been terrific. It's all been like a dream," he said, clutching his rosette. The day had been special, and not just because of the showjumping.

"This is just the start," said Daisy, gently touching Haydn's arm. "I'm sure you two have a big future together."

She reached up and gave Haydn a peck on the cheek. "I hope we can do it again."

He clambered into the cab of the wagon and quietly reflected on their achievement as Daisy drove them back. In his mind was one question: "I wonder what the future holds … for the three of us."

Chapter Eight

"I'm going to advertise for two stablehands, if you are happy with that," said Haydn.

Scott grunted. "If you think we need them, that's good enough for me. You're in charge of that side of things, you don't need my approval."

"Nevertheless, hiring and firing should be a joint decision."

"Agreed," said Scott, holding up his hand and taking a gulp of coffee.

It was eight o'clock on Monday morning and the two men were sat in the office. A bright sun shone through the windows, warming everything it touched. Outside, the clatter of hooves and the calling of cheery voices told them that the turning out of the horses was in full flow.

They met at the start of each week to chat informally about the day-to-day running of the livery yard, up and coming events they were hosting, and the occasional financial matter needing their consideration. The meetings did not normally last long. The partners agreed about most things and it was rare they had a serious problem that demanded more in-depth discussions. Usually, they decided what they had to in ten minutes and they would then relax, enjoying each other's company and sharing anecdotes, gossip and the latest horsey news.

It had seemed natural for them to go into business together. Scott was struggling financially and needed help in running the equestrian centre. Haydn had money available, after getting a one-third share of his parents three million pounds legacy, and was looking for a way to invest it as well as a new challenge.

They had hit it off immediately when Haydn first had riding lessons with the showjumper, and their friendship had gone to another level when the younger man found Paddy for Haydn, the pair quickly developing a deep trust and respect for each other.

Scott told his friend he was looking for someone to take the pressure off him at Wickham Court, explaining how he had been left to manage on his own when his girlfriend upped and left him.

"I don't want to sell but I shall have to unless I can get the help I need. It's too much for one person to run a place like this."

"What's the deal?" asked Haydn.

"Ideally, I'd like someone to come in on equal terms, a half-share in the business – they would be able to put money in to it and share any profits. And they would bear half of the responsibility for running the place."

"But it would have to be someone who knows about horses."

"That helps, but the most important thing would be to know how to look after people, and be prepared to put the time in. I've got all the knowledge about horses that's needed."

"Well, I may not be a businessman, but I know all about doing what's right for folk and I'm not afraid of hard work. And I have the money to put into it. Look no further, Scott."

And so they struck a deal for him to pay Scott half a million pounds to become an equal partner in Wickham Court. Haydn's role would be to look after the livery customers and be in charge of the day-to-day running and maintenance of the yard, while Scott concentrated on giving riding lessons and organising the horse camps and events.

Haydn accepted it was a huge investment, but he believed it was a sound one, and he had the funds to do it without compromise. His generous police pension was enough for him to live on.

And if he was to go into partnership with someone, he could not think of anyone better than Scott.

Aside of the trust they shared, they both also recognised a fellow survivor.

Haydn's devastating marriage break-up, in addition to the loss of his parents, had left him emotionally scarred. Scott too had faced the crushing humiliation of a cheating partner.

He had met Izzy West-Faraday on the showjumping circuit. They were 26 years old and both were rapidly rising up the international equestrian ladder.

Scott – tall and slim, with deep languid blue eyes and a cheeky grin – had just forced his way into the GB showjumping team and was on course to represent his country at the World Championships. He was handsome, elegant and rich – and seen as a real "catch" by the ladies.

Izzy, also from a wealthy background, and with a champagne lifestyle and supermodel looks and figure, was just as popular with the male riders.

It seemed inevitable that they would get together, and it happened in the run up to the World Championships during a training camp in Italy. Their affair was passionate and conducted unashamedly in the public gaze, to the point where the couple's romance made regular newspaper headlines. The spotlight on them increased when Scott brought home an individual bronze medal and a team silver from the Championships.

Spurred on by that success, Scott looked to use his wealth and reputation to develop his equestrian future.

He had kept his showjumpers at Wickham Court for two years. He had been aware of the equestrian centre, having been brought up in North Yorkshire, and he knew that his horses would get top notch treatment if he moved them there, and so it proved. The first-class facilities gave him the chance to 'kick on' and train himself and his horses to the highest level. The medals were his reward.

When the owners of Wickham Court – looking for a quieter life and financial security for their retirement years – put the business up for sale, Scott did not think twice about using the pot of gold, sat in a trust fund his family had set up for him, to buy it.

It was an opportunity to turn his passion for horses into a serious money earner.

But Scott found that juggling a professional riding career with running an elite equestrian centre was far from easy – even with first-rate staff to keep everything in order while he was away competing. And the cost of maintaining the place to the highest standard was more than he had imagined. Most of the prize money he won went back into the business.

He didn't mind. He was doing what he loved and he enjoyed a comfortable lifestyle.

Then his talented but temperamental stallion, Sir Gawain, threw a wobbly at a Grand Prix showjumping event – hurling Scott into a solid advertisement hoarding, and shattering his left leg.

His career was in ruins, along with his lucrative teaching commitments. He now had no earnings to put into the business.

He had been in a relationship with Izzy for four years and so she put her own money towards the substantial overheads of Wickham Court. What's more, she took time out from her blossoming career to devote herself to nursing Scott and being hands on at the equestrian centre.

Scott was under doctor's orders to stay flat on his back for six weeks while the bones of his left leg knitted back together. He was a further three months on crutches, and when he cast them aside he was still hobbling around for weeks.

Six months after his accident he was at last able to get back on a horse. But Scott knew his international competing days were over. His leg would never be strong enough for him to ride again at that level. He made the tough but inevitable decision to retire from professional showjumping and set out to make Wickham Court the best competition venue between Scotland and the Midlands.

Scott threw himself into the new challenge and was glad to be at the heart of Wickham Court. But he no longer had Izzy's day to day support. She had resumed her career, switching direction from pure showjumping to three-day eventing. She was competing all over the UK and often abroad. Scott sometimes did not see her for weeks.

Izzy was still giving financial backing, but Scott was now ploughing a lone furrow in the organising of horse camps and events, as well as looking after fifty demanding livery customers. It was exhausting. He just about kept on top of everything – thanks to a great degree to the unstinting hard work and efficiency of Daisy Langridge.

But something had to give. During a rare weekend together, matters came to a head.

Izzy, never diplomatic, got straight to the point. "It's not working between us any more, Scott. I think we've run our course."

Scott had seen it coming, but he was still shocked. "Look, Izzy. Let's not throw away our great years together just like that. We can still work it out. We still love each other."

"But that's just it, Scott. I don't love you any longer. My life has moved on. I need to be based in the south, where all the top event yards are. I'm sorry."

Within a week she was gone, along with her money. It did not take long for Scott to discover just how Izzy's life had moved on. Word reached him that she was seeing Australian eventing star Matt Kominsky. In fact, she had been sleeping with him for three months.

Scott was devastated by the betrayal. But he had to hide his hurt and get on with earning the money to run Wickham Court. He looked for new riding pupils to teach. One of those was Haydn Daniel.

"So why do we need more stablehands?" asked Scott.

"Because Alison is starting her horse physiotherapy course in Cardiff next month and Amy is moving with her family to Scotland. We can't expect the others to take up the slack."

There were a dozen stable lasses and lads – mostly young women from the ages of eighteen to thirty – who looked after the horses, mucked out, and kept the yard clean and tidy. They worked three days on and two days off in the week and alternate weekends. Daisy was in charge, working six days a week, and there was casual staff available to cover for holidays.

In addition, there was a handyman who was employed to help Haydn with the general maintenance. Scott also paid a couple of professional riders to give lessons at the horse camps and could call on part-time staff to help on the course during events. The payroll was high – the biggest cost of the business – but it could not be run without them.

"You're quite right, Haydn. A pair of stable staff it is. Anyone in mind?"

"Not really. There's nobody waiting in the wings at the moment. I'll advertise in the normal way – in the local paper, and on Facebook and Twitter. There won't be a problem."

"That's fine. Just let me know when you've fixed up someone. Any other business?"

"I don't think so."

Scott leaned back in his chair and propped up his feet on the edge of the desk. He gazed over his coffee mug at his friend. "How did you get on with Daisy at the event?"

"Great. She was a big help," answered Haydn nonchalantly.

"No doubt a few young men were casting envious glances at you," Scott smiled.

Haydn laughed nervously. "They couldn't have been jealous of some middle-aged divorcee."

"Seriously, you could do a lot worse than Daisy."

"Don't be daft. She's far too young for me. She wouldn't be interested. And anyway, I'm not sure I'm ready for a relationship."

"Only you know that. Still, never say never!"

Chapter Nine

"One hundred grand? Daylight robbery!"

Kane Weston pursed his thin lips in anger and clasped his hands in front of him on the sturdy oak desk in his study. He cracked his knuckles furiously and then pushed his wooden chair aside and marched to the window. He gazed out into the garden, but saw nothing. His eyes were clouded by a red mist. How could a two-bit Flash Harry like Johnny Smales have the cheek to demand £100,000 from Kane Weston for a downtown wine bar?

He stood there unseeing until the mist lifted and he could focus clearly again. Turning to face the room, he jabbed a finger towards Jim Lee, perched on his chair on the far side of the desk. "The greedy son of a bitch. Tell him where to stick it, Jim."

Lee was unperturbed. He was used to his boss's furious outbursts. He knew this fit of temper was not directed at him. He also knew that Kane was clever enough to see sense. "We'll get it for eighty. It's a fair price. You'll just have to make him an offer he can't refuse."

Weston narrowed his eyes and slid back into his seat. "Go on," he encouraged.

"Why does Johnny Smales want to sell the wine bar? Because he can't run a business to save his life and he's up to his ears in debt. He desperately needs the money. Make him an offer of £80,000 – and tell him he will still get ten per cent of all profits, for doing sod all. When he agrees, you can write in the small print that the arrangement lasts for twelve months.

He will have signed the contract before he notices. And anyway, he'll just be glad to get his hands on your money."

Kane considered Lee's idea. It was clever, much too clever for Smales. The wine bar, in a small town just south of Leeds, was exactly what Kane was looking for. The location was good, it wouldn't need much cash spending on it to smarten it up, and run properly it could make a lot of money. It just needed the right man in charge.

"How would you feel about managing the place, Jim?"

"It would be an honour."

"It'll be a challenge. It'll have to make good money, legitimate money."

"I know."

Kane observed his deputy. Lee was 46, of medium height and build and with craggy features. He was not a remarkable man to look at, but in his case looks were deceptive. There was nothing ordinary about Jim Lee. Like Kane, he was a Bradford lad, and had been brought up through the hard school of knocks. He was no pushover and nobody's fool. His mind was sharp and his fists were hard.

"All right, Jim. Contact Smales and tell him the deal. Let me know when it's done."

Lee nodded. He looked up and in his turn he examined the features of the man opposite. Weston returned his gaze and read the thoughts of his trusted lieutenant. He waited for Lee to put them into words.

"Does this mean we're going legit?"

It was a fair question. Lee was too smart not to realise that Kane was considering his options. He would no doubt have done the same in his position. His loyalty and reliability deserved an answer. But first Kane had a question of his own.

"Any news of the detective?"

Lee said nothing but slowly slid a folded newspaper across

the desk. Weston raised his eyes to meet those of his deputy, but they provided no clues to the answer. Lee remained poker-faced.

Kane now examined the paper. It was the local evening rag and it was open on the classified ads page. Kane saw that a particular advert had been circled in red felt tip pen. He began to read it and as he did so a smirk spread across his face, and then a chuckle gurgled in his throat, gaining in strength until raucous laughter emerged from it. He sat back and laughed and laughed, the feeling of triumphant joy taking him over. For a full two minutes he roared with laughter.

And then, as suddenly as it had begun, it stopped. Kane leaned forward and spoke quietly. "You've earned your answer, Jim, and I guess you know what it's going to be." His mind was now made up. "We're going legit."

Lee nodded, a smile now playing at the corners of his mouth.

Kane looked thoughtful for a moment. Then he said: "Bring Judd Ward to me. I have a job for him."

Lee rose to his feet and headed for the door. But Kane had one more instruction for him. "Send Keeley in on your way out."

The door closed behind Lee and Kane focused again on the newspaper advert, rereading it and savouring every word. "Stablehands needed for five star livery and competition yard, in idyllic location north of Leeds. Must be hardworking and love horses. Good rates of pay. Immediate start. Contact Haydn Daniel on ..." Kane had to break off before he could read the mobile number that followed. The excitement of seeing that hateful name again was just too much.

Daniel had been on his tail for years, from the moment Kane had left the Collins gang and set up on his own. He had been too smart for the detective, keeping his distance from the crimes he organised, like the old-style Mafia dons he so admired. But Daniel had been persistent and after much digging he decided he had enough evidence to charge Kane with conspiracy to rob.

Kane fought it, of course, and never expected to be found guilty. The robbers, bolstered by the promise of a big payout and Kane's permanent protection, swore blind they did not know him. But it was his QC – and he could afford the very best – who found a crucial loophole in the prosecution case, the failure to serve vital documentary evidence on the defence which meant it was impossible for Kane to have a fair trial. The look on Daniel's face when Kane walked free was one to treasure.

But it did not end there. The detective kept up his obsessive pursuit of his target. Perhaps Kane got over-confident. His most audacious enterprise, linking up with international drug smugglers from the Netherlands to import heroin through Manchester Airport for distribution throughout the north of England, was also his most dangerous one. There were too many links in the chain. It just needed one of the links to break to unravel the lot. When a courier, bringing part of the drugs haul across the M62 to be stored in a Bradford warehouse, was routinely stopped by police the game was up. This time cell site phone evidence, unearthed by Daniel and linking Kane to the Dutch mastermind, was damning. Even his lawyers could not find an escape route. The best they could do was limit Kane's involvement to one element of the conspiracy, rather than the whole of it. It meant he got a lesser jail sentence than the others. But Daniel had still cost him five years of his life, and for that Kane would never forgive him.

As he reflected on his enemy, the door to the study opened and Keeley flounced in. She was wearing figure-hugging T-shirt and jeans and her high heels clicked on the wooden floor.

She tried to drape herself around Kane, but he pushed her away. "Sit down," he ordered.

Keeley knew better than to protest and obediently took the seat that Lee had occupied a few minutes earlier. She cast a glance beneath her fluttering eyelashes at her husband, seeking a clue as to what might be wrong.

But Kane was in no mood to dally. "Now I'm back, things are going to have to change," he began.

Keeley wondered how any changes would affect her, but she said nothing.

Kane continued. "I have to decide who is loyal to me and who is important to me. You, of course, were both, Keeley."

She allowed herself a small sigh of relief. Perhaps things were going to carry on just as they had before. But her hopes were quickly dashed when Kane spoke again.

"I am sorry to say you are no longer loyal or important. You are a cheating whore and you will have to pay the price for that."

Keeley rose to her feet. "But Kane, you know that's not true."

He allowed her to desperately maintain her innocence, tears mixing with her mascara to carve black tracks down her cheeks, until the energy of her protestations subsided and she slumped back into the chair.

Then he calmly passed sentence on her.

"You will move yourself and your things by the end of tomorrow. I have bought an apartment for you on the outskirts of town. It's very smart with nice views of the canal. I have arranged transport."

He glanced coldly at his wife. Her eyes, now puffy and red, gazed at the floor. She did not speak. She had accepted her fate. There was nothing else to do.

"The flat is part of the divorce deal. You will have a weekly allowance, paid into your bank account. The rest is up to you. You will not contact me here. My lawyer will have the document ready for you to sign by next week."

Now Keeley looked up with anxious eyes. "What about the boys?" she asked.

"They will live here. Their grandmother will care for them. They will be taken to visit you twice a week. That can be arranged to suit, if you speak to Jim Lee. No doubt, a holiday can also be organised."

Keeley whimpered again before launching into one final plea. "Kane, please give me one last chance to be the wife you deserve." But she knew it was hopeless.

Kane eyed her with disdain. His heart was cold. "Nobody cheats on Kane Weston and gets away with it. Not even you, Keeley. Especially not you."

He turned away dismissively. "You better start packing."

There was a deferential tap on the study door and then it was opened and Jim Lee walked in. He was followed into the room by a tall, slim young man, dressed in narrow dark jeans, white T-shirt and black leather jacket. He was unshaven, had blue eyes and his short, blond hair was fluffed and curly on top. He was good-looking but more pretty than handsome, in a vaguely effeminate way, Kane thought. However, the gangster could see why his wife might find Judd Ward attractive.

Kane's eyes bore into him, but the young burglar avoided his gaze with such desperation that he might have been trying to evade being turned to stone, like the victims of the snake-haired Medusa of Greek mythology.

Kane could see that Ward's hands were trembling. It pleased him that he could instill such naked fear in the young man, merely by his presence and reputation. Ward was a promising gang member. He had been on the payroll for two years. He was only twenty-two but had demonstrated an ingenuity for breaking and entering and a willingness to learn about the more serious side of criminality – how to plan a robbery, how to threaten violence and how to make someone fear for their life. He was only starting out on the criminal path, but in many ways Kane recognised himself as a young man. Mind you, he would never have been stupid enough to bang the gang leader's wife.

Ward sat down at the table and minutely examined his long, thin fingers, looking for any blemish or speck of dirt that could distract him from the brooding malevolence in front of him.

"Look at me," Kane ordered. The young man's fear fought against it, but he was unable to resist the silent force of will that made him lift his head and meet the stern gaze. He wanted to look away but he could not. His eyes were held by those of the other man. He was in a trance, as though he was staring into the magical Mirror of Galadriel, the elvish queen from Lord of the Rings. Unblinking, Ward saw the gangster's thin lips move, exposing the brownish teeth.

"I should have your bollocks chopped off," Kane announced. "And then slit your throat with a rusty blade."

Judd shuffled in his seat. He wanted to turn and run, but he knew it would be no use. He said nothing and waited.

Kane gestured to Lee, who reached for a carved wooden box of hand-made cigars. He flipped open the lid and proffered the box to Weston. Kane took out a cigar and lit it with his favourite horse-head lighter. Then he pushed the box across the desk towards Ward. "Take one."

His hand still trembling, Ward burrowed clumsily inside eventually emerging with one of the long, thick smokes. He put it to his lips and leaned forward as Kane flicked on the lighter and held it up. The young man looked resignedly into the cold eyes and waited for the sudden movement that would switch the flame from the cigar to his face. But it did not happen. Weston flicked off the lighter, leaned back and regarded Ward, taking pleasure from the expression of relief which had inadvertently spread across his face to replace the look of terror.

"Well, Judd. Let's be grown men about all this. These things happen. It's hard to say no to Keeley, after all she is irresistable, isn't she?" Weston gave the young buck a thin, cruel smile.

"I didn't mean anything to happen, I couldn't stop it," Ward blurted.

"So you admit it? You shagged my wife?"

Judd blanched and this time avoided Weston's gaze. He stared determinedly at the ground.

"Answer."

Ward nodded his head furiously. "Yes, yes. I'm sorry, I'm so sorry."

Weston leaned forward again, his fingers drumming the surface of the desk. "You should be sorry. There is a heavy price to pay for such treachery, a painful one, a disfiguring one."

Ward felt sick to his stomach, the fear almost overwhelming him. But suddenly Kane chuckled.

"Look at me," he repeated. Ward raised his eyes, and Kane saw that they were again full of fear. Now he spoke slowly and clearly. He wanted the young man to totally understand him.

"I am going to suspend the inevitable sentence on you. I am going to give you a chance to redeem yourself. You are going to do a very special job for me. If you do it to my satisfaction, you might just keep your pretty face."

Weston tossed the newspaper, with the stablehand job advert face up, across the desk to Ward. "Read it."

Ward scanned the ad, quickly memorising the detail.

"You like horses, don't you?"

"Yes, I do."

"Good, because you're going to be working with them. Ring the number and make sure you get the job. Fail with that and your sentence will become immediately active.

"Once you're there, you are going to find out everything you can about Haydn Daniel, and I mean absolutely everything – where he lives, who he sees, what he eats, no detail will be too small. You won't arouse any suspicions and you will report every snippet back to me.

"There is no room for failure, you know the price of that."

"I won't fail, I won't. Thank you, Mr Weston."

"It's your lucky day, Judd. Now get out of my sight!"

The door closed behind the young burglar. Kane looked at Lee and screwed up his face. "Keep close tabs on the little shit, Jim. When this is all over, I'll personally rearrange his features. Now pour us a whisky. It's been a day for unpleasant business."

Chapter Ten

The last of the gleaming horseboxes trundled down the driveway, signalling the end of a successful residential camp at Wickham Court – the first one of the year. But for Haydn and his team its departure marked the start of a summer of hard work. Over the next six months it would be rare for a week to go by without them hosting some sort of equestrian event. And the high standards expected of them would have to be maintained throughout. The cross-country fences, the surfaces of the outdoor schools, and the accommodation, for horse and rider, would all have to be kept in tip-top condition. The facilities at Wickham did not come cheap and customers expected value for money.

The camp had been well attended. For four days thirty horses had been housed in the visitors stable block, adjoining the cross-country course and separated from the livery accommodation by a short drive down the track. Most of the riders, their family and friends, had slept in their smart and roomy wagons, but a handful had bedded down in the main wooden-built cabin where guests also took their showers and ate their meals.

Now both buildings had to be made perfect for the next group of equestrians.

It was early April but the abnormal heat from the afternoon sun had raised the temperature in the normally cool interior of the stable block. Haydn had stripped down to his T-shirt and jeans for the task ahead. It looked like being hot work. Daisy and two of the stable lasses, Jenny and Faye, had joined him, while new recruits Zoe and Brad were given the task of cleaning out the cabin. Haydn watched them march enthusiastically over to the building. They had proved to be keen and efficient since being set on two weeks ago. They were eager to learn and hungry for jobs to do. The only time he'd had a cross word was to reprimand Brad after he caught him on his mobile phone when he should have been mucking out. But that was on his second day and there had been no problems since. Haydn was confident he had chosen well when he took them on. He smiled to himself, knowing that a livery yard was only as good as the staff who worked there.

"Well, the sooner we start, the quicker we'll be finished," said Haydn, grabbing a barrow and a shavings fork.

He and the girls threw themselves into the clean up, clearing out the dirty beds in all thirty stables, putting down new shavings, emptying and refilling the horse's water containers, sweeping the aisles and replenishing the stocks of bedding and haylage in the storage area.

It was hard physical work but they enjoyed it, chatting together as they forked and swept, while Jenny occasionally burst into song. By teatime, everything was done and the stables and the cabin were spotless.

"Home time," said Haydn, and everyone crammed into the Mule for the two-minute drive back to the main yard.

"See you tomorrow," called Jenny, making a dash for the car park.

"We'll want to hear all about your hot date!" replied Faye.

All the livery horses had been brought into their stables for the night, so Haydn followed his usual routine and prepared to give Timmy a walk and a run in the fields. He collected the dog from a spare stable where he had been relaxing. Haydn had soon learned that greyhounds are remarkably lazy, and Timmy was more than happy to spend most of the day curled up in the barn, only stirring himself for his lunchtime and teatime walks when he would emerge and shake himself vigorously from side to side, the shavings which had covered his lean body cascading about him in a great cloud.

The hound excitedly jumped up at his master who grabbed him in a playful bear hug and then attached Timmy's lead to his collar. As he did so, he heard a voice behind him. "Can I join you?"

It was Daisy.

"We'd be delighted to have your company," smiled Haydn.

The three of them walked briskly to the nearest paddock, where Haydn let the dog off the lead. Immediately, Timmy began racing round in ever-widening loops, circling the couple as they strolled along. After a couple of minutes the dog stopped running and came walking up to join them.

"He's so funny. I thought he would run and run but he just doesn't," said Daisy.

"No, two or three minutes tearing around is all he seems to need, then he becomes comatose again! Greyhounds are really very easy to look after."

"And so sweet-natured. They do seem to be the perfect pets."

They walked across the meadow in silence, enjoying the scenery and the pleasant early evening sunshine, before making their way to the car park.

"Have you any plans for tonight?" asked Daisy.

"Just the usual. Home, a ready meal, a bottle of beer and maybe a Midsomer Murders on the telly."

"Sounds nice. But do you fancy a change?"

"Such as?"

"Well, how about a drink and a sandwich at my local? I'm not doing anything and it's a nice pub."

Haydn glanced at Daisy. It was an innocent enough

suggestion, but one she had not made before. Was there more to it? Her eyes gave nothing away. If it was innocent, all well and good. If not, how should he respond? He did not know. Still, what harm could there be in a quick drink and a bite to eat?

"That sounds nice, Daisy. I'll have to go home and feed the dog first, though."

"Okay. How about I see you there in an hour?"

The Townley Arms was a traditional country pub in the heart of the village where Daisy lived, a few minutes drive from Haydn's cottage and three miles from the equestrian centre. From the outside, with its white painted walls and black wood, the hostelry looked almost Elizabethan. It was, in fact, two hundred years old and inside it maintained its old oak beams, stone fireplaces and wooden alcoves. There were two large rooms, one either side of the main entrance, and a smaller games room, branching off from the tap room, with a pool table and darts board.

The pub was popular with villagers but also attracted customers from Leeds, as well as walkers and the odd tourist, with its real ales and home cooked meals.

As he pulled into the car park, Haydn reflected that it was just his sort of hostelry. He had been there once before, a few months ago with his detective pal Andy Watson, and was happy to be going back, even though he was unsure why he had been invited.

Haydn glanced at his reflection in the car mirror and was satisfied with the face staring back at him. He felt comfortably dressed in a white, open-neck shirt, with just the top button undone, a light riding jacket, black jeans and black shoes.

Steeling himself, he got out of the car, locked it, and strode into the lounge bar. He saw Daisy straight away and, despite an instruction to himself to stay calm, he felt a surge of excitement. She had changed into smart but casual clothes: a black V-necked cotton top beneath a light blue cardigan zipped three-quarters of the way up, tight blue jeans and sandals with little heels. She had let down her dark hair, which curled around her shoulders, and she had applied a touch of black mascara around her eyes. Haydn thought she looked very different to when she was at work, but even more attractive. She was perched on a bar stool and clutched a small glass of wine. Her hazel eyes shone as she saw Haydn approach.

"I hope I haven't kept you waiting," he apologised.

"I've just got here," she replied. "What are you having, it's my round."

He plumped for a half of Black Sheep ale. He could happily have downed a pint of the strong Yorkshire beer but he was driving.

"Let's get a table. Follow me," said Daisy.

She led them to a quiet alcove down one side of the room, slid into the long cushioned bench seat, ushering Haydn in beside her, and plonked down her drink.

Picking up the menu, she asked: "What shall we eat?"

Haydn would have been quite content to have feasted his eyes on her beauty. Instead, he strolled to the bar and ordered scampi and chips for himself and a jacket potato for Daisy. As he sat back down, Daisy raised her glass. "Here's to one of life's better days ... and to good company!"

He observed her as they clinked glasses. Her big, bright eyes looked thoughtful.

"Is there something on your mind?"

"You don't miss much, do you?" she replied. "Yes, I want to ask you something."

Haydn shuffled in his seat and tried not to let his thoughts get carried away. He must have inadvertently frowned, for she burst out: "Don't worry, it's not serious.

"I'm not working next Sunday and I have entered Des and I for a British Eventing competition. I wondered whether you might be able to come with me. It's at Northallerton, so it's not far. I understand if you are busy, but I couldn't think of anyone better to be my groom for the day."

Haydn did not know whether to feel relieved or disappointed at the question, but he was glad to offer his help. "It's my day of leisure and it would be a wonderful way to spend my time off," he answered.

"Oh! Thank you, Haydn, you're so kind," and she gave him a peck on the cheek. As she leaned over he was aware of her perfume, the same subtle scent he had noticed on her handkerchief after he fell off Paddy. He felt himself falling under her spell as he breathed in the smell of her and felt the closeness of her body next to him.

He was brought back down to earth by the arrival of their meals. As they ate, they chatted about their busy day and the happenings at the yard. When they had finished, Haydn replenished their drinks.

"Better make this the last one," said Daisy. "I don't drink much these days, I feel a bit light-headed."

She giggled. "We don't want you taking advantage of me, do we?"

Haydn laughed and said nothing. But he was thinking: "The more time I spend with Daisy, the more I want to take advantage of her!" Instantly, he put the thought out of his mind.

They talked and laughed together for another half-hour. Daisy drained her glass and pushed it across the table. "Time to go."

"How far is it to your apartment?"

"Just a hundred yards down the main street, round the

corner and I'm there," she replied.

"I'll escort you back."

Daisy smiled. "Chivalry lives on! You don't have to."

"I'd like to."

Dusk had fallen and dark shadows had begun to gather around the village. Outside it was now cool but pleasant. Daisy linked her arm through that of Haydn. "Just in case I have a wobble."

They strolled in contented silence and soon reached a modern, stone-built apartment block. The gardens around it were in darkness but a light shone in the main entrance.

"My flat is on the ground floor. This is as far as you go!" said Daisy. She turned to face Haydn. "Thank you for a lovely evening."

And then she placed her hands gently on his hips and drew him towards her. Her beautiful mouth moved towards his. Her lips parted as she prepared to kiss him for the first time.

Haydn longed to kiss her too. But as the moment arrived his strength failed him. Fear took over, fear of being hurt by another woman, and he pulled back. He saw momentary surprise in her eyes and then she quickly masked her disappointment.

"I'm sorry Haydn. It's me who's taking advantage. Too much wine, I guess. Please forget it happened."

"No, don't apologise, Daisy. I'm to blame, not you. I wanted to kiss you. I just couldn't do it."

"I understand. Your divorce must have been more painful than you have let on."

"Yes it was. I'm sorry I have spoiled your evening."

"You haven't. It was the best night out I've had in years. I'll see you tomorrow."

She squeezed his hand and disappeared inside. Haydn watched her go and cursed his stupidity. She was a lovely woman, she did not deserve to be rejected.

He walked back to the pub and wondered if he would ever kiss a woman again. Deep in thought, he was about to unlock his car when he realised the alarm was sounding. Then he noticed glass on the ground. Glancing up he saw that his rear nearside window was smashed.

"How the fuck has that happened?"

He turned off the alarm and climbed inside to check that there was no other damage and that nothing had been stolen. Being a former policeman he was particularly security conscious. He never left valuables in his car, though thieves could have targeted his radio and stereo system. But it was intact. Nothing was missing, there was just the shattered window. On the floor, behind the passenger seat, was a rock, clearly the missile used.

He swore in anger at the would-be thieves, who must have been disturbed. He could soon get the window fixed, but it was still a pain in the arse.

A wave of melancholy swept over him as he drove home. His wonderful evening had gone terribly wrong. Then a thought struck him, if the thieves had wanted the stereo, or to steal the car, why didn't they smash a front window to get in? It also didn't make sense that they would choose a car parked outside a busy pub. Maybe there was another reason for the damage.

His thoughts returned to Daisy. Perhaps she had a secret admirer, or an old boyfriend had seen them together and got jealous. Or maybe he was just being melodramatic.

Back home, he poured himself a large whisky and threw himself onto the settee.

He took a drink and smiled across at Timmy, lounging contentedly on the rug. "Oh well, tomorrow's another day."

Chapter Eleven

The next morning, Haydn took his car to the auto glass repair garage and had the window replaced. On the way back he called at The Townley Arms to speak to the manager and explain what had happened.

The pub boss was suitably shocked. "This sort of thing doesn't happen here. I can't remember a customer's car being attacked."

He said a couple of regulars having a smoke round the back had heard the car alarm. They had gone round to the front to have a look but there was nothing to be seen. He said there were CCTV cameras, but not covering that area of the car park.

"I'll check the tapes for you and let you know if they show anything, but it's unlikely. Leave me your phone number just in case."

There was nothing more for Haydn to do. He knew it was pointless reporting the damage to the police, they would not have the resources to bother with something so petty. He would just have to grin and bear the cost of the £100 bill.

He decided not to trouble Daisy with it. In the cold light of day he felt it probably had nothing to do with her. It was just one of those things, annoying and upsetting but not personal.

Back at Wickham Court Daisy was her usual self, friendly and professional, getting on with her job. She did not mention the previous night and he was glad. Perhaps friendly and professional was the way forward, he thought.

Later in the week he met Andy Watson. Andy was now his only link with the police. The pals got together every few weeks for a few pints and a chinwag. But they had not seen each other for three months, so there would be plenty to catch up on.

They arranged to meet at a large pub on the Leeds Ring Road. Haydn wanted to get off home ground after the car incident, but neither did he fancy going to their old police haunts in the city centre. He caught the bus so he could have a few drinks. He felt he needed them after a confusing and difficult week.

"How's it all going?" asked Andy as they got stuck into their first pint.

Haydn reflected for a moment before replying. "I can't say things couldn't be better, but I really can't complain."

He told his friend about the smashed window. Andy was typically robust about it. "These things happen. Villains get everywhere – even to pretty villages like yours. But it was probably some youth out of his tree."

He drained his pint and said: "Sup up. I'll get us another and then I'll tell you something you might be interested in."

When he returned he said: "Did you know that Kane Weston is out of prison?"

Haydn's body stiffened at the mention of the name. He took a swig of his pint and said: "I knew from you that he was due for release but I didn't know he had walked."

"Yeah, about two months ago. But get this – he's going straight."

"Never! He hasn't got a straight bone in his body."

"I know his probation officer and he tells me Weston is a model prisoner on licence. He is doing everything that is asked of him. We are keeping a close eye on him and there is not a whiff of any drug dealing. In fact, his whole crime operation seems to be winding down. And he has bought a wine bar south of Leeds, seems to be putting all his energy into that."

Haydn raised his eyebrows. "Maybe the worm has finally turned."

"It's early days yet," said Andy. "But all the signs are right."

"He's kicked Keeley out of the house, found out she'd been shagging one of the young gang members. He's disappeared from the scene."

Haydn whistled. "If he's any sense he will be on the other side of the world by now."

"Talking of shagging, is your love life looking up yet?"

"I can't say that it is."

"There's nobody on the scene, then?"

Haydn considered his answer. Andy was his best mate, he could confide in him. But he did not want to. He did not want to talk to anyone about Daisy right now. "Nobody," he replied.

Andy could see Haydn was not telling him something but he respected his privacy and let it pass. Instead he said: "Claire and Dave are living together."

Haydn pulled a face. "They are welcome to each other."

"Just thought you should know."

Sunday dawned bright and breezy. Haydn was up early to give Timmy a good walk before they had to leave for the yard. As he gulped down a mug of coffee at his pine kitchen table, he reflected on the day ahead. He was uncertain whether he was doing the right thing in going to the event with Daisy after what had happened between them. But the arrangement had been made before the would-be kiss. It had seemed the right thing to do at the time. Had anything really changed?

What was clear from their evening together was that Daisy had feelings towards him. Perhaps they were just physical and not a deeper attachment. Either way, it was scary. He had forgotten what it was like to be "fancied."

And what were his feelings towards her? He did not like to admit that he fancied her in return, but there was no getting round the fact that she was desirable, or that he desired her. And she was fun to be with, he was happy when she was around.

None of this took away the feeling of fear which overpowered everything else. He was afraid of rejection and worried that he would not be good enough, for Daisy or any woman. Stepping into a relationship seemed harder to him than setting foot on the moon.

But that did not mean he could not enjoy their outing, and be useful at the same time. He could not let Daisy down by backing out now. She needed a groom and he had promised to do the job, so he would.

He arrived at the yard at 8am and settled Timmy in Paddy's stable as usual. Daisy was already busy, loading her horse's tack into the wagon. Seeing Haydn, she smiled and called out: "Do you want a job?"

"That's why I'm here."

"Can you fill the big plastic tub with water and put it in the back of the wagon? Then I'd be grateful if you would give Des a good brush, he's spent the night laying on a poo pillow!"

"No problem."

While Haydn made sure the horse looked immaculate, Daisy loaded everything she needed for the one-day event. She would wear a smart white shirt, stock and pin and black jacket for the dressage and showjumping phases of the competition, and then change into her cross-country outfit. During the competition, she would have to swap Des's white dressage saddlecloth for the green one he wore for cross-country, which would mean taking off his saddle.

Shortly before nine o'clock they were ready to leave. Daisy led Des up the shallow ramp of the side-loading horsebox, span him round to face the back and deftly tied him up. They secured the doors, jumped into the cab and were off.

It was a 40-minute journey to Northallerton, mostly on main roads. Haydn felt relaxed as he chatted with Daisy about the competition and what his role would be.

"The important thing for me is that you look after Des when I'm not on him, and you give me a hand changing his tack for the cross-country," Daisy said. "The rest is up to me."

"Are you confident?" asked Haydn.

"If you mean confident of winning, then no. It's our first BE event for a year and I expect the opposition will be strong. But he's a damn good horse and I think he will go well."

"What will be the hardest part?"

"Des is an ex-racehorse, so I guess he finds the dressage the most difficult. But if we can get a decent score in that we'll be well placed for the jumping, which he likes the best. I just need plenty of time to warm him up for the dressage."

There were no hold ups en route and they arrived at the venue with more than an hour to spare.

"We'll get Des ready first, then you can walk him round while I get changed in the wagon," said Daisy.

When she emerged, Haydn caught his breath. He had never seen her dressed in her competition regalia and she looked stunning in her smart jacket, velvet riding hat, long black boots and tight-fitting white jodhpurs. He could not help but notice how they hugged her slim, toned legs and pert bottom, but he quickly focused on looking after the horse.

He held her stirrup as she lithely swung her leg over Des's back and gently settled herself in the saddle.

She smiled down at Haydn. "Wish me luck."

"You won't need it."

Soon Des was prancing elegantly around the dressage arena, his rider looking equally serene and smooth. As it was a

BE90 competition, there was a lot of cantering involved and many difficult movements and transitions to achieve. But the pair looked very good to Haydn. He knew they needed a low mark to be in the mix. A score of 31.5 meant Daisy was in eighth place out of the 24 competitors. They were in with a chance!

A lovely clear round in the showjumping lifted the pair to fifth place. But there was no time to celebrate.

"We've got the cross-country in twenty minutes, so it's a quick change for us both," said Daisy. "We'll do the horse first."

Des was soon wearing his green saddlecloth, along with jumping boots to protect his legs and a martingale added to his bridle, giving Daisy extra control. "I need it, he can get pretty strong out on the course." Then she was gone again, reappearing a couple of minutes later in a red and white cross-country shirt and a body protector.

Haydn was now getting worried. He knew this was the exciting part – but also the one with the most danger. Galloping at big, solid three-foot-high fences always had an element of risk. But he was reassured by Daisy's confidence.

"I can't wait to get going. Come on, Haydn. Give me a leg up!"

Daisy put one foot in the stirrup and offered the other foot to Haydn, who on the count of three whisked her up and on to the saddle. Des immediately marched off towards the start, clearly knowing the fun that was ahead. "See you at the finish," Daisy called back.

Haydn took up position on a little hillock between the start and finish lines, where he hoped to be able to see the pair go round most of the course. He was surprised to find his hands were trembling from nerves.

Daisy looked calm and determined as she cantered Des round the warm up area. Then her name was called and they walked purposefully into the start box as Haydn watched anxiously.

Suddenly they were off and cantering swiftly towards the first fence, a large and wide wooden barrel. Haydn heard the crackling commentary blaring around the course and was confused when the loudspeaker announced that Daisy Langridge was riding Secret Desire. Then he remembered that it was Des's competing name.

He watched the pair blaze a merry trail over the jumps until they disappeared behind a belt of trees on the far side of the course. It was bad enough for Haydn to watch Daisy tackling the big obstacles, fearing all the time that something would go wrong and they would have a horrible fall. It was far worse now he could not see them. He imagined Des tripping over a fence and launching Daisy head first into the ground.

He listened intently to the commentary and was relieved to hear that Secret Desire had "flown over the big table in great style."

Then it was announced that they were heading for home. Haydn suddenly spotted them steaming downhill towards him and let out a whoop of joy. Des leaped over a big log and splashed through the final water complex beyond it before surging through the finish. Haydn took a deep breath. They were back safe. Thank God!

He found himself running as fast as he could to greet them. He punched the air in a mix of delight and relief as Daisy pulled up her snorting steed. She wrapped her arms around the horse's neck before jumping off him. Haydn grabbed the reins and patted Des down the neck. Daisy crouched down, the palms of her hands resting on the grass, catching her breath after the exhilarating ride. She was tired but ecstatic.

She looked up at Haydn. "That was such a thrill. He was awesome."

"You were both awesome," he replied.

Wearily, she got to her feet. "We need to get his tack off, wash him off and walk him round," she said. Her only thought was to look after her horse.

Twenty minutes later Des was tied up in the wagon and, his breathing already back to normal, was munching on a haynet. Finally they could relax.

They sat together on the wagon ramp. Daisy had removed her body protector and hat and loosened her hair. Despite her exertions, she looked radiant. She glanced up at Haydn. "Thanks for all your support today. I wouldn't have blamed you for not coming after what happened, but I couldn't have done it without you. I'm glad you were here to see us in action."

Haydn reached down and squeezed her hand. "I'm glad too. Shall we go and see what colour rosette you have won?"

"I'll go. You stay here and keep an eye on Des."

The results had just come in. Daisy knew she had been placed, but in what position? She went into the officials tent to collect her prize and was handed a blue rosette – for second.

"Oh my God!" she said, clutching the ribbon to her. "I can't believe it."

She dashed back to the wagon, calling out to Haydn and waving the rosette: "Look what we've got!"

Her hair was awry and she was damp from her efforts on the cross-country course. Haydn thought she looked especially sexy.

She excitedly flung herself into his arms and clung to him, celebrating her success with him. "I can't believe it," she repeated.

Like the other evening, Haydn was only too aware of the smell of her and the proximity of her body. He could feel the swell of her breasts pressed against his chest. The sensation became overpowering, and to his alarm he felt a sudden stirring in his own body.

But just at that moment Daisy stepped back from him, her eyes shining with the excitement of her success, and he regained control. She leaned forward, kissed him on the forehead and said: "You're my lucky omen. You'll have to come with me every time I compete from now on."

She checked that Des was settled and, satisfied that he was, jumped into the cab.

"Come on, Haydn. Let's get going. I need a shower and a glass of Prosecco."

She reversed the wagon out and pointed it in the direction of Wickham Court.

Chapter Twelve

Judd Ward sat patiently in the reception room at Sicily House, Kane Weston's imposing fortress-style home. He glanced across at the grandfather clock in one corner. It told him the time was 11.20am. Judd had been waiting for twenty minutes. He had arrived promptly after he was summoned to the meeting with Weston. Jim Lee ushered him into the reception room, sat him down and left him. The minutes ticked by. Judd had amused himself by strolling round the room and trying to appreciate the lurid David Hockney paintings on the walls, but they left him cold.

After a while he took a seat and contemplated how the meeting with the gangster might go. It was the first time Judd had set foot in Weston's stronghold since his terrifying experience a month earlier when Kane had confronted him over the fling with his wife. He had left the house feeling thankful to have got out in one piece and knowing what he had to do to stay that way.

Judd had landed the stablehand job without any trouble, his genuine love of horses coming through clearly at his interview with Haydn Daniel.

His first impression of the former detective was of a decent, honest man, albeit somewhat serious, and Judd was surprised to find himself liking him.

He had used the false name Brad Smith and told Daniel he had worked previously at stables but had been out of a job for six months after suffering a shoulder injury. But Daniel was satisfied about his fitness when Judd demonstrated that he could carry hay bales across the yard. He started work at Wickham Court the next day and quickly fell into the yard's routine, enjoying being around the horses and the bevy of young female colleagues.

But he knew the real reason for him being there and set out from the word go to keep his eyes and ears open. He was soon picking up snippets of information from the stable girls' chit chat, as well as his own observations.

The grandfather clock chimed, announcing that it was now 11.30. Judd had expected to be kept waiting, as a test of his nerve, but he was surprised by how calm he felt. The prospect of another grilling from Weston did not instill the fear in him that he naturally felt on the last occasion. Perhaps his change in lifestyle had altered his own outlook.

The door to the study suddenly opened and Jim Lee appeared. Lee had noticed the change in the young man. Not only was he dressed differently – blue jeans tucked neatly into short riding boots, and a checked shirt beneath his designer riding jacket – but there was an air of self-confidence about him now. His hair was neater and he'd had the fluffy curls clipped off the top of his head. The young man seemed to have suddenly grown up.

Lee jerked his head toward the doorway and grunted: "Come through."

Judd rose to his feet and walked purposefully into the study.

Weston was sat behind the oak desk. He watched Ward stride in and sit opposite him. As before, he fixed the young man with a steely stare. But this time Ward returned his gaze, perhaps not as an equal but certainly without fear. Noting the look, Kane wondered if he had been right to delay Ward's punishment. He continued to look into the piercing blue eyes. At last, Ward dropped his gaze.

Kane got up, walked to the window and turned to face the room. Without preamble, he said: "Well, Judd. What have you learned so far?"

Ward looked at him. He saw a man in his prime. A man of power and menace. Kane Weston was thirty-six years old, six feet tall and muscular. His body rippled with muscle, aided by gym sessions and his use of steroids. But his face was thin, the cheeks slightly sunken, and the cruel thin lips and narrow slitty eyes made his head almost ghost-like on top of a super hero's trunk. Ward had no doubt that the man in front of him would do whatever it took to get what he wanted. Now he wanted information.

Judd took a deep breath and launched into a detailed account of the set up at Wickham Court and the role of Haydn Daniel. For ten minutes he spoke about where the horses were kept, how the equipment was maintained and what Daniel did when he was there.

Weston began to look bored and waved his arm to signal Judd's silence. "What about security?"

"It's good. There are CCTV cameras everywhere, an electronic gate at the entrance and the perimeter fences are electrified. It's a posh place."

Kane nodded. "So what can you tell me about Daniel. What's his security like?"

"He lives in a village ten minutes from the equestrian centre. His cottage is burglar alarmed and has a couple of cameras, but there's nothing special. It's tucked away."

Weston nodded again. He appeared to be pleased by Judd's information. Boosted by his approval, the young man continued: "He drives a silver Land Rover Freelander with a personalised plate, H8DN72. He keeps it on the drive in front of the house."

Kane glanced up, pleasantly surprised by the level of detail

Ward was providing. Masking his approval, he rolled his eyes and sighed: "Ah yes! The Land Rover that had its window smashed. Was that you, Judd?"

The young man perceptibly bristled with indignation, but he kept his answer calm and to the point.

"No, Mr Weston. But I saw it happen. I had tailed Haydn Daniel to the pub and was keeping watch. I was hiding behind a tree when this guy appeared. He just threw the stone through the window and ran off into the darkness."

"I see." Kane was well aware that Judd had not caused the damage to the car. Indeed, he knew perfectly well who had done it, for he had ordered them to do so. But he was taken aback by the depth of Ward's inquiries. The kid was trying. He still would not escape his punishment, but he was doing such a good job he had certainly bought himself more time. Weston decided to offer him some encouragement.

He took out his wallet, drew out £50 in notes and tossed it on the desk. "Have yourself a night out on me, Judd. You've done well, keep it up." He turned back to the window in a sign of dismissal.

Judd pocketed the money but hesitated before leaving. "There's one more thing, Mr Weston."

Kane swivelled round.

"He's getting close to the head girl at the yard. He went to the pub with her that night and then walked her home. She's called Daisy Langridge."

Weston watched the young man leave, then slid into the chair at his desk, reached for his pen and notepad and wrote Daisy's name on it.

Judd sat outside a supermarket in his VW Polo and counted out the £50 he had been given. It was a lot of money to him and he wondered briefly how he should spend it. His mind made up, he went inside and bought the most expensive bottle of champagne he could find. He got back in his car, took out his mobile phone and sent a text: "On my way round. Xx"

Fifteen minutes later he parked up outside a three-storey complex of swish waterside apartments. Clutching the bottle, he sprinted up the stairs to the top floor, walked down the corridor to the end flat and rang the bell.

The door was opened by Keeley Weston, who greeted Judd with a squeal of joy. She leaped into his arms and wrapped her legs tightly round his waist, urging: "Carry me over the threshold!"

He staggered with her into the living room where they fell in a giggling heap on the sofa, Judd still gripping the precious bottle of bubbly with his outstretched hand.

Keeley lifted her head and passionately kissed him on the lips. Finally noticing the champagne, she asked: "What are we celebrating?"

"Being together," he replied, leaping up and heading off to the kitchen for a corkscrew.

He filled two glasses and joined her on the sofa. She was reclined against the side with her back against the cushions, her long legs, exposed by the short white skirt she was wearing, drawn up under her chin. They linked arms and sipped the champagne.

This was his third visit to her flat. The first time he had been reluctant to go, fearing the consequences of Kane finding out that he was continuing the relationship with his wife. But she had begged him.

"I feel so alone. There's no-one I can talk to, no-one I can trust."

He had not been able to resist her allure. He stayed for three hours and they spent most of it in bed. A week later he spent the night there and had to drag himself exhausted off to the stables the next morning after hours of lovemaking.

Now she drained her glass and placed it on the floor next to the sofa. She pulled Judd to her and began to kiss him, probing his mouth with her tongue. At the same time she drew her legs apart and placed his hand between them.

The sex was frantic and prolonged but finally their passion was satisfied. Keeley lay naked, her sexual energy briefly spent. She watched contentedly as her slim young lover refilled their glasses. Then she said: "Have you seen my husband?"

Judd did not answer at once. She had not talked about Kane since he kicked her out of the marital home. He did not know if she was still in contact with him. And he was uncertain whether he could trust her. After all, she was Mrs Weston.

Seeing him hesitate she said firmly: "Judd, I never want to see him again. I hate him."

He looked at her and saw a woman who was telling the truth.

"Yes. I saw him this morning. He gave me some money. I used it for the champagne."

"Why did he give you money?"

Judd had not said anything about his secret assignment at the stables. He had simply said that Kane had given him another chance.

"I'm doing a special job for him. He seemed happy with how it was going so he gave me the money."

"What is the job you are doing?"

"I can't say."

A sudden chill ran through her. "Judd, whatever it is, be careful. You can't trust him. There is nothing he would not do."

"It's okay."

Her eyes pleaded with him. "I know him, better than anyone. He is dangerous. Do you think he has forgiven you for what we did, what we are doing? He never forgives. He never forgets. You're a marked man. We're all marked."

She began to weep. Judd was instantly at her side and took her into his arms. "Everything will be all right, I promise you," he said.

She cried for a full ten minutes, holding him close for protection. Finally her crying stopped. She wiped away the tears and gazed at him, hungry for him again. She kissed his mouth and then his neck. Slowly her lips made their way down his body.

Chapter Thirteen

It was the beginning of June. The past few weeks had been a blur as the team at Wickham Court hosted a series of events. There were five more horse camps, two dressage competitions and three one-day events.

Scott's organisational skills were put to the test, but they were up to the task and everything went well. The only hiccup was when a competitor had to be airlifted to hospital after fracturing his pelvis and ribs in a somersaulting fall on the cross-country course. But that was a normal hazard of equestrian competition and could not be blamed on the fences they had built.

Haydn had thrown himself into the livery side of the business, keeping the customers happy and the stables and fencing up to scratch. The new recruits, Zoe and Brad, had fitted in well and were already established as valuable members of the team.

Haydn had put his competing with Paddy on hold to concentrate on his work. But he was riding his horse regularly and still having lessons with Scott and Daisy. The bond between horse and rider grew stronger and Haydn knew there was no need to rush their competitive journey together.

His relationship with Daisy remained friendly, but no more than that. After the embarrassment of the rejected kiss, Haydn had taken a subtle step back. He had gone with Daisy to another British Eventing competition, where she finished sixth, and it had been an enjoyable day out. But there had been no hugging this time.

Nor had there been any more meets at the pub, or other time spent together outside work. Haydn knew Daisy was giving him space after he confessed to the pain of his divorce. He was grateful for it. He had felt suddenly overwhelmed at the speed at which they seemed to be heading into a relationship. His feelings toward her were unchanged but he was relieved they had put the brakes on the budding romance. He needed to be very sure before he committed himself, if indeed he ever could.

Haydn now had another personal matter to occupy his mind. His daughter, Emily, was coming to stay for the weekend and they needed to talk about her 21st birthday, which was only two months away.

He was deeply proud of Emily. She was halfway through a four-year Veterinary Nursing and Bioveterinary Science course at the University of Bristol and working hard for her degree. Her love of animals had driven her ambition to be a vet and she was dedicated to achieving her aim.

She enjoyed living away from home for the first time, sharing a large terraced house with three other female students, but did not let it interfere with her strong work ethic or detract from her goal. She was shocked when her father told her that he and her mother had split up. He did not tell her the reason why, believing it was Claire's responsibility to explain and not wishing to influence his children's judgment. But Emily was a strong and balanced woman and had seemed to deal well with her parents' marital breakdown. Nor did she take sides.

His son, William, who had always been close to his mother, had struggled more with the situation. He was studying history and politics at the University of Newcastle and it seemed he had thrown himself into the night life of the city. But, by all accounts, he was bearing up as well as could be expected.

Haydn planned eagerly for his daughter's visit. He had not seen her since last Christmas and was excited at the prospect of having her around for a couple of days. He picked her up from Leeds City railway station on Friday teatime.

Emily dropped her bags when she saw her father on the platform and hugged him happily.

They stepped apart and cast a critical eye over each other. Haydn was impressed. Emily looked fit and well, she had a healthy colour to her cheeks, her fair hair tumbled around her shoulders and her smart, casual clothes looked clean and tidy. She was happy that her dad looked much more relaxed than the last time she had seen him. The haunted look and stress lines had disappeared. He looked five years younger.

Grabbing her bags, he announced: "Come on, Em! Let's get back to the cottage. I thought we'd have a Chinese takeaway and a bottle of Prosecco to celebrate."

Later, as they tucked into sweet and sour chicken and beef in black bean sauce, Emily told her dad all about her course and excitedly explained how she would spend the third year of her degree on placement at a veterinary practice in the Bristol area.

"I'll be able to get properly hands on with the animals. I can't wait."

Haydn felt warmed by his daughter's happiness.

"At the end of June I will be heading out to Portugal to do the volunteering work I told you about at a horse sanctuary. That's really important. The work they do there for those poor animals is amazing."

"How long are you there for?"

"Six weeks. But I'll be back in plenty of time for my birthday. Do you want to talk about that?"

"Yes, of course."

Emily was aware this was not an easy subject for her dad.

There had been a big family party to mark her eighteenth birthday. This time, things were different.

"To be honest, Dad, it isn't such a big deal. I've so much else going on in my life, I thought I would keep it low key; perhaps a do with my friends in Bristol, and then maybe just a meal out with you and something separate with Mum. How does that sound?"

"As long as you're happy, it's fine. But a meal out together sounds lovely."

"There was a really good Italian restaurant down in Ilkley. I thought perhaps we could go there. It's traditional and cosy and the food was wonderful."

"Yes, I believe it's still open. Who do you think should go?"

"Well, maybe just us – and a couple of guests."

"Did you have anyone in mind?"

"Actually, there is somebody I would like you to meet."

"Go on."

Emily took a deep drink from her glass of Prosecco. "He's called Nathan."

"Okay. Tell me about him."

"He's on my course. He's a year older than me. He loves animals. Obviously he wants to be a vet. He's kind and caring and good fun. He's really nice."

"Good. And how long have you been seeing him?"

"Six months. But we're just taking things slowly. We're both young and we are focused on our course. We help each other out with the work."

Haydn smiled at his daughter. "You're clearly very happy. I'm pleased for you."

"Thanks Dad."

Emily paused. "So how about if he came to the meal?"

"I'd like to meet him. I think he should be part of the occasion."

Emily tried to look nonchalant before asking: "So what about you, Dad? Is there anyone you would like to bring?"

Haydn knew what she meant, and that the question was driven by her desire for him to be happy. But it was not a conversation he welcomed, so he dodged the query. "No, not really. I was wondering if Scott might come. We could ask him at the meal tomorrow."

"Yes, let's. Now what about another glass of Prosecco?"

Haydn had arranged for Scott to join them for a meal at the cottage the following evening. Haydn enjoyed cooking when he had the time to do it, and he had decided to serve up his speciality dish, chill con carne.

In the afternoon, father and daughter rode out together at Wickham Court. It was the first time they had done so. Emily had not ridden for three years but she had been a talented teenage horsewoman, having lessons with a Pony Club enthusiast who tried to nurture her talent. But then her studies had taken priority. In those days Haydn had not even sat on a horse and now he relished the opportunity to hack out with Emily.

Haydn let her take Paddy, while he borrowed Scott's horse, Lord Percy. They chatted happily as the horses walked along the tracks and paths around Wickham Court, before they marched on to the cross-country course.

They stopped to examine the fences.

"They're huge," gasped Emily. "You wouldn't catch me jumping them."

"Nor I," said Haydn. "But people leap them all the time in the competitions we host. There are some brave folk out there."

"What are your plans with Paddy?"

"We're still getting used to each other. But I hope we'll be doing one-day eventing in a year or two. We've started showjumping already. We came third on our debut. Daisy thinks we can go a long way."

Emily glanced across at her father. "Who's Daisy?"

"Oh, er, she's our head girl. She's been teaching me."

Haydn quickly looked away. "We better head back to the stables. Do you fancy a canter?"

As they clip-clopped back on to the yard, Emily noticed a young woman carrying two big haynets into Paddy's barn. As she dismounted, the woman emerged from a stable and smiled. "Hi! You must be Emily."

"Yes, that's right."

The woman held out her hand. "I'm Daisy. Pleased to meet you."

Emily smiled back. "Ah, Dad was telling me about you."

Daisy looked startled. "Really?"

"Yes, he said you had been very supportive with his riding. I'm glad he's around horses. He seems so much happier."

Daisy relaxed again. "Horses make the world seem a better place."

"I'm sure Dad's in a better place now."

Scott scooped up a last mouthful of food, pushed his empty plate to one side and stretched out contentedly in his seat. "Haydn, you make a mean chilli! What's for afters?"

Haydn laughed. "Glad you enjoyed it. I thought we'd have something healthy for pudding ... chocolate ice cream!"

"And another bottle of Prosecco to go with it," said Scott, leaping to his feet.

They settled in the cosy chairs in the living room, Timmy the greyhound curling around Scott's feet, hoping for – and getting – his ears tickled.

"How was your ride today?" Scott asked Emily.

"It was wonderful to get back on board after so long – and

lovely to ride out with Dad."

"Yes, he's turning into a good jockey. It's a shame he didn't start riding sooner. He could have been a superstar!"

"I'm getting a lot of help," said Haydn.

"But you're a willing pupil. Daisy agrees," Scott added.

"I met Daisy today," said Emily. "She looks like a proper horsewoman."

"She's a very talented rider, and a wonderful worker," said Scott.

"She seemed really nice, and she's really pretty too."

"I keep telling your dad that but he takes no notice," said Scott, with a grin.

"Now Scott..." Haydn protested.

"They went for a drink together, you know," said Scott, seeking Emily's support.

"It was just a friendly thing after work," said Haydn. "Anyway, I'm her boss. You can't get too close to your employees."

"Rubbish!" said Scott, pouring himself another generous glass. "Daisy is head girl. She's in a position of authority. Anyway, you're both grown ups, you're both single. What's to stop you? What do you think, Emily?"

She turned to her father: "I just want you to be happy."

Emily stood in the dark and stared thoughtfully out of the window in the spare bedroom of the cottage. Scott had headed back to Wickham Court in a taxi. She had kissed her father on the forehead and wished him goodnight before retiring to bed. She left him standing at the back door, waiting for Timmy as the dog had a wee in the garden.

Emily could see that her dad was happy and it was clear to her he had everything he wanted – except for one thing, a partner to share in all the good things he now had; his horse, his dog, and his pretty little cottage. She understood how hard it must be for him to move on from such a terribly painful end to his marriage. She refused to blame her mother – but she desperately wanted her dad to find that extra happiness. And if Daisy might be the one to provide that, then she would do all that she could to try and make it happen.

As she stood at the window, Emily saw Timmy patter into the kitchen and heard the door slam shut and then the bolts fall into place. She walked across the room and switched on the bedside lamp. She returned to the window to draw the curtains. But as she reached up to tug them closed, her eye was caught by a sudden movement in the garden, near to the apple trees. She peered into the gloom and then gasped in alarm. She could just make out a figure, lurking among the trees. It looked like a man, hooded and cloaked in dark clothing. For an instant she caught a glimpse of a pale face staring towards the house. Then the figure turned away and was gone.

Chapter Fourteen

The next morning, as they sat at the pine kitchen table eating boiled eggs and toast, Emily told her father what she had seen.

"It was really scary. What would anybody be doing in your garden? Has it happened before?"

"No, it hasn't, and I don't know why they would be there. Are you sure it was a person?"

"Positive. They looked to be up to no good."

"Well, I can't explain it. Don't worry, I'm sure it doesn't mean anything. But I'll keep an eye out."

They rode out together again during the day and then it was time for Emily to pack her bags and head back down south. Haydn dropped her at the railway station and they hugged.

"Keep in touch," said Haydn. "I'll see you in a couple of months. I'll book a table at the Italian restaurant."

"For four?"

"I guess so."

"Good. I hope you bring Daisy. Take care, Dad. See you soon."

Haydn watched her train pull out and disappear down the tracks. "They're all ganging up on me, taking it in turns to be matchmakers," he thought. "Perhaps they are right and I am wrong." He shrugged and slowly turned to go.

On Monday morning, Scott and Haydn had their usual weekly briefing. After discussing the horse camp due to start the next day and the arrival of a new livery customer, they fell into their normal leisurely chit-chat.

Then Haydn said: "Emily thought she saw a prowler in the garden after you left on Saturday night."

"And did she?"

"She said she did. I've no reason to doubt her."

"That's a bit odd in this neck of the woods. Do you think they were spying on her?"

"How would they know she was there? She'd only been here two nights."

"Unless you'd been followed."

"Who would want to follow us? That's for the big, bad cities, or detective novels."

"It's only a few weeks since your car window was smashed." Scott suddenly grinned. "Maybe you were too good at being a detective and someone's got a contract out on you!"

Scott was only joking. But Haydn looked thoughtful. He had forgotten about the damage to his car. This was the second strange thing to have happened to him in a short space of time. Perhaps someone was out to spoil his happiness. But why would they do that? Haydn brushed the thought aside. It made no sense.

He stood up. "Better get cracking. I need to go round the cross-country course and rebuild some of the fences after the weekend event."

"Have you got some help?"

"Yes, young Brad is going to give me a hand."

"How's he doing?"

"Really well. He's a hard worker and a quick learner. You can't ask for much more. He doesn't say a lot, but maybe I'll get to find out more about him if I'm working with him."

Haydn drove the Mule at full throttle down the track and steered it into the cross-country field. Beside him, Judd Ward stared excitedly at the big fences dotted around the course.

Haydn noticed his eager look and said: "Have you ever fancied riding round something like this, Brad?"

Judd had always loved horses. He had spent many happy hours as a teenager hanging round the gipsy cobs tethered in fields around the city estate where he was brought up. He had even jumped on the back of one of them and ridden round in a circle until it reared up and chucked him off. It hadn't put him off horses but he hadn't ridden since and the inclination to do so diminished when he got himself involved in criminal gangs. But now Kane Weston had given him the chance to be around them again, and he was loving it.

"If I could ride and I had a horse, I guess I might," Judd replied. "But I can't and I haven't, so that's that."

Haydn glanced at the young man, trying to work him out. He didn't give much away and that created the impression that he didn't have much to say for himself. But when he did speak he did so with meaning. Haydn felt there was more to Brad than at first sight.

"Scott would teach you to ride. He'd give you a big discount as you are a member of staff."

Judd looked wistful. "But I haven't got a horse."

Haydn felt a sudden urge to help. He was warming to the young man and he had a strange feeling that their destinies were somehow linked. He remembered how Scott had let him ride his horse when he did not have one of his own.

"If you really want to have lessons, you can ride Paddy," said Haydn. "He'd be the perfect horse for you, and he could do with the extra work."

Judd was shocked by the offer, but he had no hesitation in accepting it. What a wonderful opportunity this was for him. A lovely horse, a top teacher. Who would have thought Haydn Daniel would be the man to provide it for him.

Judd smiled to himself. And then another thought crossed his mind: "I can't wait to see Kane Weston's face when I tell him."

Judd's head was spinning. His latest meeting with Kane Weston had been going well. But then the gangster had asked: "When is Daisy Langridge next competing?"

The young man was instantly on the back foot. He did not know the answer. What's more, he knew the question was a loaded one. What lurked behind it?

Judd had succeeded so far in providing good information to Weston. What he then planned to do with it was not Judd's concern. What mattered was that he kept coming up with the goods. But this question troubled him, and not just because he did not have the right response.

It was no use trying to bullshit the criminal. Judd decided to gamble. "She is going to an event next month. Haydn Daniel will be going with her. But she has a couple of options, she hasn't decided which one yet."

Weston seemed convinced. Then he rapped his knuckles on the desk. "Find out where she is going and when," he ordered. "I need to know well in advance so I can plan a nice surprise for the happy couple."

Judd felt confused. His duty was to save his own skin by giving Weston what he wanted. But now he wondered about the consequences. Kane's "nice surprise" – whatever it might be – was hardly likely to be much fun for Haydn and Daisy.

For the first time, Judd questioned where his loyalty lay. Haydn had gone out of his way to be friendly and helpful towards him and had presented him with the chance to ride.

Scott had already given him two lessons on Paddy and Judd was pleased with how they had gone. Haydn could not have been more encouraging. As well as loaning him his horse, he had provided Judd with a spare riding hat and his body protector. Judd had worn a T-shirt, jeans and yard boots for his first lesson.

"They'll do for now," Haydn had said. "But if you keep on with this, we'll fix you up with a pair of proper riding boots and some breeches."

When he first got on Paddy, the young man asked Haydn to "stay close, just in case." It was a compromise between confidence and caution, as well as a reflection of the trust he had in the older man.

Daisy, too, had been supportive, advising Judd on his riding and guiding him in his new job. It was a new experience to have people show him concern and consideration. They did not deserve to be shafted.

But Judd realised he had no choice. It was his neck on the line. If he failed in the task Weston had set him, he knew only too well what the consequences would be.

Chapter Fifteen

Daisy reversed her smart little wagon out of its parking spot at Wickham Court and prepared to load Des.

It was a sunny Sunday morning in early July and the pair were going showjumping. The weather forecasters had predicted a hot day and the temperature was already climbing, but Daisy felt cool in her thin, short-sleeved showjumping shirt as she fetched her horse.

She was travelling alone to the event. With no dressage or cross-country involved, she could manage on her own and this time Haydn wouldn't be there to help.

"I've promised to hack out with Brad to help build his confidence," he said when Daisy mentioned it. "I can change the day, if you like."

But she had told him not to worry and promised to phone to let him know how they had got on.

Daisy could not help but feel disappointed. She had allowed things to cool between them when she realised how emotionally wounded Haydn was. She hoped that by giving him time he would be able to reciprocate her feelings towards him. But the weeks went by and he remained aloof. She was beginning to wonder if that would ever change.

Oddly, she thought, Haydn seemed more intent on devoting his spare time to helping young Brad. He had taken him under his wing, going out of his way to guide him with his riding and his work. It seemed silly, but Daisy was starting to feel envious.

Brad was a good worker and a pleasant lad, though Daisy felt there was something about him that did not quite add up. She could not put her finger on it, but she detected another layer to his character. The way he avoided eye contact or talking about himself suggested there was something in the background that he was keeping hidden.

She liked him nonetheless. He never shirked anything and seemed genuine about his love for the horses, which was everything in this job. He was a good-looking lad, though not her type at all. She preferred the older man with more rugged looks – like Haydn. Daisy needed no reminder of the pitfalls of going out with a younger man. She had experienced at first hand how fickle they could be and how easy they found it to cheat on their partners. Brad appeared to be no different. He had not disguised his physical interest in the young stable girls and Daisy suspected he had been dallying with Faye.

Daisy had even caught Judd casting hungry eyes towards herself. The thought had crossed her mind that she could use that to try and reignite the flame of Haydn's desire by making him jealous. But she quickly dismissed the idea. She could not partake in such cruel games, and anyway it might have the opposite effect and drive Haydn away forever.

She attached a rope to Des's head collar and walked him to the wagon. As she did so, Haydn appeared.

"Do you need a hand?" he asked.

"I'll be fine. But you could just check everything is fastened properly when I have got him on board."

"Of course."

Daisy was grateful for a second pair of eyes making sure that all was safe and secure for the journey. Haydn had already checked the wagon's tyres and oil and water levels for her.

"You're good to go," he said. "Have fun and bring some rosettes back with you."

She smiled. "We'll do our best."

Haydn watched the little wagon disappear down the drive and felt saddened that he wasn't going with Daisy. Deep in thought, he turned and went to find Brad.

Their ride out was pleasant. They hacked out at a leisurely walk, along lanes and woodland tracks and across a gentle stream, enjoying the wonderful scenery and the soothing rhythm of the horses. They rode in silence at first but then Haydn drew the young man into idle chit chat.

As they clip-clopped along, Haydn said: "You ride Paddy well. I like the way you relax with him, he seems very happy with you."

"He's a lovely horse, Mr Daniel."

"Look, Brad. I know I'm your boss, but please call me Haydn. There's no need to be formal. Okay?"

Judd nodded. "Okay."

Now the young man was more relaxed Haydn decided to see if he would open up about himself. "Where is it that you are living?"

"I've got a flat just off the Leeds Ring Road."

"Is it rented?"

"Yes."

"And do you live there on your own?"

"Yes."

"There's no girlfriend, then?"

"Nobody serious."

"I'm surprised you're not taking out one of the girls at the stables."

"I'm not sure it's a good thing to mix work with pleasure."

Haydn considered Brad's answer. It was something which had niggled him about getting involved with Daisy. Was it the right thing to do? Or was he using it as an excuse to hide from his fear of rejection. Scott had said it was not an issue, and Emily had seemed to agree. But here was Brad making the same argument.

Just then, Haydn's mobile phone whistled, indicating he had received a text message. Holding both reins with one hand, he used his free hand to fish out the phone from his pocket and clumsily prodded the keypad with one finger until he could see who the text was from.

His young companion leaned across eagerly to try and catch a glimpse. "Who is it from?" Brad asked.

Surprised at his interest, but not offended, Haydn replied: "It's from Daisy."

"What does she say?" came the instant response.

Haydn glanced across, struck by the anxious tone in Brad's voice, and saw that it was matched by the young man's expression.

"I'm sure it's nothing to worry about. Daisy will just be letting me know how they have done in the showjumping. Let's stop while I have a look."

They pulled up the horses on the woodland path and Haydn settled Lord Percy's reins on his neck so he could use both hands and ensure he did not drop the phone.

He did not understand why Brad seemed so concerned. Perhaps he had feelings for Daisy, though they probably would not extend beyond the purely physical. Still, the last thing he needed was a young rival.

Haydn opened Daisy's text message. It read: "Hi. Good day so far. Second in the 85 cms and third in the 95. Will finish while we're on top. See you back at the yard. x."

He smiled proudly at her success. Then he said: "It's as I thought. They have had a second and a third and are heading home."

Haydn could not fail to see the look of relief that briefly lit up Brad's face. "Hmmm," he thought. "Maybe it's time I sorted things out with Daisy. I might not lose her to Brad, but I could to somebody else."

He quickly tapped out a reply: "Proud of you both, well done. See you soon. Xx" He wondered if two kisses was one too many, but after a moment of consideration he sent the message, telling himself "faint heart never won fair lady."

Picking up the reins, he squeezed Lord Percy forward with his lower leg and turning to Brad said: "Let's get back."

Haydn was lifting the horse's saddle on to its rack in the tack room when his mobile phone rang. He finished putting the saddle in place before reaching for the phone, which continued to shrill insistently. He saw that it was Daisy calling.

He jabbed the green phone icon to answer but before he could speak, he heard Daisy's voice. It bore the high tone of panic and the quaver of upset. "Haydn, Haydn, you've got to help me, PLEASE," she implored.

Inside, Haydn was instantly in turmoil. What was wrong? Had Daisy had some sort of accident? Was she hurt?

But on the outside he remained calm, his many years of experience as a police officer kicking in. "Daisy," he said, quietly but firmly. "Take a deep breath and tell me what is wrong."

"Oh my God, Haydn, it's been awful. Please, come quick. Oh God!" Her voice was tremulous and she was clearly tearful. Haydn needed to calm her down quickly.

He said: "Daisy. I am going to come and help you. But I need to know where you are and what has happened. Can you tell me."

The measured delivery of his words seemed to sink in. He could hear Daisy taking gulps of air, trying to get control of herself. After a few seconds she spoke again, but this time her voice was calmer. "I am on the A61, north of Harrogate. I've crashed the wagon, Haydn. It's in a ditch. There was a tyre blowout."

Haydn took a deep breath. His heart was racing but he had to guide Daisy through the crisis. He could not understand why a tyre should have blown, he had checked them before she left. But there was one thing he needed to know more than anything.

"Are you injured?"

"No, I'm fine. Just in shock."

He thought: "Thank God!" Then another concern crowded into his spinning brain. "What about Des?" he asked.

"He's okay. We'll need to get the vet to check him over but I've had a look and I can't see any injuries on him. He panicked at first and was jumping about in the back of the wagon, but he's settled down now."

"All right, Daisy. The most important thing is that you are both unhurt. Anything else we can sort out. Is the vehicle safe where it is?"

"It's not ideal. It's half on and half off the road. But another horse wagon was passing. They stopped and have blocked us off with their hazard lights flashing. Someone has called the police.

"Haydn, we need to get Des off here and get him safely back home."

"I know. Try not to worry. Scott and I will come up in his wagon straight away. We'll be with you in half an hour. Now is there someone who can stay with you until then?"

"The people from the other horse wagon say they'll wait until I get sorted out. They are very kind. It's funny, the young lady beat us in the 85cms class."

They were silent for a moment, both of them physically and emotionally catching their breath. Then Daisy said simply:

"Don't be long."

Haydn tried to reassure her, before ending the call. He rushed out of the barn and headed to the office, hoping to find Scott there. As he dashed across the yard, he noticed Brad was hovering near to the entrance to the barn. The stablehand was still holding Paddy's saddle. A slightly guilty expression was on his face. Haydn got the impression he had been listening to his phone conversation. But he might just have been waiting to ask what to do with the horse's tack.

Haydn shouted across to him: "Put the saddle in the usual place. Can you make sure Paddy has got everything he needs? I have to fetch Daisy. She has had an accident."

Brad looked alarmed. "Is she …? How is she?"

Haydn felt a pang of unjustified anger. Why should it matter so much to Brad? It was he, Haydn, who really cared. But when he spoke it was to answer with gentle reassurance. "Don't worry, Brad. Daisy is not injured, and nor is her horse. Everything will be fine."

Brad turned and stumped into the barn with the saddle. It seemed to Haydn that the young man had a weight of worry on his shoulders. But that was not his concern. All that mattered was Daisy. He must get to her side. That was where he should be.

Scott turned on to the A61 and smoothly went through the gears into fifth and put his foot almost to the floor. With no horse on board, he was able to drive his large wagon faster than normal in a bid to reach Daisy as quickly as possible.

He had been horrified when Haydn burst into the office and told him about the incident. Without hesitation, he grabbed his keys and said: "Come on, let's go and get them."

The normally placid Haydn had been literally shaking with worry. Now he sat rigid and silent in the cab, staring at the road ahead, as Scott sped to the rescue. Before leaving Wickham Court, Scott had alerted a recovery company to head to the scene.

He glanced at Haydn's troubled face. "Soon be there, mate. Then we'll get everything sorted." Haydn nodded in reply.

Ten minutes later they came upon a queue of traffic, the tailback from Daisy's accident. For fifteen minutes they crawled along, until up ahead they could see blue flashing lights.

"This must be it. The police are obviously here, so they will have made the scene safe," said Scott.

Haydn peered ahead, desperately looking for the wagon and a glimpse of Daisy. Then he saw the horsebox. It was perched on the edge of the road, to the offside, on a diagonal slant. The cab appeared to have sunk down into a shallow ditch beyond the grass verge, and just in front of a bushy hedge. The back end of the horsebox was angled into the road. The vehicle appeared to be leaning slightly to the left. A police car was parked in front of it with its blue lights flashing, and another one was stationed just down the road on the other side. Two officers were alternately stopping or waving through the two lines of traffic. The people in the other horse wagon had driven away when the police arrived.

Haydn's eyes swept the scene like radar, seeking out Daisy. But she was not to be seen. As they approached, Scott switched on his hazard lights and wound down his window. At the head of the queue he brought the wagon to a stop and the nearest police officer walked up to the cab.

"We've come to take the horse off the wagon," Scott told him.

"Okay. Pull up over there behind it." The policeman waved his arm towards the back of Daisy's vehicle.

Now Haydn called out from the depths of the cab. "Where is the young lady? Is she all right?"

"She's okay now," replied the officer. "She's in the back, with the horse."

Scott expertly manoeuvered his great horsebox into position and switched off the engine. Almost before it had stopped, Haydn was out of the passenger door and jogging over to Daisy's wagon. The back door to the compact living area was open and through the gap, to his great delight, Haydn could see Daisy. She was standing with her back to him, in front of the horse partition. Des's head was resting over her shoulder and her arm was around his neck as she stroked him soothingly.

Haydn called her name and at once Daisy released her arm and turned to face him. "Oh Haydn, you're here!" she said, and her anxious face broke into a smile of relief and joy. She emerged from the back and they embraced, clinging to each other for much needed comfort and both refusing to let go.

At last they pulled apart and looked into each other's eyes.

"I knew you'd come," she said. "It just seemed to take forever."

"For me too," he replied. "But I should have been with you from the start."

"No."

"Are you sure you're not hurt?"

"Yes, I'm sure. It was just so frightening. The tyres blew and the wagon slewed across the road. We're so lucky there was nothing coming the other way at the time. We could have been dead. Instead, it just slid into the ditch."

"Thank God!" Haydn muttered, and clung to her again. Then he gently kissed her on the forehead and stepped back once more.

And now he reflected on her words. "Did you say tyres... more than one?"

"Yes, two on the nearside, one at the front and one at the back. They went off like a couple of explosions, one after the other. There was nothing I could do."

Haydn considered this. Tyres did blow out, but two at once? That was unusual. Had Daisy run over something, like nails?

"Did you see anything in the road before it happened?"

"No, but I wouldn't have done from the cab."

"I'll make sure the police do a proper search of the surface. They may find something that would explain it."

Scott now appeared and gave Daisy a hug. "The recovery people have just arrived," he said. "I've given them instructions to take the wagon to Jack Holford's place for him to look at. I'll pay for the recovery. I've had a look at it and, apart from the tyres and a few scrapes underneath on the nearside, the wagon seems to be undamaged."

He put his hand on Daisy's arm. "Come on, let's get you and your horse back home."

Haydn parked his Land Rover on the street outside Daisy's apartment block. "I'll see you to the door," he said.

He had persuaded Daisy to let him drive her home. At the yard she had been trembling with the after-shock of the accident and he was concerned that nothing else should go wrong. "I'll pick you up for work in the morning," he promised.

Now he put his arm around her shoulders as he escorted her to the front entrance. She rested her head against his arm as they walked.

As they reached the big glass doors, she fished out her fob to let herself into the building.

"Now look after yourself and try to relax," Haydn said.

Daisy smiled up at him. "Don't worry. A hot shower, a gin and tonic and an early night and I'll be as good as new."

He gazed into her eyes. They had lost their haunted look and now shone again. For the first time in hours he felt reassured.

"Thank you for everything you've done today, Haydn," she said, placing her hand on his arm. "I knew I could rely on you to ride to the rescue!"

It was time to go. Their eyes met again. They were both reflecting that this was where their relationship had stumbled on the rocks of Haydn's uncertainty all those weeks ago. Now, finally, both were ready. Suddenly she was in his arms. Then they were kissing, tenderly and yet with deep meaning.

After a few seconds, they separated. They did not speak. No words were needed.

Daisy reached up her hand and gently stroked Haydn's cheek. "Good night," she said, and turned to go.

Chapter Sixteen

Haydn was out of bed early the next morning. He had arranged to pick up Daisy at 7am. Soon after six o'clock, already showered and shaved, he was walking Timmy through the woods. As usual, it gave him time to think.

He had slept badly. The significance of his kiss with Daisy, which should have filled him with happy thoughts, had been eclipsed by his concerns about her crash. He lay awake until the early hours, trying to fathom out what had gone wrong. All the time a nagging fear disturbed his mind. Why had it happened? The tyres had looked perfectly normal when he checked them at the start of the day. It didn't add up that two of them should explode, unless she had driven over something in the road... or they had been sabotaged. That was the unnerving thought that refused to go away. But why should anyone deliberately vandalise Daisy's wagon? Did they not understand that they could have caused a fatal accident? And why her? There was no logic to it.

And yet, he found it impossible to dismiss the absurd idea. He could not ignore that this was the third incident that had affected him; first there was the smashed car window – another act of vandalism – then the prowler in the garden under cover of darkness. Now this. But this was far more serious. This time the woman he now knew he loved could have been killed. Were they just coincidences? Or was there something more? And if so, what?

He had found no answers and, at about 1am, he had

dropped off into a troubled sleep.

He woke to the pleasant memory of their kiss, and leaped out of bed to face the day with new resolve.

Striding through the woods, with his greyhound beside him, the birds chirruping above, and a pale, weak sun chasing away the dawn, he recalled their parting of the night before. Had it really happened? Of course it had, and in the light of the morning he felt confident it was the right thing to have done. The terrible doubts and anxieties that had dogged him for so long had been banished, like the dark of the night, by one simple act of affection. And more than that, he knew there was no going back. He accepted that she was the one for him, and understood too that he was the one for her.

That seemed to be confirmed half an hour later when she emerged from the flats. She dashed over to his waiting car, climbed in the passenger seat, flung her arms around his neck and kissed him full on the lips. "Good morning," she said.

"It certainly is," he replied, her presence warming his whole being.

She looked into his eyes, and holding his gaze, said simply: "No regrets?"

"None."

"We'll take things slowly. I don't want you to feel we are rushing anything. As long as we are agreed about where we are going."

"There's no doubt about that, Daisy. I felt like jelly when you called yesterday after the accident. I was so scared I was going to lose you. I knew then what I wanted."

She reached out and took his hand and they sat for a moment, quietly reflecting on how lucky they were to have found each other.

Then Haydn said: "You're right, though, about taking our time. We can enjoy being together, without getting ahead of ourselves."

"Yes, it might be more fun to let things unfold and see where the road to romance takes us!"

As if to demonstrate, she pulled him towards her and kissed him passionately. Then she shuffled back into her seat. "You better get driving. I've got work to do!"

They travelled the short journey in a cosy silence, each comfortable in the other's presence. As they waited for the electronic gates at Wickham Court to open, Daisy reached out and touched his hand. "I guess this is where we act professional," she said.

"I guess so. But people will soon find out. You can't keep secrets in the equestrian world."

He parked up, but paused before getting out of the car. "I'll ring Jack Holford later this morning and see what he has found."

"A few nails or screws embedded in the tyres, I should imagine," she replied.

"Let's hope it's no more than that."

It was Jack Holford who called Scott first. "I think you should have a look at the tyres, and perhaps the police ought to as well."

"We'll be right over."

Haydn was sat in the office with Scott when the call came in. He knew at once who was ringing, and why. "Let's go and inspect the damage," he said resignedly. "I'll let Daisy know, but there's no point her coming too. She might as well carry on working and I'll ring her from Jack's."

Jack Holford's vehicle repair yard was situated on a sprawling site close to a railway station in a small town about a fifteen minute drive away. He had run his business for thirty years and specialised in the repair and rebuilding of horseboxes. He had a reputation for being the best in the region and nearly everybody at the yard went to him when they had a wagon problem.

Jack was in his early fifties, short and squat, with wavy iron grey hair and rosy cheeks. He was a jolly soul with a permanent smile on his face. Today his smile was missing.

He shook his head at Haydn and Scott. "This doesn't look good, gentlemen. Come and see."

Jack led the two men to his main workshop. Daisy's wagon was cranked up on the big ramp. The nearside wheels were bare. Propped up against a wall were the two burst tyres. They each had great holes in them but enough of the structure remained for a thorough examination to be made.

Jack picked up one of the tyres and spun it round. Pointing, he said: "Look here. That's a cut."

They could see that down one side the tyre had been ripped in a straight line about four inches in length.

Jack said: "The other one is exactly the same. The cuts are precise. If she had run over something in the road the damage would have been more random. There is a clear pattern to this. It was no accident. The tyres have been slashed with a sharp instrument."

Haydn felt sick. It seemed obvious that someone had tried to injure, or even kill, Daisy, either deliberately or – to use legal terminology – being reckless as to whether life would be endangered.

He turned to Scott. "I don't understand."

"We have to inform the police," Scott replied. "This is serious."

"I know. Daisy will have to report it. But I'll also get hold of my detective pal and see what he can find out."

Jack said: "I'll keep the tyres in my workshop. Get the police to contact me when they want to examine them. I'll put new ones on the wagon and give it a good check over. I'll let Daisy know when it's ready."

"I doubt she'll be going anywhere until this is sorted out," said Haydn.

That afternoon the vet arrived at Wickham Court to see Des. After a thorough examination he gave the horse a clean bill of health. Daisy tried to be positive about the traumatic incident. Some idiot had slashed her tyres, for some inexplicable reason. But she and her horse were fine and her wagon would soon be fixed. Perhaps everything would soon be sorted.

When the vet had gone, she called the police non-emergency number. But she was soon feeling frustrated. After an interminable wait for someone to answer, during which a recorded voice persistently told her her call would be dealt with shortly, she at last got through to a rather brusque woman switchboard operator, who refused to transfer her to an officer. "I can take the details and they will be passed on and allocated to someone," she insisted.

After Daisy had explained what had happened, the woman told her: "An officer should be in touch with you in the next couple of days." And that was that.

It was three days before Daisy received a call on her mobile phone.

"Miss Langridge?" a man's voice said. "I am PC Adam Jones. I am in charge of your case. Could you come to Otley police station so I can take a statement from you?"

"Yes, of course," said Daisy. "I can come tomorrow."

"No, I'm off duty for the next three days. How about next Monday?"

"Can nobody else take the statement before then?"

"I am sorry. I am the officer in the case. Nobody else will be able to deal with it, I'm afraid. Can you make 2pm on Monday?"

"Yes, all right."

Daisy felt annoyed. She thought: "Someone tries to kill me and the police can't be bothered to see me about it."

She asked: "When will you take the tyres to examine them?"

"If you can provide me with the details of the garage, I will arrange for them to be collected as soon as possible."

Haydn went with Daisy to her appointment at the police station.

PC Adam Jones was a quietly-spoken officer in his early twenties. He was clean-shaven, with a fresh complexion, neat, dark hair and a firm handshake. He gave the impression of being correctly efficient.

PC Jones led Daisy to a small, bare interview room at the back of the old-fashioned building. Turning to Haydn, the constable said: "I am happy for you to sit in, if you wish. If there is anything useful you think you can add, I can take a note."

Haydn thought the young man's tone was slightly condescending, but he recognised the mentality of playing strictly by the rules which was drummed into police recruits these days. It wasn't personal, he was just doing his job. Haydn nodded and smiled and took a seat next to Daisy.

PC Jones sat opposite them, his notebook open and his pen poised. "First of all, we have managed to make a preliminary examination of the two tyres and the indications are that they were vandalised, so at this stage we are treating this as criminal damage."

"Who would do such a thing?" said Daisy.

"That's what we have to try to find out," the young officer replied. "I am going to ask you a few questions now, and then I'll take your statement. Okay?"

"Yes," said Daisy.

"Right, so can you just tell me about the accident?"

Daisy described how she had been driving back from the showjumping competition when the two tyres burst and the horsebox slid off the road into the ditch.

"We found no sharp objects in the road which could have caused this, or within the tyres," said the constable. "It seems clear they were damaged deliberately. Did you see anybody hanging around the wagon, either at the venue where you were competing, or at the yard where you keep the vehicle?"

Daisy said: "I was on my own at the event, so I was busy, and when I was riding my horse I wasn't near the wagon. But I didn't notice anything strange."

"So could anyone have tampered with the vehicle before you set off from your yard?"

Haydn interjected: "Nobody would ever have done anything like that at Wickham Court. And anyway, the tyres would have blown when Daisy was driving to the event, not on the way back from it. They must have been slashed at the competition."

"I agree that is the most likely explanation, but we can't rule anything out."

"I checked the tyres myself before Daisy set off, and they were fine. They could not have been damaged there."

PC Jones said: "I will make inquiries at the event venue to see if anyone witnessed anything suspicious, or saw someone they did not know. If there is anything to tell you, I will be in touch. I will take your statement now, Miss Langridge."

When the statement was signed, they left the police station and Haydn drove them back to Wickham Court.

That evening they went to the pub. They chose to go to Haydn's village local, the Kestrel.

As they sipped their drinks, Daisy said: "I can't believe the police aren't doing more to investigate who did this. And why are they only treating it as criminal damage, Haydn? I could have been killed."

"I know. It's all about resources, and evidence, Daisy. They haven't got enough staff to put the man hours into the investigation that you might expect. And I agree it deserves a more serious charge, putting your life at risk like that. But it's a question of proof. It's easy to prove the criminal damage – but much harder to prove that someone wanted to cause you harm."

He sat back and took her hand. "I know it's frustrating. I'm as desperate to find out who is responsible as you are. But it won't be easy."

"If the police haven't the manpower, or won't make the effort, then we'll never know who did it. That's scary," said Daisy.

She added: "PC Jones is nice enough but I have no confidence in him finding the culprit. What do we do now?"

Haydn sat deep in thought for a while. Then he said: "Maybe I should use my old detective skills on the case."

"Oh no, Haydn. I'm not having you put yourself at risk."

"I wouldn't be. Anyway, for now I'll just have a chat with my mate in CID, see what he can turn up."

He added: "I think it would be wise to keep our eyes and ears open and our wits about us for the moment."

Chapter Seventeen

Keeley Weston stretched out contentedly on the bed, her hand resting on Judd's shoulder and her tousled blonde head nestling into his chest. As usual, their sex had been passionate and energetic and now she basked in the warm glow of its aftermath.

Judd was silent, staring unblinking at the ceiling. She looked up into his eyes. His thoughts seemed far away.

"What's wrong?" she asked.

Judd stirred and gently stroked her face. "Nothing that need trouble you."

"It's something to do with Kane, isn't it?"

Judd might not be in love, but he cared deeply for Keeley, for her personality as well as her body. He recognised that she wasn't the most intelligent woman he had ever known, but he admired her simplicity, her directness and her devil-may-care attitude. She was also intuitive, in a way that only a gangster's moll could be. And so she always seemed to know what he was thinking, which was a little unnerving.

He sat up in bed. "Yes, it is, but I can't talk about it."

"You can talk to me, babe."

He hid his annoyance at her pet name for him. He might be ten years younger but he wasn't anyone's babe! "Talk is dangerous."

"No-one can hear us."

"You don't know that for sure. How do you know he hasn't bugged this place?"

Judd did not really believe that, but how could he be certain? Keeley herself had said her husband was dangerous. Daisy's 'accident' had proved it.

"You can't be too careful, Keeley. I don't want anything awful to happen to you. I can't protect you when you are here alone."

"I can look after myself," she said. Slipping off the bed, she added, with a giggle: "I'll show you."

She wiggled her way across the floor to the white, modern dressing table and opened a bottom drawer. She burrowed inside and pulled out a plain dark wooden box, around six inches long, four inches wide and three inches deep. Keeley returned to the bed and placed the box on it, in front of Judd. Handing him a small, golden key, she said: "Open it."

He unlocked it and slowly lifted the lid. For a moment he held his breath as he saw what the box contained. "Wow!" he said. "Is it real?"

"See what you think."

Judd reached inside and, using both hands, carefully removed a small revolver. He held it in front of him and studied it.

It was a lady's gun, small but perfectly formed. His knowledge of such weapons was limited but he had learned enough to guess that it was something like a .38 calibre revolver, probably made by Smith and Wesson. It was light to handle and had a deep, ebony black handle and a two-inch-long silver-grey barrel.

"Where the hell did you get this?" he demanded.

"From Kane. He gave it to me as a birthday present a couple of years ago. He said I could pretend to be Miss Fisher. I didn't know who she was but he said she was a woman detective on the telly. I thought it was pretty."

"Is it loaded?"

"No. But he gave me a single silver bullet to go with it. I keep it in a little jewellery box. So you see I am perfectly safe."

"But you wouldn't know how to use it, even if you needed to."

"Oh, it would be easy. All I'd have to do is point it and pull the trigger. Bang, you're dead!" She laughed.

But Judd looked serious. "You should keep it locked away and don't touch it. It could go off and kill you if you messed about with it."

"Don't worry, Judd. It's just something nice to look at. A bit like you!"

Kane Weston got to his feet, drank deeply from his flute of champagne and raised his glass. Addressing the small but select audience in front of him, he said: "Thank you all for coming and celebrating with me my latest business venture. I hope that it will put the town on the map."

He was where he wanted to be – standing at the centre of the stage at Kane's Wine Bar, with fifty invited guests before him all keen to listen to every word he had to say.

Weston had transformed the bar from a dingy and gloomy premises attracting too many alcoholics to a light and bright upmarket establishment which now drew quality customers from the smart suburbs of Leeds, successful business people with connections and pretty young girls who wanted to have connections.

He had persuaded Johnny Smales to sell for £70,000, telling him the building needed £10,000 spending on it, and threatening to tell the authorities about his tax evasion if he did not agree to the price. He had smartened the place up at a fraction of the cost, brought in existing gang members and their families to staff it, and was soon making a healthy profit. The business was legitimate, apart from his subtle sideline in prostitution. He convinced the young girl customers, teenage but legal, with stars in their eyes that their desire to be rich and famous would benefit from them sleeping with the well-to-do, older, married male clients. At the same time he persuaded those men that if they wanted some illicit sex, he could arrange it – at a price. All he then had to do was match up the couples, provide them with a key to the flat on the top floor of the building, and pocket his handsome arrangement fee.

Although the wine bar had been trading for a few months, tonight was the official opening. Some of those businessmen were present – knowing that to accept the invitation and to keep spending money there would ensure their guilty secrets stayed safe – along with a couple of local politicians who were under Weston's influence, and dignatories and business leaders who were able to see at first hand how Kane was transforming the local economy. A professional photographer, also loyal to Weston, was there to capture the occasion in its all glory for distribution with a glowing press release to the regional media.

Kane's speech was short and to the point. He could get his positive message across without boring everyone silly.

"I believe this is just the beginning of a success story for this town," he concluded. "And I intend to continue to lead the way in that success story."

He raised his glass again. "To success."

His toast was echoed from below and, without more ado, he strode off the stage and into the office, set back behind the bar. He was joined almost immediately by Jim Lee.

"Whisky, Jim?" Weston shoved a bottle of malt and a glass across the desk. Lee helped himself.

"That went well," Lee said. "It should get a good show in the local paper."

"Yes, it's a good PR exercise. But the point is, we wouldn't be in a position to get good publicity if you weren't doing such a bloody good job in running the place."

"That's what you pay me for."

"Well, you earn every penny."

Lee inclined his head in acceptance of the praise. Then he said: "Have you thought any more about expanding? Another bar?"

"Maybe in another six months, there's no rush. Anyway, I'd need to find someone as good as you to run it. Any suggestions?"

Lee shuffled in his seat, in an unusual show of nerves. "Yes, but I don't think you'll like my idea."

"Try me."

"Judd Ward."

Weston stared incredulously at his deputy. "Damn right I don't. Explain."

"I know how you feel about him and I understand why..." Lee began.

"Do you?" Weston growled menacingly.

Lee ignored the interruption. "But he is the future of our organisation. He has the right image – clean cut, bright, hard working – and he would fit in well with the direction we are going in. He has proved himself in the job you have given him. In fact, he has surprised you by just how well he has done, hasn't he? To get you the information he has without blowing his cover has been no mean feat."

Weston grunted. "Yeah, the kid's done all right. But he is still paying his debt. And I need him where he is."

"Yes, but for how much longer? Surely his job is done now, after the horsebox incident."

"I think the success of that tells you why he should stay where he is, Jim. That must have caused Daniel some real grief." Weston guffawed.

"But it nearly went badly wrong, Boss. If the girl had been

killed it could have ruined everything we are starting to achieve. After all, we are pretty much legitimate now."

"But not completely. Anyway, it wouldn't have come back to me."

"But is it worth the risk? Hasn't Daniel paid the penalty yet?"

"Daniel will never have paid his penalty. It's just a question of when I am satisfied – and I'm not yet."

Lee subsided into silence as Weston poured them another whisky. Then Kane sat back. "However, Jim. I have to accept there is sense in what you say, as always. I will have to draw a line under my revenge at some point, and transfer my malice elsewhere, as they say, wherever that may be. But the time is not now.

"And if Ward is to come back into the fold and take a more important role, he will have to stop shagging Keeley. He's still at it, the little bastard."

"I am sure he will see the wisdom of that."

"He's not off the hook yet, Jim. And nor is she. I think it's time she got the message that her behaviour is unacceptable. I want you to get our lawyer to write to her and inform her that she will not be allowed to see the boys unless she ends the affair with Ward, as it is not good for their emotional and moral well-being. That should put a stop to it.

"In the meantime I need to plan one last surprise for the detective."

Chapter Eighteen

July was drawing to a close. It was three weeks since Daisy's crash and a fortnight since she had made her statement to the police. She had heard nothing from PC Adam Jones. In truth, she had not really expected to. It seemed to her that her case was of little importance to him, or the local police generally. They had more to keep them occupied than some rich horsey woman with more money than sense, or so she suspected was their opinion.

Haydn tried to reassure her that the boys in blue would be taking it seriously, but she knew he had turned his back on his policing career because he was disillusioned with the service that was being provided to the public and she had no reason to think it was any different now.

They were in the Kestrel one evening when Haydn said: "I know you're frustrated with the police. I'm going to see my mate, Andy Watson, tomorrow. He might know something."

"I'm not sure it will do any good, Haydn," she replied. She reached for his hand and said: "Whatever information he may have, you are not going to act on it on your own. I forbid it."

Since their first kiss, on the evening of Daisy's accident, they had been out on a date half a dozen times. Mostly, they had gone for a drink at a pub or a wine bar. But they had also enjoyed a walk round a reservoir and been to the cinema, where they watched the new James Bond film. They regularly held hands, and kissed at the end of their romantic meets but they had gone no further physically. Both were content for their relationship to build steadily and they were just happy to spend time together.

However, it was clear to them both how much they already meant to each other, and Daisy was determined to prevent Haydn putting himself at risk.

"I'm not going to do anything stupid," he said. "I just want to find out who did this to you."

"And what then?"

"Inform the police, of course, and let them do their job."

Now they changed the subject. There was nothing to be gained from venting their frustrations on the police.

"I think I am going to enter Des for the one-day event we are hosting next week," Daisy said. "It's time he did some more competing."

At the height of a warm and relatively rain-free summer, Wickham Court was holding events every week. It was the busiest time of year for Scott and he was mostly to be observed as a human whirlwind, breezing between different areas of the equestrian centre as the competitions took place. He had little chance to stop and chat, but Haydn knew he would make time if it was needed.

Daisy sipped her half of lager and said: "Why don't you and Paddy have a go?"

"We're a bit short of practice. We have done hardly any jumping for months."

"It doesn't matter. I'll give you a jumping lesson, you'll soon get back into it. You could use the event to gain experience and have some fun. At least you'll know the course."

"You're right, Daisy. I've nothing to lose and it would take my mind off things. Perhaps we could have the lesson at the weekend?"

"Perfect."

"I need to think about Emily's birthday, too. It's only three weeks away now."

"Isn't she bringing a young man to stay?"

"Yes. She was very keen to introduce me to Nathan. She wanted us to go out to that nice Italian restaurant in Ilkley."

"I know the one."

"She said she would like you to come along to the meal."

"Me! Whatever for?"

"Well, Scott was a bit naughty, suggesting I should ask you out. Emily seemed to agree."

Daisy giggled. "They must have seen the writing on the wall!"

"More than I did, perhaps. Anyway, how about it? Will you join us?"

Daisy now looked serious. Was it too soon to turn up as Haydn's girlfriend at his daughter's 21st birthday celebrations? But then, Emily had encouraged it. Daisy decided. "I would love to."

Haydn put his arm round her. "That's fantastic. I better book it tomorrow. The restaurant is small and it gets very busy."

Haydn reserved a table the next day, before setting out to meet Andy Watson. As usual, they had a jovial time, swapping stories and jokes. But Haydn was disappointed that his friend had not turned up anything positive on Daisy's case.

"They're doing their best, Haydn. They are actually making an effort. PC Jones is a good young officer who wants to make a difference. But they haven't anything to go on. Nobody at the riding centre seems to have witnessed anything untoward and there is no CCTV. Daisy saw nothing. It's a blank canvas. They can only spend so long on a case that is going nowhere."

"I just don't understand why anyone would target Daisy," said Haydn.

"Maybe she wasn't targeted. Maybe it was just random vandalism."

"Yes, like my damaged car. It seems we have been unlucky."

Andy hesitated. Then he said: "There is another possibility. Perhaps someone is targeting you through Daisy. There must have been a few villains who were pissed off that you locked them up. Or maybe it's a jealous rival from the horsey set!"

"It's possible someone has got it in for me, I suppose. But I really don't imagine any of my old criminal adversaries would be bothered to try and exact some kind of petty revenge. They'll be more intent on evading my replacement."

"I'll keep my nose to the ground for you, Haydn. But I guess you're right. That sort of thing doesn't happen in the real world."

"Well, you know where I am if you pick up on anything."

Haydn's jumping lesson with Daisy went well, and under her tuition he and Paddy were soon showing signs that the old team was back. Haydn was determined to follow Daisy's advice and enjoy the event. He had no expectations about getting a rosette. He had had little time to practice the dressage test and their showjumping was bound to be a bit rusty. This was simply about taking part.

Haydn felt relaxed as he brushed Paddy on the morning of the competition. It had rained heavily overnight, but now the sun shone from a cloudless sky and his whole being was warmed by the occasion.

With Haydn and Daisy both competing, Scott had recruited a small army of volunteers to help with the running of the event. Marshals in fluorescent jackets guided competitors in their smart horseboxes down the drive to the large wagon park. A paramedic car arrived, followed soon after by a local vet.

Daisy joined Haydn in the stable to check on Paddy's

mane, which she had plaited the previous evening.

"His plaits are pretty much intact," she said. "He's a good boy. Some horses make such a mess of them in the night you have to do them all over again in the morning. How are you feeling?"

"Great. I'm really looking forward to it. My only problem is tying my stock."

"Don't worry, I'll do it."

Daisy took the white cravate and expertly fastened it round Haydn's neck, attached the silver fox head stock pin to it, then stepped back to examine her work. "You'll do," she said. "Now don't get over ambitious. Look after yourselves."

"We will. I'll see you later – when you have won your class!"

With a wave and a smile Daisy was gone, to get her own horse ready.

Haydn had entered the smallest class, which was still a decent height for him at 70 centimetres, while Daisy was tackling the more challenging 90 centimetres.

As he checked the tightness of the girth on Paddy's saddle, Haydn heard his name called and turned to see Scott peering round the stable door.

"Can't stop, I've lots to do," Scott said. "Just wanted to wish you good luck. There's twenty-four in your class and rosettes to tenth, so you've every chance."

"We'll see. It's just nice to be competing again."

Haydn mounted his horse and rode off to the warm up area. It was dressage first and Haydn's big concern was that he would get the test wrong and be disqualified. But his memory did not let him down and they reached the end of the test without a hiccup. Their performance had been pleasant on the eye, if not outstanding, and they were lying in twelfth place after the dressage phase.

It was showjumping next, and here their lack of practice

showed as they had three fences down, putting them right out of contention.

But Haydn was not concerned and vowed to have fun in the cross-country, the third and final part of the competition.

He cantered Paddy round, warming him up for the task ahead, and then pulled up and gazed across the course. Although he knew the fences inside out – after all he had helped to build many of them – he had jumped few of them. Now, as he prepared to set out on his round, they began to look daunting. For a moment he felt troubled and wondered if he was doing the right thing.

Suddenly, he noticed Daisy riding towards him on Des. She trotted up until they were separated only by the taped fence around the warm up arena.

She looked anxiously at him. "Are you feeling all right?"

"A little nervous, but I'm okay."

"Take a few deep breaths and keep relaxed," she advised. "Believe in yourself and your horse and you'll be fine. I've got my dressage in ten minutes. You'll be back safe by the time I've finished that."

A couple of minutes later Haydn was called to the start box. This was a new experience for him and his horse, to wait inside a small grassed area, enclosed on three sides by a wooden fence, until the starter pressed the stopwatch and allowed them to go. The commentator's voice resonated from the loudspeakers on the course. Haydn could feel Paddy was on edge, the atmosphere of the occasion starting to get to him. The horse pawed the ground and shook his head in excited anticipation.

And then the starter counted them down: "Three, two, one, go! Good luck!"

Haydn let Paddy go and the horse immediately sprang forward and started galloping towards the first fence, a solid-looking log. Haydn's control of his steed was limited but he put his faith in Paddy. The horse saw a good stride to the obstacle and took off, soaring over it in fine style.

He continued to gallop along, but Haydn was beginning to relax and be more in charge of the partnership. By the time they had jumped the third fence he had brought Paddy back to a fast canter and the pair were thoroughly enjoying themselves.

The next fence was one which had caused Haydn some anxiety when he walked the cross-country course the previous day, to examine the ground and work out the route he intended to take between the jumps. It was a substantial, gnarled log, very solid and very wide. It was an inviting fence to jump, but the sort of obstacle that could look scary, to both horse and rider, and he and Paddy had never jumped it before. Haydn had decided to let Paddy run at it and trust him to see a good stride.

As they approached the log, Haydn felt Paddy's body tighten as a wave of uncertainty swept through him. The horse did not like the look of it. Haydn realised he would have to take charge. He tightened his hold on the reins and gave Paddy a kick in the belly, urging him to take on the fence. But at the moment of take off Paddy lost his nerve and tried to pull out. Haydn kicked again and their momentum took them into the bottom of the big fence. Paddy bravely tried to get his front legs up to leap the log, but he was too close to it. He clipped the top of it and keeled over to one side, like a sinking ship, all four legs off the ground. For one terrifying moment, Haydn thought Paddy was going to somersault completely over, putting him at risk of the horse falling on top of him, but somehow Paddy managed to keep himself on an even keel.

But the horse could not prevent the inevitable fall. He crashed sideways to the ground, hurling Haydn out of the saddle, their landing mercifully cushioned on a surface softened by the soaking from the overnight rain.

Haydn lay momentarily stunned. Then his brain came alive

and he began to think about the danger he might be in. He was sprawled on his back. He had been thrown just clear of Paddy, above the horse's head and back and with his legs pointing towards him. Paddy was laid on his side and Haydn felt sick with worry that his beloved horse might be badly injured. But then Paddy began to struggle to his feet and Haydn had an overwhelming feeling of relief.

It was quickly replaced by a sense of alarm. As Paddy stood up, Haydn found himself being dragged towards him across the ground. He put his hands down to stop himself but he could not arrest the momentum and suddenly found himself dangling upside down from the horse, with his right leg in the air and his head and shoulders on the grass. He tried to yank his leg back but it did not move. Looking up, Haydn realised to his horror that his right ankle was wedged firmly in the stirrup iron. He tugged again but the grip on his leg was vice-like. There was no escape.

Paddy snorted and shook his head, clearing it from the fall. And then he took two paces forward. Haydn found himself being pulled along. He started to panic. "Paddy, stop, stop!" At any moment the horse could gallop off, dragging Haydn with him across the ground and causing him terrible pain and injury, and he was powerless to stop it.

He frantically shouted for help as Paddy began to trot, but suddenly the horse came to a stop. Haydn heard a man's soothing voice: "Steady Paddy, it's all right."

Haydn twisted his head round and saw Brad. He was stood at Paddy's head, clasping the reins with one hand and stroking the horse's neck with the other while speaking quietly and reassuringly to him. Paddy already seemed calmer.

"Thank God you're there, Brad," Haydn gasped.

"Don't worry Mr Daniel. Everything will be all right now. I'll have you free in a moment."

Brad continued to soothe Paddy. Then he put his arm through the reins, keeping control of the horse, while at the same time he used both hands to unbuckle the stirrup leather, letting it drop to the ground, and with it Haydn's leg. He was free.

Now Scott came running up and took hold of Paddy. Haydn sat up in bewilderment, his emotions running riot. He knew he'd had a narrow escape and he had Brad to thank for sparing him serious injury, and perhaps worse.

"I'll take Paddy to be checked by the vet, but he looks none the worse," said Scott. "Are you all right, can you walk?"

Sitting on the ground, Haydn could now get the leverage to haul the stirrup off his foot. He stood up. "Yes, I think so. I'm just shaken up. It was a near thing."

"Yes. It's a good job for you that Brad was on hand."

Haydn turned to the young man. "I thought I was in trouble there. You could have saved my life."

Brad looked slightly embarrassed. "I just did what I had to do. I'm glad I did."

He turned away and began to walk back to the yard. Haydn watched him go. It seemed he had been right about their destinies being linked. Brad had been there when he needed him most. Deep in thought, he set off after him.

Chapter Nineteen

Haydn steered his Land Rover into a space at the Leeds railway station car park and switched off the engine. He checked his watch. It told him the time was just after six o'clock in the evening. Emily's train was due to arrive in less than half an hour.

He turned to Daisy, in the passenger seat. "We're in good time. Shall we get a coffee?"

Daisy nodded, squeezed Haydn's hand and kissed him on the cheek. She knew how nervous he was. Not only was he meeting his daughter's boyfriend for the first time, but – even more worrying for him – he was bringing along the first woman in his life since her mother. He was desperate that nothing went wrong.

Daisy was anxious to get the right balance between respect for the father and daughter relationship and her right to be Haydn's girlfriend. After her initial acceptance of his invitation to join the birthday party, Daisy had begun to have doubts about her decision to go. When she tentatively mentioned it to Haydn she saw a brief look of hurt in his eyes, telling her how important this was to him and strengthening her resolve to go ahead with it. She understood what a huge step it was for Haydn to make, and when he told her he would be picking up Emily and Nathan from the station, she insisted on going with her.

Haydn was comforted by Daisy's presence. He felt that if she was by his side, all would go well. Now he strode confidently on to the platform to greet his daughter, hand in hand with the woman he loved.

As the train pulled in, Daisy released her grip and stuffed her hands in the pockets of her fleece top. She did not want to overshadow Emily, so had decided to be casually smart in jeans, a black T-shirt with a gold horse embroidered on the front, and the fleece. Her hair was tied back in a ponytail.

Haydn spotted Emily straight away as she emerged from the train. He waved and she returned the wave enthusiastically. He waited, Daisy at his side, as Emily walked briskly towards him. In her right hand she clutched a smart, canvas Joules bag, decorated with colourful designs of horses and equestrian equipment. Her left hand was held firmly by that of a tall, slim young man, with a thin beard and moustache, a mop of wavy, brown hair, and small, John Lennon-style spectacles.

Emily rushed into Haydn's arms and clung to her father for a few seconds. Then she said: "Dad, this is Nathan."

The young man proffered his right hand, together with a warm and genuine smile. "Pleased to meet you, Mr Daniel."

His handshake was firm and Haydn instantly felt comfortable with him. He said: "Please, call me Haydn."

Nathan nodded and smiled again before releasing Haydn's hand and stepping back.

Daisy had been standing unobtrusively to one side. Now Emily came to her with her arms outstretched. "Hello, Daisy," she said and, without hesitation, hugged her. "It's good to see you again."

Daisy shook Nathan's hand and the four then walked together to Haydn's car, as natural as any happy family who had known each other for years. Haydn was delighted. The first meeting, which had loomed so scarily in his mind, could not have gone better.

They called for a quick drink at the Townley Arms, before

dropping off Daisy at her flat, and it reinforced the bond that had already formed between them.

When they reached Haydn's cottage he carried their bags through to the spare bedroom. Here he faced another challenge. For the first time Emily would be sharing her bed, under Haydn's roof, with another man. His little girl had suddenly grown up. He told himself she would be twenty-one in a few days, but it still felt awkward.

Emily was not blind to her dad's uncertainty, however hard he tried to hide it. "Nathan can sleep on the settee in the living room, if that's easier," she said tactfully.

It was a thoughtful offer, but Haydn knew it would be ungracious to accept it. "There's no need. You'll both be more comfortable in here. I'll make us all a hot drink while you unpack."

As he stirred the boiling milk into the mugs of hot chocolate, Haydn recalled how embarrassed he had felt as an innocent teenager when he first brought Claire home to meet his parents. The courting couple were only at the kiss and cuddle stage but he had felt sick with fear. But his mum and dad had welcomed Claire and put them both at ease. Thirty years on, he was determined to replicate his parents.

In truth, he was more worried about how Emily would deal with his affair with Daisy. But she had literally welcomed her with open arms and the two women seemed to like and respect each other. The meal tomorrow night would tell him a lot about the future for all of them, but there seemed every reason to be positive.

The next day passed peacefully. Emily and Nathan took themselves off for a trip to the Yorkshire Dales, after tucking in to Haydn's full English breakfast. They had all slept soundly, though it had taken Haydn a little while to drop off. His head was full of anxious thoughts but the house was silent, except for the deep ticking of the grandfather clock in the living room, and he eventually drifted off to sleep and had pleasant dreams about running, barefoot and hand in hand with Daisy, through an endless cornfield.

It was a normal working Saturday for Daisy, while Haydn spent several hours preparing the cross-country course for the next horse camp, which would start on Monday. In the afternoon he drove to Ilkley and collected Emily's birthday cake from a specialist shop which baked and decorated them. He drove to the Italian restaurant to deliver the cake, so it could be kept cool and ready to be presented during the evening. Satisfied that all was in order, he drove back to Wickham Court and sought out Daisy.

He found her in a barn, hanging up haynets for the horses at the end of her shift. It was a warm, dry day and she was wearing a T-shirt and shorts. Haydn halted in the entrance and gazed in admiration at her slim figure as she stretched up to tie a knot in the final net.

She sensed his presence and turned towards him. "I hope you're not ogling me!" she said, in mock anger.

"No, no! I was just watching you work," he said, unable to repress a blush.

"I don't believe you. Come here!" she said, gripping the open neck of his shirt and pulling him to her. "In future, don't just stand there." And she kissed him on the lips.

Then she said: "Tell me about tonight. How will we all get to the restaurant?"

"I've been thinking about that and I've decided to drive us. It will make it easy and I don't want to be drinking. I want to appreciate her birthday properly, not have some vague recollection of it because I had too much to drink."

"Okay. So will you pick me up from the flat?"

"Yes. Shall we say seven o'clock? The table is booked for eight. I'll drop you home afterwards."

"Right. I better get off and start titivating!"

She kissed him again and headed for her car.

Haydn stared critically in the bedroom mirror and smoothed down with his hands his short-cropped fair hair. Odd flecks of grey were starting to appear, but Haydn hoped they merely gave him a more distinguished look.

He glanced at the clock. It was 6.45. Time to go. He had decided to wear smart charcoal grey trousers with a white, open-neck shirt, a light tweed jacket and black shoes.

He walked into the living room where he found Nathan sat in a cosy chair. He was stroking Timmy, who was curled happily round his feet. The greyhound looked up expectantly at Haydn, with one ear pricked and the other half-cocked in the unusual style of the breed.

"Quiet night for you, Timmy," said Haydn. "We'll be back later."

Turning to Nathan, he said: "How is Emily doing?"

"About ready. In fact, here she is now."

Emily appeared. "How do I look?" she asked anxiously.

She was wearing a cream blouse, with matching jacket, a black skirt which was above the knee but not outrageously so, and high heels. She had put on a little make up, but only enough to make her look natural, and was holding a small, black clutch bag.

"Perfect," said Haydn, and meant it.

It was two minutes past seven when they parked up outside Daisy's flat. She was waiting in the doorway to the building and immediately stepped forward to the car and got in to the front passenger seat. She was wearing a knee-length, deep rose red dress with short sleeves and a V-neck top giving the slightest hint of cleavage, and strappy black shoes. Her legs were bare. A thrill of excitement swept over Haydn as he took in her beauty.

Emily took the words out of his mouth. "You look stunning, Daisy."

"And you look gorgeous, Emily."

The passengers chattered excitedly as Haydn drove them to the restaurant.

"Your birthday is actually on Monday, isn't it?" Daisy asked Emily.

"Yes it is. I can't believe I'll be twenty-one. It only seems five minutes since I had my eighteenth birthday party. That was a good do."

"So what will you be doing on the big day?"

"Nathan and I are travelling to Edinburgh. We've booked in for a couple of nights at a nice hotel. It's our first time away. Then we have to get back to Bristol and start preparing for a big year ahead."

"Yes, it's hard work qualifying to be a vet, but worth it. It's a wonderful career."

Now they were in Ilkley and soon they were being shown to their table. The restaurant was very traditional, run by an Italian couple originally from Florence. The wooden tables were covered by red and white checked tablecloths, black and white family photos adorned the walls and the menus were chalked on blackboards.

The owner came to each table with his board and explained, with typical Latin animation, what ingredients were in each meal and how they were cooked.

They were spoiled for choice but soon they were tucking in to perfectly cooked Italian cuisine, accompanied by wine. By the time they were scraping up the last morsels of the cake and ice cream desserts, it was well after nine o'clock.

"What a wonderful meal that was," said Emily.

"Shall we finish with a liqueur? And there's a birthday surprise to go with it," said Haydn.

Soon after, the owner appeared from the kitchen. He was carrying the cake. It was square, measuring a foot in both directions, and covered in thick, white icing. On the top, in the centre, had been shaped the figure of a woman surrounded by a horse, a dog and a cat. Round the edge, in blue icing, were the words: "Happy 21st birthday, Emily." A dozen small candles flickered around the outside of the cake.

Her eyes shone. "It's absolutely beautiful. Thank you so much, Dad."

"You deserve it," he said. "You know you are getting your main present tomorrow, but here's a little something to keep you going!"

He handed her a small package in brightly coloured birthday wrapping. Emily eagerly ripped it open. Inside was a box containing a delicate chain with a silver horse pendant.

"Oh, Dad. That's gorgeous." She stood up and put her arms round him. "Thank you, thank you."

As she sat back down, Daisy, sitting next to her, pushed another little package in front of her. It was wrapped in shiny silver paper neatly tied with a silver bow. "I hope you don't mind, Emily, but I wanted you to have something from me."

Emily took hold of Daisy's hand and squeezed it. "Of course I don't mind. I'm very touched you should have bothered."

"Open it then!"

This time Emily was more careful to unwrap, believing the gift might also be fragile. The package contained a similar box. Opening it, Emily discovered a pair of little silver pearl ear rings. "Oh wow!"

"I thought they might go with the silver chain."

"Definitely. They are beautiful. It's so kind of you." And Emily flung her arms around Daisy. "I ought to have a 21st birthday every year if I get presents like this!"

Now Emily blew out her candles, wishing for happiness for herself, Nathan, her dad and Daisy. At her request, the owner took a photo of the four of them, with the cake, on her phone.

Then she said: "I won't eat it here. Let's get it back to Dad's and keep it safe. I'll cut it up tomorrow and share it out."

The evening was drawing to a close. All were reflecting on what a wonderful night it had been. The ladies were feeling a little merry after the two bottles of wine and the liqueurs, but they both sensed they had created a close friendship which would last. Nathan was glad to be part of a happy occasion with such nice people.

Haydn's joy that everything had gone so amazingly well was matched by the pride he felt in the two women who meant so much to him. To see them hugging each other was a delight he could not have hoped for so soon.

It was almost eleven o'clock when they arrived back at the cottage. While Haydn unlocked the door and let Timmy out into the garden, Nathan and Daisy carefully carried the cake into the kitchen and placed it in the fridge.

Emily yawned. "I'm ready for my bed. Thank you, everybody, for a wonderful birthday celebration. It's been amazing."

She hugged them all.

"I'll drop Daisy home. I won't be long," said Haydn.

Emily turned to Daisy. "Aren't you staying?"

"Not tonight."

Emily looked thoughtful. "Another time, perhaps?"

"Perhaps."

Emily hugged her new friend again, then turning away, she

said: "Take your time, Dad. Make sure she's safe. She needs looking after."

Haydn parked up outside Daisy's apartment block. He turned towards her, her beautiful face illuminated by the security lights. "Thank you for tonight. You were perfect."

"It isn't quite over yet," she replied. She pulled him to her and kissed him passionately. "I hope you are going to be a gentleman and see me to my door."

"Of course."

She fished out her fob and let them into the building. This was the first time Haydn had been inside. It was clean and smart. They strolled arm in arm down a corridor until Daisy stopped outside a plain blue door. "This is it."

She placed her hands on his hips and drew him to her, rather as she had done months ago when he had first escorted her home. On that occasion he had rejected her advances, and regretted it almost immediately. This time he returned her kiss.

Daisy took a deep breath. It was one of desire. She unlocked the front door and opened it. "Come in."

Haydn hesitated but she tugged his jacket and he found himself following her over the threshold. The hall of the flat was in darkness but she led him firmly by the hand into the living room. A table lamp in the corner cast a gentle glow across the room. He could see a flat screen TV in the opposite corner, landscape paintings on the walls, an oval mirror above the hearth where there was a modern gas fire, and a large leather settee in the centre of the room. French windows looked out on the garden.

Daisy went to the windows and closed the curtains. She kicked off her shoes and returned to Haydn in the middle of the room and slipped off his jacket. Her inhibitions had been removed by the alcohol. Her physical urges had taken over.

Haydn could see the desire for him in her eyes and it made his hunger for her all the greater. Yet, still he was unsure, still there was the lingering fear of rejection.

But Daisy was not going to be refused this time. Turning her back to him, she whispered: "Unzip me."

Haydn's hands were trembling, but he took hold of the zip at the back of her dress and drew it down her back to her bottom. She turned to face him again and, gazing into his eyes, she slipped the red dress from her shoulders, let it fall to the ground, stepped out of it and stood before him in her black lace underwear.

His heart was pounding, pumping the blood into his penis, making it grow. She put her hands behind her back, unclipped her bra and removed it, exposing her small, pert breasts to him for the first time. He was mesmerised, but she took his hands and placed them over her breasts and he began to play with her thin, dark brown nipples, squeezing them so they stood out hard.

She was losing control and pulled him to her. She kissed him, exploring his mouth with her tongue, and at the same time tearing at the buttons of his shirt until they were all undone and she could remove it. She ran her hands over his bare chest and flat tummy, then grabbed his bottom and shoved him closer to her. She could feel his great erection pressed against her through his trousers. Haydn could no longer control his desires. He slipped one hand down the back of her panties and caressed her bottom, while stroking the inside of her thigh with his other hand.

Haydn's penis was thrusting against her stomach. She was desperate to see it, to touch it. Dropping to her knees, she unfastened his trousers and in a moment had yanked them down to his ankles with his boxer shorts. She gasped as his huge, thick cock sprang to attention. She took hold of it and felt it pulsing in her hand and then she leaned forward, wrapped her lips around it and began to suck it. Haydn let out a mighty moan as the pleasure he had not known for so long flowed through his body, making it shake.

Daisy knew it would not take long for Haydn to orgasm. But she wanted him inside her. She too was almost there.

She pushed him on his back onto the settee and whipped off her knickers, soaking with her lust. Slowly she lowered herself on to his twitching cock and it was her turn to moan.

"I'm sorry, it will be quick," he gasped.

"I don't care, I just want you," she breathed.

She felt his hardness reaching every secret place. And then he came deep inside her in a violent explosion of pleasure which sparked her own shuddering orgasm.

She collapsed trembling into his arms, his still erect penis filling her body. They clung to each other and their intimacy gave them comfort. They felt certain that together they could face anything that was thrown at them.

Chapter Twenty

Haydn awoke in his own bed. He was alone.

For a moment he was confused. He recalled a vivid dream in which he had passionately made love to Daisy. And then he realised it was not a dream but a reality, and the memories of the night before came flooding back.

They had lain contentedly together for what had seemed a long time. Occasionally she stroked his cheek or gently kissed him on the lips, while he held her tightly to him. They spoke little, no words were needed.

After a while Daisy desired him again, and her hands and mouth soon had him erect. This time he was able to keep himself under control and spend more time pleasuring her, bringing her to two powerful orgasms before his own.

He reluctantly left her soon after 1a.m. and drove home, creeping into his own house so as not to disturb Emily and Nathan, like a teenager trying not to wake his parents after staying too long in the pub.

Haydn now considered what it felt like to have someone he could properly call his lover. His passion had seemed strange at first, but Daisy had put him at ease and he now felt reassured that he was wanted in that way.

He knew also that this was not just a physical love. Their sex had reinforced how much they cared for each other in so many different ways. He loved her body and soul.

He asked himself whether he had any regrets, and the answer was a resounding no.

The grandfather clock rang out eight chimes. It was time to begin a new day and his daughter would be the focus of it. Emily and Nathan were heading off after lunch. They were having a meal later with her mother and would stay there overnight before travelling to Edinburgh. But Emily wanted to have a ride and show Nathan the horses before they left.

Haydn climbed out of bed and hurriedly got showered and dressed. Timmy would be waiting for his walk.

When he entered the kitchen, Emily was cooking breakfast. He called Timmy and reached for the dog's lead.

"Don't worry, Dad. We've already taken him for a long walk. We had a good night's sleep, so we were up early. Unlike some!"

"It's early enough for a Sunday," he protested. "It's my day of rest."

"Well, if you will come in at all hours..."

"It wasn't that late."

"Wasn't it? Anyway, how was Daisy?" she said mischievously.

"She was fine. Everything was fine."

Emily stopped frying for a moment and looked at her father. "I'm glad. You are made for each other, you know that don't you?"

Haydn smiled. "She certainly means a lot to me, I'll admit that."

After breakfast, Emily divided her birthday cake into quarters. "One for you, one for Daisy, one for us and one for Mum, all the people that matter to me," she said.

Before heading to Wickham Court, Haydn produced a large, square box, decorated in green wrapping paper and tied up with a matching bow. He placed it on the kitchen table.

"Happy birthday," he said.

Emily ripped open the package and unfastened the box.

Her eyes wide, she drew out a long, turquoise satin evening dress. It shimmered as she held it up.

"Oh Dad, it's gorgeous."

"I thought you could wear it for the posh do's you're bound to be going to at university."

"I'll be working too hard for those," Emily laughed. "But I'll definitely wear it tomorrow for our evening meal at the hotel."

She flung her arms around her father. "I'm so lucky. It's been a wonderful weekend. Now let's go and ride!"

Haydn and Emily enjoyed a leisurely hack out together, finishing with a flying gallop in the cross-country field, while Daisy showed Nathan round the equestrian centre and introduced him to some of the horses.

When it was time to go, Haydn drove the young couple to the local railway station. He and Daisy warmly shook hands with Nathan and hugged Emily.

"Thanks for everything. We'll see you at Christmas," Emily said. As they walked away with their cases and packages, Daisy turned to Haydn and said: "They make a lovely couple, don't you think?"

Haydn nodded in agreement. "Everything seems to be going so well."

Daisy linked arms with him. "Still, it will be nice to have an evening to ourselves. How about a night in with a Chinese takeaway?"

"Sounds perfect. Your place or mine?"

"Oh, yours. I want to try out your bed!"

Haydn lay on his back and looked up at the bedroom ceiling. Daisy was asleep next to him. She was breathing softly, one arm wrapped around him and her head on his chest.

They had had a lovely evening together, eating and

watching TV, before going to bed and making love.

Haydn reflected on how his life had changed. The way his close friendship with Daisy had suddenly become a deep and passionate love affair seemed so natural. He had never felt happier. He had a woman who he truly loved, and who loved him; a relationship with his daughter and her boyfriend that could not have been better; a nice home, a wonderful horse and a fulfilling new career. All the bad things that had happened to him were fading to a distant memory. Even that awful recurring nightmare seemed to have gone away, he had not had it for at least three months. It seemed that his new-found happiness had driven it off.

So why did he feel troubled? Was it simply that it was all too good to be true? Did his unhappy recent life history – his cheating wife, his shattered ego, and the violent death of his parents – mean that he subconsciously expected something in his perfect new world to go wrong? Or was there something else? An unexplained, lurking threat to his cosy existence that simply would not go away.

Daisy stirred in her sleep, curling herself even more tightly around him, and he felt once more at ease. There were no demons here after all. His mind relaxed and he drifted off into a gentle slumber.

Haydn sat bolt upright, suddenly very much awake in the darkness. The quiet of the night was broken by the strange sound of Timmy barking, unusual because greyhounds do not normally bark. Haydn could also hear the troubled meowing of the cats. But it was not the noise of the animals that had registered in his brain and dragged him from his sleep. Haydn knew he had been woken by the sound of a shot.

Beside him, Daisy raised herself on one elbow and sleepily murmured: "What is it?"

He cupped her cheeks and gently raised her head so that she looked at and focused on him in her half-wakefulness. "Daisy, stay where you are. I'm going to have a look round. Just stay in bed."

"What's wrong? What has happened?"

"I don't know. But you mustn't move until I have found out."

She nodded, still half-asleep, and watched anxiously as Haydn slid out of bed, put on his dressing gown and slippers and quietly opened the bedroom door.

She sat up, rubbed her eyes and glanced at her mobile phone. It showed that it was two o'clock. Seeing it was still the early hours and hearing Timmy for the first time, Daisy was now fully awake and aware that all was not normal. "Be careful," she called out.

Haydn paused in the doorway, listening for any sign of intruders. But all he could hear was the dog and the cats. Timmy had stopped barking and was whimpering.

Haydn paced down the corridor, switched on the kitchen light and marched into the room. The cats were stood together in their basket, still meowing furiously. The dog was cowering on his cushion, his tail between his legs. The kitchen looked entirely normal. There was nobody in it.

He strode up to Timmy, who came to meet him and leaned his body anxiously against his legs. Haydn stroked and soothed him, at the same time doing a quick examination of the dog with his eyes and hands. Timmy appeared to be uninjured, just shaking with upset and worry. Haydn continued to stroke him until Timmy began to relax and he was able to coax the hound to lie back down on his cushion.

He silently moved to the living room, pausing outside to put his ear to the door. Satisfied that there was no sound from within the room, he pushed the door open and flicked on the light.

Haydn saw that the room was empty. But on the floor beneath the window there was broken glass.

He walked over, carefully avoiding any of the sharp slivers, and pulled open the curtains. More shards of glass were scattered on the sill and there was an uneven hole on the left edge of the top pane of double glazing. The outside window was shattered.

Haydn stared in disbelief at the damage. He was in no doubt it had been caused by a gunshot. It seemed his hidden fears had been justified.

He heard a noise behind him and span round in alarm, then breathed a sigh of relief as he saw Daisy framed in the doorway. She had wrapped a bath towel around her and was barefoot.

"Don't come any nearer. There's glass on the floor," he warned.

"I don't understand. What's happened, Haydn?"

He looked blankly at her. "I don't know, Daisy. I'll have to call the police. The window has been shot through."

"Is someone trying to kill us?"

He walked across and hugged her. "No, they're not. Why would they? It's just a warning."

"A warning about what? Why would anyone do such a thing?"

"I don't know, Daisy. Go into the kitchen and make us a mug of tea while I get hold of the police."

Before making the call he unlocked the front door and stepped outside. He needed to know that the gunman had gone. He felt certain that he would have discharged the weapon and jumped straight into a getaway car and driven off. That was what always happened in such incidents. But he had to be sure. Peering down the short length of the quiet cul de sac, he could see no sign of either a strange car or a mystery person, though he did notice the curtains twitching at the nearest house to his.

They must have been woken by the gunshot. Perhaps they had seen something? It reminded him he needed to get the police on the scene as quickly as possible. He knew how vital it was in firearms incidents to gather evidence early.

But first he walked round to the back of the house and checked there was nobody hiding in the garden. He was reminded of the time Emily had seen a cloaked figure lurking there. He had dismissed it as a youthful prank. Now it took on a more sinister meaning. Suddenly worried about Daisy, he dashed back into the cottage and secured the door behind him.

Then he dialled 999 and was quickly put through to a police switchboard operator.

"Can I help?" inquired the woman on the end of the line.

"There's been a shooting at my home. A window has been damaged."

"Is anybody hurt?"

"No, it's just the window."

"Is the gunman still at the scene?"

"I don't believe so. They've gone. It doesn't need armed response."

The operator took details of the address. "Someone will be round within the hour."

Haydn ended the call. Fat lot of good them turning up in an hour, we'll be dead by then if the shooter comes back, he thought. But he knew that he wouldn't. He had disappeared into the night, his mission accomplished. There was no point in him returning.

Twenty minutes later a police patrol car pulled up outside and two uniformed officers got out. Haydn met them at the door. One burly, serious-looking constable went plodding off round the garden to double check that there was nobody else around, while the thinner, cheerier sergeant entered the house.

He examined the damaged window and then turned to

Haydn. "There's no doubt it's been caused by a gunshot. Probably a shotgun."

"Single-barreled, I would think, and likely to have been sawn off," Haydn replied.

The sergeant raised his eyebrows. "You seem to know about such things."

"I used to be a detective."

The sergeant grinned. "Well, there's your motive!"

He walked into the kitchen and sat down at the pine table. Haydn sat opposite.

"Seriously, apart from you being a former cop, can you think of any reason why anyone should do this?"

"Nothing that makes sense. But there is something going on. This is not the first incident. I suppose I have been in denial, but things are clearly escalating and it's starting to get frightening, especially for my girlfriend."

Haydn told the sergeant about the damage to his car, the intruder in his garden and the horsebox accident.

"You're right that the last two incidents are more serious. And your girlfriend seems to be linked in to what is going on. Could she be the reason? There's no husband involved?"

"No, no, she's not married."

"What about a jilted boyfriend or jealous rival?"

"I don't think there's anything like that. But it's a new relationship, we're still finding out about each other."

"Well, it might be worth sitting down with her to chat about previous relationships."

The officer stood up to leave. "There's no more we can do tonight. We'll have a patrol keep an eye out for the next few hours. If you and your girlfriend can come in to the station at your convenience in the morning we'll take statements. And a forensic team will do a full examination of the scene as soon as it is light."

He handed Haydn a card with his contact details. "Don't hesitate to call if you think of anything."

Haydn looked thoughtfully at the card. "I have a pal in Leeds CID, a detective sergeant. He knows all there is to know about me. Do you mind if I contact him about it?"

"Not at all. Get him to call me if you think it might help."

Haydn nodded. "Thanks."

"If I were you I would lock up and try to get some shuteye."

"Yes. Goodnight."

Haydn locked the front door behind the officer and then leaned his back against it, staring blankly at the wall, questions about what was going on chasing each other furiously round his brain. But so far he had no answers.

Chapter Twenty-One

Haydn sat in the kitchen of Scott's bungalow and sipped from a bottle of beer.

Scott joined him at the table and drank deeply from his own bottle. Then he turned to his friend. "So what are you going to do?"

It was Monday afternoon. Neither Haydn, nor Daisy, had managed to get much sleep after the shooting, their minds alert with worry and confused thoughts. At eight o'clock the police forensic team had arrived. They spent three hours meticulously examining the living room, garden and street, removing evidence and putting it in bags. It included contaminated particles of glass and gunshot residue. The early indications were that a single shot had been fired, almost certainly from the edge of the garden.

When the forensics officers had gone, Haydn drove Daisy to the police station and they gave their statements. Afterwards he dropped her at her flat, insisting that she took the rest of the day off to recover from the shock of the shooting.

Haydn then headed to Wickham Court, determined to carry on as normal and have the weekly meeting with his business partner. It was Scott who had suggested they held it at his bungalow, tucked away between the stable blocks and the entrance to the equestrian centre, so they could discuss in private what had happened.

Haydn had raised his concerns for Daisy and queried whether he was leading her into danger through their relationship. Now he answered Scott's question.

"I need to speak to Daisy, but I am inclined to suggest we don't see each other for a while, until all this is sorted out. I can't put her at risk."

"But wouldn't she be at risk anyway, and without you there to protect her?" Scott replied.

"It seems we are both in danger, but I do think Daisy is less so on her own."

"She wasn't when her tyres were slashed."

"I know. But it's my window that's been shot at."

"Well, see what she thinks. But it seems a shame if you were to be apart when you have only just got together."

"Daisy's safety has to come first."

Scott looked thoughtful. "Is there anything I can do to protect you?"

"I don't think so. The security at Wickham Court is great already. I can't see them targeting me here."

"And who is 'them?'"

Haydn shook his head. "I wish I knew."

That evening he met Daisy at the Townley Arms. He had decided it was safer to see her there than at his cottage or her flat. They chose a quiet corner table. As they sat down, Haydn found himself surreptitiously eyeing the dozen or so customers scattered around the pub, subconsciously assessing whether any of them could be a gunman. But they were clearly harmless locals merely enjoying a couple of pints.

Haydn had never asked Daisy about her previous relationships. Now he nervously broached the subject. To his relief, she was not offended.

"There's not much to tell," she said. "I had the usual teenage experimental experiences and a couple of flings in my twenties. But most of my energy and love went into horses.

There wasn't a serious relationship until I met Jason."

"So who was Jason?"

Haydn didn't really want to know, but the question had to be asked.

"I met him two years ago. He was a new stable hand at Wickham Court. He had just finished a college equestrian course and wanted a career with horses. He loved them and was really good with them."

She hesitated. Neither of them wanted to talk about this, but it had to be done.

"Go on," Haydn encouraged.

"Well, he was a bit of a flirt and a good-looking lad. He was ten years younger than me, so when he made a play for me I suppose I felt flattered and I fell for it. We started going out.

"After six months I discovered he was seeing another of the stable girls behind my back. She told me he was also having an affair with a girl in the village. I was pretty devastated that he had been cheating on me and I ended it there and then. After that I threw myself into my job and forgot about blokes – until you came along." She squeezed his hand.

Briefly, Haydn's uncertainties had returned as he absorbed Daisy's account of her relationship with a younger man. But, looking into her eyes and seeing only genuine affection in them, his doubts dispersed. Now he focused again on the reason for the conversation.

"Do you think he would want revenge for you ditching him?"

"Look, Haydn. I obviously didn't mean that much to him. He was just getting what he could wherever he could get it. Anyway, he left Wickham Court. I think he found himself a job at a racing stables down at Newmarket. I haven't seen or heard of him since. I really don't think he is responsible."

Haydn accepted that made sense. But it brought them no

nearer to knowing who might have it in for them. Now he reached for Daisy's hand.

He said: "I hate to say this, but I think we should stop seeing each other for a little while. I'm really scared that something awful is going to happen to you if we don't, and I couldn't bear that."

She squeezed his hand. "I knew that was coming, and I can see why you are suggesting it. But wouldn't we be better facing whatever this is together?"

"I would love us to do that. But I think it is too dangerous. I believe the time has come for me to do what I do best and investigate, find out who is responsible for doing this to us and make sure they are brought to justice."

Her face clouded over. "You promised me you would not take the law into your own hands."

"And I'm not going to. I will work with the law. But if I just sit back and do nothing I fear what the consequences will be."

They both fell silent, reflecting on the unhappy prospect of being apart. Then he said: "We'll keep in regular contact by phone and we'll see each other every day at work. We just have to be patient. But it's not the end of anything."

"I hope not, Haydn. You mean too much to me for that. I can't lose you when I have only just found you."

"You won't. I promise. I could not bear to be without you."

He drew her to him and they clung to each other as though their lives depended on their embrace.

Chapter Twenty-Two

Judd Ward gazed out of the front window of his flat and watched the peak time traffic crawl its way past.

But his mind was not on the lines of cars and their occupants slowly making their way home. What troubled him was the news that someone had shot out a window at the home of Haydn Daniel.

It had not come as a surprise to him when the rumours about the shooting began spreading like wildfire around the yard. Nothing stayed secret for long in the equestrian world – everyone had known that Haydn and Daisy were an item within hours of them getting together – and then Scott had got all the staff together to give them brief details about the incident and to reassure them that they were perfectly safe.

It was not unexpected because, of course, Judd knew who was behind it and why it had taken place. What had taken him aback was the nature of the incident, the firing of a shot.

Judd was not privy to the intimate details of Kane Weston's desire for revenge, only to the fact that it was there and that the gangster was prepared to act on it. Judd knew he was not trusted to be told exactly what would happen and when. His job was simply to keep supplying information back to the spider's lair. He did not know the spider had struck until after the victim had suffered the bite.

As he stared unseeing from his window, those thoughts were making him feel uneasy. The use of a gun had changed the whole perspective. Judd had never fired a gun, or even handled one. But in his short criminal career he had seen them both carried and used. He was well aware of the damage and pain they could inflict – even death.

And he knew he did not want any of that to be visited on the bright new world he now inhabited. Deep down, he had known for a while that he preferred the life he was leading at Wickham Court to the very different one he had as part of Kane Weston's gang. Now he was forced to openly admit that reality to himself.

And with that acceptance came a further realisation, that he cared for the people he now worked for, those who had given him the chance to do something worthwhile and satisfying, and had supported him with it. That meant Scott, and it meant Daisy, and it meant Haydn Daniel.

The fact that a gun had been used against them, even to simply cause damage, now filled him with horror. And he asked himself: "How far is Kane Weston prepared to go?"

Judd turned away from the window and stood in front of the large, oval mirror on the living room wall. He looked into it and found himself struggling to meet the gaze of the anxious eyes staring back at him. He had deceived Haydn, and the others, by giving himself a false name and pretending to be someone he wasn't. How would he be able to look himself in the eye if they were injured, or even killed, because he helped a gangster in his malice against them?

But what was the alternative? Kane Weston was a ruthless and powerful man who ruled by fear. He saw everything and his control over others knew no bounds. Nor did his cruelty.

Judd felt an urge to tell all to Haydn, to tell him the truth about who he was and why he was there. But did he really have a choice?

The bitter truth was that Judd was in Kane's debt. He owed him. He owed him because he had slept with the gangster's wife and it was still payback time. If he stopped paying back, the debt would be forfeit and he knew what that would mean.

He had not seen Keeley for weeks. Jim Lee had told Judd that Kane knew about the continuing affair and ordered him, in no uncertain terms, to put an end to it or face the consequences, and he had. He knew he had left his brains in his pants but there came a time when every hot-blooded lothario had to see sense.

Keeley had tried to call him and sent him text messages for days but he had ignored them. It had taken great discipline, she was an amazing lover and he did care for her. But he had been compensated to a degree by a fling with Faye at the yard.

Now, as he wrestled with this seemingly impossible conundrum, his thoughts turned again to Keeley. Not this time because he wanted her body, though he always did, but because he had nobody else he could talk to. Keeley would understand his dilemma. She would help him find the right answer.

He picked up his mobile phone and dialled her number.

When Judd arrived at Keeley's apartment she flung herself naked at him and tried to drag him straight to the bedroom.

But for once he denied her. He held her gently at arm's length and said: "I need to talk to you."

"Oh, how disappointing, babes!" she trilled. But seeing his serious expression she covered her nudity with a dressing gown and led him by the hand into the living room. They sat side by side on the sofa.

"I don't quite know where to start," he said.

"Before you do, I want to know why I haven't seen you for ages. I've had to look after myself, which isn't the same."

Ignoring her suggestive remark, he said: "It's all part of it, Keeley. I'm sorry to be so serious but I've got a big predicament."

She stroked his thigh and said: "I love it when you have a big predickament!" Then, wrapping her gown tighter around her she urged: "Go on, Judd. I'm listening. It's about Kane isn't it?"

"Yes." He hesitated. "Look, Keeley. Anything I say can't go any further."

"Fucking hell, Judd. You should know by now that what is between us, stays between us. I've as much to lose as you have, probably more. Kane sent me a solicitor's letter telling me I wouldn't be allowed access to my boys if I didn't stop seeing you. I guessed he'd got at you as well."

"The heartless bastard. But, yes. I had the word of warning, and I'm sorry but I felt I had to listen to it."

This time she caressed his hand. "I don't blame you. I missed you, that's all. So what else is there?"

"Kane sent me to an equestrian centre where Haydn Daniel, the old copper who put him away, works. He's a part owner there. Kane wanted me to spy on him and feed back information, which I did. He said it was my chance to redeem myself for sleeping with you.

"He then got someone to cause damage to Daniel's car and to his girlfriend's horsebox, which could have been really nasty. But then last weekend someone shot a hole in Haydn's living room window. I just think it's getting scary. I don't know what's going to happen next."

"This is the guy that Kane vowed revenge on, isn't it?"

"Yes. But how far is he going to go before he stops? I feel guilty about passing back information because I don't know where it's going to lead to any more."

"Kane's an evil bastard, but he's not stupid. I can't see him having an ex-cop bumped off. They'd be bound to find out he had ordered it. Anyway, why do you care so much? As long as you're safe that's all that matters."

"But it isn't. Daniel's been really good to me, they all have. I don't want anything to happen to them, and me be the reason why."

"Then the only thing to do is to tell this Haydn Daniel everything. If you did that, they could put Kane away for life. We could all be free of him."

"I don't think I can do that, Keeley. If it didn't work, I'd be a dead man."

She tenderly touched his cheek. "Judd, sooner or later you are going to have to choose – Kane or the cop."

"I know," he said gloomily.

Then he shrugged his shoulders and smiled at Keeley. "I'll sleep on it."

She got to her feet. Unfastening the belt of her dressing gown she let the garment fall to the ground and stood before him naked. Holding out her hand she said: "Now take me to bed."

Chapter Twenty-Three

Haydn sat opposite Andy Watson and stared thoughtfully into his beer. He looked up and smiled thinly at his friend. "Thanks for coming at such short notice. You must be busy."

"I've always time for my best mate," Andy responded.

He had agreed to see Haydn at the pub on the Leeds Ring Road, which had become their regular meeting place. It was big enough for them to find a quiet corner to chat privately on a midweek afternoon, and anyway, the beer was good.

Haydn had called Andy that morning, after the cheery sergeant, Max Bannister, had contacted him with the forensic results. He wanted to run them past him, as well as see if he had gleaned anything about the investigation.

"I finish my shift at two o'clock. I can be there by half past," Andy told him.

He was inevitably delayed by a briefing and it was after three o'clock when he got to the pub, but Haydn was just grateful that he had made it. He immediately turned to business.

"The forensics people have established that a single-barreled sawn off shotgun was used to blast my window."

"A known weapon of violent criminals," Andy stated.

"Exactly."

"Which begs the question, why would such a person shoot at your house?"

"Why indeed. Any ideas, Andy?"

"To answer the why, you first need to know the answer to who."

"But wouldn't the why give you the who?"

"It might. But I believe that if you determine who did it, you will know why they did it."

"I suspect that finding out who was responsible would be like looking for a needle in a haystack."

"Perhaps not in your case."

Haydn took a gulp of his beer. "Sounds like you have a theory."

"I do." Andy leaned across the table conspiratorially. He lowered his voice. "Kane Weston."

"What makes you say that?"

"Process of elimination, my dear Sherlock. Nobody else has vowed revenge on you, like Weston did the day he was sent to prison."

"But surely that was a show of defiance, an act of bravado. I never believed he meant it."

"Maybe he did, maybe he didn't. 'I'll make you pay for this, I promise you.' Those were his words, I heard them too."

"But you said he was going straight. It doesn't fit with that."

"Running a legitimate operation wouldn't necessarily stop him from wanting to avenge you for what he perceives as your unforgivable behaviour. Anyway, we are keeping an eye on his property and there are still plenty of comings and goings which suggest not everything connected to that place is above the law."

"But if it is him, he seems to know a lot about me – where I live, who I am dating. It's a stretch of the imagination."

"He was part of an international drugs ring. Is it so fanciful he could find out what was happening so close to home?"

"You have no evidence, Andy?"

"No, it's just a theory. But I think it's a good one."

"So, if I accept your theory, what do I do now?"

"YOU, Haydn, don't do anything. You leave it to us. I'm

going to set up an urgent meeting with Max Bannister to discuss this. First and foremost, we need to look at your safety and take whatever precautions are needed to protect you, and those close to you, like Daisy. How is she?"

"She was shocked at first, but she's a strong girl. She'll be fine. We're not seeing each other at the moment."

"I'm sorry. Did she think you were too dangerous to be around?"

"No, it was my decision. I thought it was for the best. It's just temporary, I hope."

"I'll talk to Max about protecting her as well. And I'll step up our observations of Weston and his cronies."

"Don't you think we are over-reacting a bit?"

Andy stared into Haydn's eyes. "You spent all those years pursuing Weston and making sure you put him away for a good stint. You did that for a reason, didn't you? No, I don't think we are over-reacting."

Watson stood up. "I have to go. Keep an eye out, you can't be too careful."

He paused. "Maybe you should think about having Daisy under the same roof. It seems she's at risk anyway, at least you'd know she was safe."

After he had gone, Haydn reflected on their conversation. He had not given any thought to Kane Weston, let alone considered he might be responsible for what had been happening. But now he could see the logic of Andy's argument. It still seemed incredulous, and yet it was possible that the gangster had uncontrollable vengeful thoughts driving him. If that was so, where and when would they end?

He could not contemplate that Weston would try to have him killed – for of course he would not do any of the evil deeds himself, he would keep a protective distance from them. But he had employed the use of a weapon once, what was to stop him doing it again?

Haydn was reassured that Andy was taking a positive stance and upping the investigation. But he could not help feeling frustrated that he was not involved. The temptation to take action himself was strong. Once a detective, always a detective.

But he knew that, for now, he had to leave it to others and put his faith in them.

Haydn was clear in his rejection of Andy's suggestion that he and Daisy should live together. Again, he could see why his friend had made it. But Haydn firmly believed that Daisy would be in greater danger if she was with him. At the end of the day, Weston's malice was aimed at him, not Daisy. But the sooner it was resolved the better, he was already missing her.

Chapter Twenty-Four

"It's Jim Lee."

The call, as always, was unexpected.

Although Judd knew he would be phoned by Kane Weston's deputy from time to time, he was still not prepared for it when it happened. Increasingly, the calls, and the instructions that came with them, were unwelcome. Judd just wanted to ignore the phone, and its complicated intrusion into his life. But he knew he couldn't.

"Hello, Mr Lee."

"Kane wants to see you at the house. In an hour."

There was a click as the line went dead.

Judd scowled and cursed. He flung down the shavings fork he had been using to muck out. For a moment he considered phoning back Lee to say he could not make it. But he dismissed the idea as pointless. There was no debate to be had. He had got his order and that was that. He would have to go.

Judd was thankful that it was mid morning and the challenging job of turning out the enthusiastic horses had been done. The staff were now busy cleaning out the stables and making the horse's beds. It was hard work and he knew it would mean extra graft for his colleagues, but he had no option.

He sought out Daisy and when he found her he clutched his stomach and grimaced. "I'm sorry, Daisy. I'm going to have to go. I've been sick and I've got awful gut ache. I think I must have food poisoning."

Daisy looked less than impressed but could not argue

against his apparent agony. Five minutes later he was driving towards the big city.

Judd was ushered into the opulent study at Sicily House. Kane was leaning back in his chair at the far side of the big desk. Silently, he gestured to Judd to sit opposite him. Weston studied the young man and noted he looked more pale and drawn than when he last saw him. Some of the confidence he had been brimming with before had evaporated, the gangster thought. He wondered what the reason for that might be. Nothing had changed that he was aware of.

Judd did not look at the imposing man in front of him, gazing instead over his shoulder at the window into the garden. He's something to hide, and I know what, thought Weston.

Then the gangster spoke. "How is my old friend? Has he got over his shattering experience yet?" He curled his lip in a snarl of triumph.

"I don't know, I haven't seen much of him since," Judd hedged.

"Ah, playing it safe," said Kane, leaving the young man to figure out who he was referring to. "And what did you make of what happened, Judd? How did you like the shooting?"

Judd had expected that question and had been rehearsing his answer. "It was a surprise, but it was a serious statement of intent and very impressive."

"I'm glad you're impressed. Because if something similar were to happen again, I thought you might like to play a part. Perhaps at the home of the girl next time. What do you think, Judd?"

Kane opened a drawer and removed a dark grey revolver from it. He slid it across the desk to the young man.

Judd stared at the gun. He was horrified. He had hoped that Weston's lust for revenge had been sated by the shooting, that there would be no more firearms incidents. The last thing he had expected was to have his own finger put on the trigger. His thoughts tumbled around his confused head. He said nothing.

"Well, Judd. I'm waiting."

Still he remained silent, his brain refusing to send the right words to his voice.

Weston laughed. "I see you're not up to the task after all. How disappointing."

Then he said: "Put the gun in your pocket, in case you change your mind. But be careful what you do with it, it's loaded."

He swivelled in his chair and stared out of the window. Then he turned back to study the young gang member. Judd looked petrified. "Don't worry, Judd. I have another job for you, one that doesn't involve guns."

Judd was unable to stop a long exhalation of breath as relief swept over him.

Now Kane got to his feet. He nodded his head at Jim Lee who, awaiting the signal, poured two glasses of neat whisky from a decanter on the desk. He placed one before his boss and pushed the other in front of the young man.

Kane picked up his glass and indicated that Judd should do the same. "Drink," he instructed.

Judd sipped the whisky and waited.

Then Kane spoke. "I have a proposition for you. Your time with Haydn Daniel is over, your job there is done and you have done it satisfactorily. You are ready for the next step."

He paused for effect, while looking for signs in Judd's face of what he was thinking. The young man's anxiety and uncertainty was transparent.

Kane pressed on. "I am going to give you another opportunity, one which give you a greater role and responsibility in this organisation. I am not certain you deserve this chance, but I am advised you are the man for the job." He cast a sidelong glance at Lee.

"I have purchased a wine bar in the centre of Bradford. It is my second one, I am sure you are aware of what a good job Jim Lee is doing with the first."

Judd nodded his acknowledgment.

"It is vital to me that this new enterprise is a success, for that will breed more success and pave the way for a chain of wine bars in my name with the earnings to match. It is imperative I have a manager there who will ensure that it will be everything I want it to be. You, Judd, will be that manager."

Kane returned to his chair, drained his whisky and stared at Judd over the empty glass. "So, what do you say?"

For a second time, Judd was lost for words. He had never imagined being offered such a position. In fact, he had felt certain he was on borrowed time with Kane Weston. When the gangster had told Judd he was no longer needed at Wickham Court, he had feared the worst. Now, here was a lifeline. And yet, he was in two minds. This unexpected offer did not alter the gratitude he felt towards Haydn Daniel and his team, nor did it take away the thrill of working with the horses. But if Kane's campaign of hate was truly over, perhaps Judd was left with no choice but to return to the fold, his future secure and his sexual treachery forgiven. It was decision time.

He became aware of Kane's eyes burning into him, seeking his answer. But he could not deliver it. "I don't know what to say," was all he could manage.

Kane smiled and it seemed to encourage rather than to mock. "You don't have to say anything now. I will be opening the bar in two weeks time. I expect you to be in charge when I do. You have seven days to decline the offer. If that is what you choose to do I will have to reconsider your position. I hope that won't be necessary. You may go now."

The meeting was at an end. Judd left the room. His mind was in a whirl. He had to talk to someone about it and he knew who it must be.

Weston turned to Lee. "It will be very interesting to see what he decides. The kid was shitting himself. I'm not convinced he's up to the job."

He added: "Have him followed. I want to know where he goes next."

Chapter Twenty-Five

It was lunchtime and Haydn was riding his horse in one of the outdoor schools.

Since his conversation with Andy Watson he had thrown himself into his work, trying to forget about everything else that was going on. There was plenty for him to do. It was now September and drawing towards the end of another long season, but horse camps and competitions were still being held and the cross-country course, outdoor arenas and stabling and accommodation for the visitors had to be maintained. Then there were the livery customers to keep happy.

There never seemed enough hours in a day to do all the jobs he wanted to. But there was always time for him to fret about the unpleasant events which had turned his perfect new life on its head.

He was in a permanent state of frustration; frustrated that he couldn't be involved in bringing to justice whoever was trying to wreck his life, whether that was Kane Weston or somebody else. And frustrated that he could no longer be with Daisy. He saw her most days working round the yard and they had a chat when they could, and even held hands when they were sure no-one else was near. But he missed the closeness they had developed so quickly, the support they gave each other simply by holding each other tight. His cottage now seemed empty and his life without her mirrored that.

Haydn decided the best way out of this malaise was to get on his horse and test their dressage skills. He was determined to push himself. Paddy recognised they had work to do and tried his hardest to achieve the difficult movements being asked of him.

As they did a tricky half-pass across the arena, Haydn noticed they had an audience. Daisy was standing at the wooden fence around the school. She was watching them closely.

Haydn rode across and halted Paddy next to her. "I didn't see you there."

She smiled. "I haven't been here long. The pair of you are working really well. I've never seen you look so good in here."

Haydn glowed inside from her praise, which meant so much to him. He studied her in turn. She was wearing a pink T-shirt and thin black leggings and he found her as attractive as ever. But he thought she looked tired and troubled.

"How are you?" he asked.

"Missing you," she replied.

"Me too."

"What, you're missing you as well?!" Her face momentarily lit up at her joke.

They laughed together. Then she said: "Have you found anything out?"

"Nothing new since the forensic results. Andy Watson is meeting the police sergeant today to discuss the case, and to review our security."

"You haven't changed your mind about us being together?"

"No, Daisy. I firmly believe you are safer where you are. I know it's frustrating."

"You must do what you think is best." She stared thoughtfully across the fields.

"Is everything all right at your flat? Nothing unusual?" he said.

"No. It's all normal. I just don't know what to do with myself."

They fell into a reflective silence. Then she said: "I'm entering a one-day event at Northallerton. It will be my last one of the season. It will give me something to look forward to. It's two weeks on Sunday, I don't suppose you'll come along, will you?"

"I think it would be unwise." Seeing the disappointment in her face, he quickly added: "But I'll consider it, Daisy. It might be safer for me to be with you."

"Well, let me know, Haydn." Then her eyes brightened and she blew him a kiss. "Must get back to work, and let you dressage divas get on with it."

He watched her walk away with a mixture of sadness and admiration and prayed that Kane Weston would not ruin their relationship.

Later that afternoon, Haydn took a call from Max Bannister. The sergeant was his usual cheerful self. "How's you and that horse of yours?"

"Both fine. What news have you?"

"Andy and I have had a good old natter and we're singing from the same hymn sheet on this. However, we are limited on what we can do by a lack of evidence. I've heard of this Kane Weston character, I know he's a bad 'un. But at the moment we've nothing to link him to anything. Do you really think he's responsible?"

"Well, I hadn't thought about it until Andy came up with the idea. But now I can see it makes some sort of sense. Certainly, nothing else does. What do you think?"

"I agree, he's a strong candidate. But proving it is the problem. What interests me is the level of knowledge he has about you. For instance, how did he know Daisy was going to that particular event in time to get one of his gang there to slash her tyres? Someone is feeding him information."

"You mean somebody at the yard?"

"Probably. Certainly it has to be someone who knows you pretty well. Anyone spring to mind?"

"Not immediately. I can't think of anyone who would want to do that to me."

"Well, get your old detective radar switched on and see what you can come up with. In the meantime, we are going to fit panic alarms at your place and Daisy's, just in case. Patrols will drive by your homes as and when they can for the moment. Andy will keep doing his stuff at the other end. It might help if you can send him photos of your staff for him to check against police records. You never know."

He added: "Don't worry. If Kane Weston is responsible, we'll catch him out. Until then, watch your back."

The next day Haydn set himself the task of cleaning out the water bowls in the horse's stables. It was a simple enough job, but with around sixty to do it would be arduous and time consuming. Each bowl had to be unplugged, allowing the water to empty into a large bucket placed beneath it which then had to be dragged outside and emptied. The metal bowls would be scrubbed clean before being allowed to automatically refill.

He sought out Brad to help. It would lighten the load and speed up the process, allowing Haydn to get on with other things in the afternoon. It would also be more fun to have a companion to chat to during the hard physical work.

It was a chilly morning and Haydn wore a zip-up fleece top over his casual shirt. Summer could often come to an abrupt early end in the Yorkshire Dales and the dip in temperature gave the first sign of the approaching autumn.

He found Brad returning with the other stable staff from the fields where they had just finished turning out the horses.

Haydn called out to Daisy, who was in charge as usual. "Can

I borrow Brad from mucking out duties to help with changing the waters?"

"I suppose we'll have to manage," she smiled.

"Come on, Brad. It's better than shovelling shit!"

The young man smiled thinly and said nothing. He followed Haydn into the nearest barn.

"Grab that big bucket and we'll make a start."

He picked up the bucket and joined Haydn in the first stable. He stood silently as Haydn prepared to release the plug at the bottom of the bowl.

Haydn glanced back. "Let's have it underneath then."

Brad stirred himself and put the container in place.

Haydn observed the young man as the water poured noisily into the bucket. He seemed distant, as if he was pre-occupied with something.

"Anything wrong, Brad? You seem a bit quiet today."

The stable hand focused his attention on the bucket, avoiding eye contact. "No, nothing. I'm just tired."

"It's Saturday tomorrow. You've got the weekend off, haven't you? Have you got anything planned?"

"Nothing," Brad repeated.

"Well, put your feet up and catch up on some sleep. This is a tough job."

Brad merely nodded in reply.

Haydn gave up on his attempts at conversation. It was clearly a waste of time. Brad was never much of a talker but today he could barely manage a sentence. He was obviously not in the mood for chit chat, for whatever reason.

The truth was that Judd was finding it increasingly difficult to be Brad. The fact that his time in that role was almost certainly drawing to an end made it even harder for him to continue to play it. More and more, he was feeling like a fraud.

After his meeting with Kane he had gone to see Keeley, first carefully concealing the revolver in the boot of his car. But she had just reiterated that he had to choose between the gangster and the detective. He knew that was a decision that only he could make, and he felt completely unable to do so. He did not mention the gun.

The following day he phoned Jim Lee to beg for time.

"I think it would help if I could have a break before starting the wine bar job," he told the gangster's deputy. "I want to be fit and ready to do it justice. I know how important it is to Mr Weston."

"I'll see what I can do," Lee growled.

An hour later, Lee called Judd back. "Okay. I've spoken to Kane. You've got a week's grace. He'll delay the grand opening until Monday, September 30. You will start on that day."

It had bought Judd some breathing space, a little more thinking time. But that date was only seventeen days away and he was no nearer to making his mind up. The pressure was mounting with every passing day. He had accepted Kane's offer. To renege on that would put him at the mercy of Weston's wrath. And he knew that Kane's anger would be all the greater the nearer it got to the grand opening.

If he did pull out, how could Haydn Daniel protect him from Weston? How could anyone protect him? His heart told him to unburden himself to the detective. But his head insisted the only sensible thing to do was to take the olive branch that Kane had offered.

Chapter Twenty-Six

Haydn was sat at home when his mobile phone rang. Timmy, who was stretched out comfortably on the rug in the living room, raised his head to look towards the sound. The greyhound settled back down as Haydn reached out for the phone and answered it.

"Hello pal." Andy Watson's name had flashed up on the console.

"I think we've found your mole," Haydn's friend announced.

"I'm all ears."

"Your young stable hand, Brad Smith?"

"What about him?"

"He's actually called Judd Ward. And guess who he works for?"

"Kane Weston," Haydn stated with sad resignation.

"You got it."

"Are you sure?"

"He was seen going into Sicily House by our 'obs' team. They photographed him and we saw that it was the same guy as the one in the photo you provided. We identified him from our records, he has a couple of minor convictions for theft. We made some inquiries and discovered he has been on Weston's payroll for a couple of years. He's well down the pecking order and hasn't been involved in anything big. But get this! It turns out he was the one shagging Weston's missus while he was in prison."

Haydn pondered what he was hearing. "So Weston sent him here to spy on me and feed back what he found out."

"Yes. It would seem it was either that or face whatever punishment Kane chose for him dallying with his wife. He certainly had plenty of incentive to come up with the goods."

"And all of that means you were right, Andy. It is Kane Weston who is behind this."

"Now all we have to do is prove it. What are you going to do about the spy?"

"I need to think. But perhaps he is the key to getting the proof we need. We may yet get Weston locked up for many years to come."

"I'll have a word with my probation pal. It's time he knew about our suspicions. Maybe we could get Weston's licence revoked while we investigate."

"I think we'll need evidence before they do that. But there's no harm in putting probation in the picture. I'll let you know about Brad."

"Judd."

"Yes. It's a shame. I was getting to like him."

"Maybe you'll find the feeling is mutual."

Judd sat on the old leather sofa, beneath the far wall in the office at Wickham Court, and stared out on to the busy yard. It was Monday morning and staff were scurrying about with wheelbarrows and forks, preparing to muck out the stables.

Judd should have been among them but Daisy had called him over and told him: "Haydn wants to see you."

It was an unusual request and Judd immediately wondered why he had been summoned, but he trudged obediently across to the office. It was empty when he got there so he sat on the sofa and waited. As the minutes passed, he mused about what he might have done wrong. Maybe Haydn had interpreted his mental lethargy as diminished enthusiasm for the job and wanted to give him a kick up the backside. Or perhaps he had discovered Judd's habit of smoking cigarettes behind the stables – clearly in breach of the yard's safety rules. He could not imagine he had been called in to be praised.

At last the door opened and Haydn walked in, followed by Scott. Judd's anxiety increased with the presence of both business partners. Scott sat behind his big oak desk, while Haydn pulled up a chair alongside him. Before seating himself, he boiled the kettle and produced three steaming mugs of coffee, handing one of them to the stable hand.

"There you are... Judd," he announced quietly.

Judd almost dropped the mug as a wave of horror swept over him. His mouth opened as if to speak and then closed wordless. Shakily he placed the drink on the wooden floor, reaching down to wipe up spilled coffee with his sleeve. He stared at the ground, refusing to look at what he knew were now his inquisitors.

Then Haydn spoke again. "Judd, look at me."

Judd continued to gaze at the floor.

Then again, but louder and more firm: "Look at me."

Slowly Judd raised his eyes and with a great effort turned them towards the older man.

"Don't be afraid," Haydn said. "You are not going to be punished. I am not Kane Weston."

Judd blanched at the sound of the name. He felt sick to the stomach that it had been uttered in these circumstances, at this place.

He forced himself to speak. "What do you know?"

"All that I need to know. That you work for Kane Weston, that he sent you here to spy on me and he used you to find out about me and perhaps cause me harm."

"I didn't know what he was going to do."

"I know. I said he used you and I accept that is what happened. That is what Kane Weston does – uses people for his own ends."

Haydn paused. He could see Judd's torment and felt sympathy for him. "I do not blame you for what you have done. The damage and fear does not lay at your door."

"But if it hadn't have been for me, none of this would have happened."

Now Scott spoke for the first time. "Perhaps, and perhaps Weston would just have got someone else to do his dirty work and it would have happened anyway."

Judd glanced at Scott, understanding that he was right, and then turned back to Haydn. "What happens now? I suppose you will take me to court and I will lose my job here."

"The answer is no to both. You have done nothing wrong in the eyes of the law so there is no question of you being prosecuted. And as for the job, it is still yours if you want it."

Judd stared incredulously at Haydn. "Why? Why would you want to keep me on after this?"

"You are a bloody good worker, you fit in well and you love the horses. Why wouldn't we want to keep you?"

"Because I betrayed you. Because I was responsible for putting you in danger."

"I honestly don't believe you wanted to do what you did. Recently you have not been yourself and I think you have been having serious doubts about it all. Maybe it was the shooting that changed things for you."

"Yes, it did make a difference. I didn't want you to be harmed."

"But you felt trapped."

"Yes."

"Kane had you over a barrel because of your relationship with Keeley."

Judd spluttered. "How did you know about that? You can't say a word to anyone about it. He'd kill me."

"He might kill you anyway. But don't worry, there's no need to mention it."

Judd leaned forward, his head in his hands. The fact that Haydn knew so much was overpowering. He wanted to curl up into a tiny ball and hide from the world. "I don't know what to do anymore," he murmured.

"Then let me tell you, Judd. First of all, you carry on working here. That's what we all want, including you, I think."

"I've loved it here. Everyone has been so kind to me and being with the horses is just amazing."

"The second thing you have to do will take some courage. You will have to be strong and brave."

Judd sat up straight on the sofa. He thought he knew what was coming next.

Haydn continued. "You are going to have to tell everything you know about Kane, what he has ordered you to do and why, all that he has said to you about it. You will have to make a statement and perhaps give evidence at court."

"I knew I would have to do this if I made the choice. But I haven't chosen it and I just don't think I can do it."

"We will support you, and the police will support you. You will have all the backing you need."

"And what happens if he is found not guilty? I'll be dead."

"You won't. He will be convicted, with yours and all the other evidence, and he will be put away forever."

And then another thought struck Judd. "How can I make statements and help the police when I am back working with him again?"

"What do you mean?" said Haydn, perplexed.

"I've told him I will run a new wine bar for him. He's pulling me out of here, he says my job is done."

Haydn stared at Judd, comprehending what he had just said. If that was the case, it meant that Weston's revenge was now complete. It was over. "Judd, does he have anything else planned for me?"

"I don't know. He doesn't tell me what he is planning. But after the shooting of your window he suggested I could do the same at Daisy's flat. When I didn't reply he offered me the wine bar job."

Haydn was horrified. "Do you think he was serious?"

"I think he was just testing me out. He probably didn't mean it. But I don't know."

Haydn sighed. If Weston did mean to attack Daisy's flat, she was in grave danger, and he had been wrong about her being safer on her own. Clearly, Kane knew where she lived. He did not need Judd to tell him that. Haydn reminded himself that the first attack, on his car, had taken place as he was walking her home. Maybe Weston had simply transferred his malice to Daisy in order to get at Haydn.

He thought quickly. Then he asked Judd: "When do you start your new job for Weston?"

"Two weeks today."

"Look, Judd. We have to avoid Kane getting suspicious about you. He has to believe you are firmly on his side. You must start at the wine bar when he expects you to, in two weeks time, unless we have resolved matters before.

"We must now act fast, but it may be that we won't be in a position to arrest Kane until after that date, so you will have to go through with it. We will get your full statement from you before that. Are you willing to do that? Are you willing to stand up against Weston and get him convicted?"

Judd still felt afraid. But his mind was made up. He had made his choice and he would not change it. "I am willing."

Daisy was finishing her shift when Haydn called her over. "Come into the office. We need to talk."

Closing the door behind them, Haydn told her about his conversations with Andy and Judd. Daisy listened intently and then breathed a sigh of relief. "So the nightmare is coming to an end," she said.

"Not quite, but hopefully the end is in sight. But what is clear is that you must come to live with me. You may be in peril at your flat. I was wrong to leave you there on your own, Daisy."

"You did what you thought was right and I supported your decision, much as I did not want to be apart from you. But do you really think this gangster would attack my home?"

"Anything is possible with Kane Weston and I am not prepared to take the chance. We must go back to your place straight away, pack your things, and move you in with me tonight. I am not leaving you alone for a moment longer."

Daisy stepped toward him and hugged him tightly. "There is nowhere else I want to be."

Chapter Twenty-Seven

It was eight o'clock in the evening and darkness was falling on the yard. Scott emerged from his bungalow and set off on the short walk to the stables to make a last check on the horses. He did this without fail every night, ensuring that all the animals were safe and well and showing no signs of illness or injury, that they had enough to eat and their mechanical water bowls were working and full. His tour took him half an hour. It was essential for the welfare of the horses, but it also gave Scott a pleasant and relaxing end to the day.

Tonight it was fine and dry, if a little cool. The sky was clear and there was a gentle breeze. It was a perfect evening.

As Scott strolled to the barn where his own horses, and those of Haydn and Daisy, lived, he was stopped in his tracks by a pungent smell. He sniffed the air, seeking to confirm his immediate suspicion. There was no doubt about it, he could smell smoke.

He broke into a jog and dashed inside the barn. There was nothing unusual there, certainly no sign of his biggest fear – a fire. But the whiff of acrid smoke was more powerful. The horses could smell it too and were restless, roaming anxiously round their stables and neighing.

Scott switched on the main lights. "Don't worry, girls and boys, everything's all right," he called out reassuringly. But the horses neighed even more.

As he penetrated deeper into the barn, the smell grew stronger. It seemed to be coming from the rear of the building.

Scott headed to the big metal double doors at the back and hauled them open. At once he was confronted by a great plume of dark grey smoke to the side of the exit. As he ventured outside, the fumes hit him, almost immediately making his eyes and throat sore. Against the outer wall of the barn, a few feet from the back doors, were piled half a dozen straw bales where they had been stored until there was room for them inside. The straw was on fire and flames, already three or four feet high, were licking against the building.

The lower half of the barn was constructed from concrete, but above that it was made from wood. The flames were reaching up towards it, like long fingers stretching out to grasp it within its fiery grip.

The stables were also mainly built from wood and Scott had a very real fear that the fire could spread to them, putting the horses in terrible danger.

He pulled his mobile phone from his pocket and dialled 999. Within seconds he was through to a fire control room operator.

"I am Scott Stevens from Wickham Court Equestrian Centre. There is a fire which is spreading to a barn where the horses are." As he spoke he dashed back inside the barn, pulled a hosepipe from the wall, turned the tap on full and ran back outside, unfurling the hosepipe as he went, the phone cradled between his ear and his shoulder.

The operator was calm and efficient. "I am sending a number of fire appliances out to you now. They will be with you in just a few minutes."

"Tell them to be quick. I am tackling the fire with a hosepipe."

"Please keep well clear. You must not put yourself at risk. The firefighters will be there very soon."

"Okay."

Scott ended the call and concentrated on fighting the fire. The hosepipe only just reached outside the doors, but the water pressure was good and by aiming the end of the pipe in the air Scott was able to cascade a fountain of water on to the flames, which were creeping inexorably nearer to the wood.

Holding the hosepipe in his right hand, he took hold of his phone in his left hand. There was one more call he needed to make.

Haydn had just served spaghetti bolognese for himself and Daisy when his mobile phone rang. He saw that it was Scott calling. As he answered, he could hear a strange crackling sound in the background.

"It's a bad line, Scott," he said.

"Haydn, get here quick. Our barn is on fire. I'm fighting it now. The fire brigade are coming. We may need to evacuate the horses."

"I'm on my way."

He ended the call and turned to Daisy. "There's a fire at the yard."

"Oh my God! Are the horses all right?"

"I don't know."

"Come on Haydn. We need to get there – now."

Reassured that help would soon be at hand, from both the fire brigade and Haydn, Scott focused his full attention on firefighting. The hosepipe was still propelling a strong spurt of water at the barn, but try as he might Scott was slowly losing control of the blaze. The flames were growing bigger and inching their way towards the wooden part of the building. The smoke was thickening and wafting on the breeze into his face, coating him in a dirty, smelly ash skin. The fumes gripped his throat, making him cough, and he tried to cover his mouth with his free hand. At one point, a tongue of flame spat out towards him, singeing his hair. But he still trained the water on the blaze. He could hear the sound of the agitated horses inside getting louder.

"Please hurry up and get here," he called out to the world.

He felt as if he had been placed in hell and left alone to face the unquenchable heat. Suddenly the flow of water from the hosepipe reduced to a trickle. It barely reached the flames any longer. It seemed to Scott an eternity since he had called the fire brigade. Now he feared that death and ruin were almost upon him. At that moment he heard the uplifting sound of sirens. He flung the pipe to one side and ran to meet his rescuers.

It took Haydn less than ten minutes to drive to Wickham Court. As the electronic entrance gates swung silently open, he glanced in his mirror and to his delight saw blue lights approaching behind him. He became aware of sirens shattering the silence of the night. Haydn pulled his car to one side to allow the fleet of four fire engines to pass through.

The driver of the first appliance stopped and wound down his window. "Where are we headed?"

"Straight down the drive and its the first big barn on the right," said Haydn.

The firefighter gave him the thumbs up and led the cavalcade onto the premises.

Haydn followed, his heart pounding in fear of what he would find. He was terrified he would discover his horse burned to death in his stable. Then a guilty thought hit him: what about Scott? He had been all alone to fight the fire. What if he had been trapped by the flames, or overcome by the fumes?

As he jumped out of the car he saw a welcome sight. Scott

was standing in the yard. He was in deep conversation with a senior fire officer in a white helmet, and pointing towards the barn. Other firefighters were dashing into the building, unfurling thick hose reels which had already been attached to a water hydrant on the yard. A generator on the first fire engine hummed into noisy life.

The smell of smoke pierced the air and Haydn could see a grey cloud billowing into the sky behind the stables. He stood in shock, gazing at the awful scene, until he felt his arm being tugged. Daisy was next to him. "Come on," she said. Roused from his stupor he ran with her on to the concrete yard and shouted to Scott, who turned towards him.

He saw that Scott's face was blackened and his hair appeared to be singed.

"My God, are you all right?"

"I'm fine. But we need to get the horses out of their stables and into the outdoor arenas."

"Are any of them hurt?" asked Daisy.

"No. But we have to move them or they will be. The fire has spread to the back wall and is threatening the stables. I managed to hold it back for a while but I ran out of water. The fire brigade were here in the nick of time. They'll sort it out now. But it's hot in there and the horses are getting stressed."

The three of them raced into the barn and grabbed a handful of head collars and lead ropes. They could see two firefighters with a large water jet outside at the back of the building. Another pair of firemen were poised with a similar hose inside the barn. One of them shouted across. "You need to get this row of horses out fast or they will get soaked and debris may fall on them."

Four of the stables were close to where the fire now raged. Those horses had to be evacuated first. They worked together, Scott going in to the stables and putting the head collars on the animals, then passing the lead ropes to Haydn and Daisy, who led them two at a time out of the barn and across the yard to the outdoor schools. The horses snorted and skittered but Haydn and Daisy had a firm hold of them, and in two minutes all four animals were safely contained in the arena.

Five minutes later the rest of that row of horses had been removed from the building and the trio turned their attention to the ten animals in the row opposite, furthest away from the fire. These included their own horses.

Haydn had wanted to rush straight to Paddy when he first entered the barn but he knew his duty was to the horses in more immediate danger. Now he went to his own. Paddy was clearly unsettled by what was happening, neighing repeatedly and rushing round his box. But Haydn reassured him and slowly Paddy started to calm down. Fastening the head collar, Haydn looked into Paddy's eyes and said: "Come on, mate. Let's get out of here."

In less than fifteen minutes, all the horses had been moved into two of the big outdoor schools, the wooden gates secured behind them. Some of them had been so scared they jumped on the end of their lead ropes, but Scott, Haydn and Daisy reassured them with pats and kind words and for the most part the horses stayed calm.

Soon after, the fire chief strolled over to announce that the fire was under control.

"It will take a few more minutes to put it out and then we will have to spend time damping down to make sure there are no little pockets of fire that could ignite again. But basically the scare is over. Are all the horses safe?"

"Yes," replied Scott.

The fire chief looked at him. "It's a good job for them that you were here. If you hadn't have got that hose on it when you did the whole building could have gone up in flames, and the horses with it."

He cast an eye over Scott. "I'll call an ambulance, get the paramedics to check you over. You've had a close shave – literally, looking at your hair."

Now Haydn spoke. "I suppose it's too early to speculate on a cause?"

"Yes it is. At the moment we are still in the firefighting phase. We will have to come back in the morning to see what daylight tells us. But it's clear where the fire started, in the straw bales. It's just a question of how."

By ten o'clock the fire brigade had reduced the number of appliances at the scene to one. The crew of that engine continued to damp down behind the barn. The all clear was given for the horses to be returned to their stables. They were now settled. Three of them needed to be temporarily rehomed because of water, ash and bits of fallen wood in their stables, and Haydn and Daisy led them down the track to the barn for visitor's horses for the night, ensuring they had comfortable beds, fresh water and plenty of hay.

Meanwhile, Scott had been given a clean bill of health by the paramedics and had been for a hot shower to get rid of the soot and grime.

The three of them then gathered at Scott's bungalow to discuss the dramatic events of the evening over hot drinks.

As they settled wearily into cosy seats in the front room, Scott voiced what was in all of their minds. "Do we think this is something to do with Kane Weston? An arson attack?"

"I said the place was too secure to be targeted. Now I'm not so sure," replied Haydn.

"I thought Judd was onside. Why would he pass on information now?" said Scott.

"Yes, but can we trust him?" said Daisy doubtfully.

Haydn sat back. "Yes we can, and anyway, he wouldn't need

to feed back fresh information. Weston would already have all the details he needed to organise this. I'm just surprised anyone could get in to do it – and get out again without being seen. But I don't believe for a moment it is anything to do with Judd."

"I agree," said Scott. "It doesn't make sense for him to betray us now."

"Something else doesn't make sense to me," said Daisy. "If you were going to start a fire, wouldn't you set light to the bales stored inside? It would be more likely to burn down the barn."

"Perhaps they didn't want to harm the horses."

"But the fire chief said the building would have been engulfed anyway if you hadn't discovered it," Haydn responded.

"Yes, but wouldn't they know I'd be here?" said Scott.

They lapsed into silence. They were going round in circles and no nearer to an explanation. Then Haydn got up to go. "Just when I thought the whole nightmare could be over, this happens."

"It's terrifying, I know," said Daisy, getting to her feet and grabbing Haydn's hand. "But the horses are safe, that's all that matters right now."

"True," said Scott. "And tomorrow we may have some answers."

The final fire crew departed at around midnight and after a last check round the barn, Haydn and Daisy headed home.

"I'll have a look and make sure everything is okay at about 2am, I don't think I will sleep much tonight," said Scott. "We'll see what the morning brings."

Chapter Twenty-Eight

The fire investigation team arrived at nine o'clock the next morning. There were four of them, led by Station Officer Baines, a large man with a ruddy complexion and a determined air. They immediately began a painstaking examination of the seat of the fire.

As soon as the horses had been turned out, Scott and Haydn called the staff into the office to explain what had happened during the night. Judd could not take his eyes off Scott's singed hair as he stood and outlined the events.

"We don't know what caused the fire yet, the fire brigade are trying to establish that now. But it may have been arson. So if anyone knows anything at all which could help, please tell us," Scott concluded. He cast his eyes around the room and noted that everybody met his gaze, bar one.

After the meeting, Scott and Haydn discussed what impact it might have on the investigation into Kane Weston if it was arson.

"We'll have to see if the fire team comes up with any evidence. But even if they do, it's not going to link to Weston," said Haydn. "We'll be in the same position. Our strongest hand will be the testimony of Judd."

"If he gives it. I don't trust him, Haydn. He wouldn't look at me just now."

"I don't think he has a choice. He knows the only way to stay safe is to go with the protection we can offer him. Anyway, I don't think he has the heart for Kane Weston's empire anymore. He wants to be here."

"We'll see."

By lunchtime the fire investigation was complete. Station Officer Baines had a surprise for them. "It's pretty straightforward," he said. "And it's certainly not arson."

"NOT arson?" Haydn raised his eyebrows.

"Definitely not. We found no evidence of any accelerants, like petrol or paraffin, whatsoever. What we did find was a number of cigarette butts. Someone has been smoking round there and there is no doubt that is what set light to the straw.

"The cause is clear, accidental ignition due to a carelessly discarded cigarette. I'll send you a copy of the report when it's ready. It will contain recommendations. But the lesson is obvious – do not allow your staff to smoke around the stables. Next time you might not be so lucky."

He left with a cheery wave, but Scott looked solemn. Tapping his desk, he said: "Three guesses who is responsible."

"I'll fetch him," said Haydn.

Judd was hard at work mucking out when he saw Haydn approaching. He knew at once why he was there. "Now I'm getting the sack," he said.

"Come to the office."

Judd trudged after him, his head bowed, his mind in despair. What a fool he had been and what a mess he had made of his life. So many mistakes. And now the biggest of the lot, just when he had been given the chance to make something of himself.

He slumped on the sofa and before either Haydn or Scott could speak, he said: "It was me. I'm responsible. I've been smoking behind the barn."

"Thank you for your honesty," said Haydn. The young man hung his head in shame. "It was a stupid thing to do, you know that. The horses could have been killed. You should never smoke around hay and straw and wooden stables."

"I'm sorry. I would have killed myself if the horses had been hurt."

"There's no need to talk like that. The point is, they weren't. Just don't let it happen again. If you have to smoke, do it off the premises."

"Well, I'll be on my bike anyway now, so it doesn't matter."

"No, you won't. You've made a big mistake, but it wasn't deliberate. We can put this behind us and carry on as before. I believe we are agreed, aren't we Scott?"

Scott pursed his lips and replied curtly: "We are."

"So get back to your mucking out and think about that statement you are going to give to the police."

Judd left in a daze. He felt humbled and undeserving of the second chance he had been given. He wondered why Haydn was being so supportive. "He needs me against Kane," he mused. "But I need him just as much."

But Scott was unimpressed. "I don't know why you are sticking your neck out for him. He doesn't deserve it," he told Haydn.

"I know, and I can't explain it. Something is telling me to do it."

"Well, it has to be his last chance, Haydn."

Two days later Judd was seated in an interview room at Harrogate police station. Max Bannister and Andy Watson sat opposite him and Haydn was next to him.

When Haydn confirmed the interview was arranged Judd had panicked and decided he was not going to turn up. But when Haydn opened the passenger door of his car to take him to the station, Judd climbed in. Now he was grimly determined to do what he must.

Andy led the interview, which was being recorded, and began by chatting casually to Judd about his job at the stables. Then he became serious.

"For how long have you worked for Kane Weston?"

"Just over two years."

"And how were you recruited?"

"I was recruited by his deputy, Jim Lee. He sent a message through a friend, who was a part-time member of Kane's gang, that they wanted to see me."

Judd was surprised by how easily he was able to discuss his time working for the gangster.

"Why did they want to see you?"

"I suppose they had heard about me and thought I could be useful to them."

"Useful in what way? Because you had a criminal record?"

"I got involved in crime when I was eighteen, just petty stuff, nicking and some breaking and entering. I didn't have much money and I just got in with the wrong people."

"Who thought you would be useful?"

"Kane, I suppose."

"Even though he was in prison at the time?"

"It was Jim Lee who I dealt with, but I know he was acting with the authority of Kane."

"So what work were you doing for them?"

"Mainly housebreaking and acting as a lookout for robberies. Nothing really serious."

"It depends what you mean by serious. I'm sure decent people who have had their homes ransacked would not find it a laughing matter."

Judd bowed his head.

Andy now moved to more personal matters. "Tell me about your relationship with Keeley, Kane's wife."

Judd had been dreading this. "You know about the

relationship."

"I need you to tell me. How did it begin?"

"I used to see her up at the house sometimes. I thought she looked really fit. She was always flirting with me, winking at me and rubbing herself against me when she walked past. Then one day I went to see Jim Lee, but he wasn't there. Keeley came downstairs in a tiny mini dress. She crooked her finger at me and said: 'Judd, I need you to do a bit of breaking and entering for me.' I knew what she meant. She led me upstairs to the bedroom, closed the door and was all over me. It happened regularly after that."

"Kane was still in prison, but didn't you think he would find out? Didn't you worry about having sex with his wife?"

"I was terrified about what he would do if he found out. But I was a young lad, I couldn't resist her."

"He knows now though, doesn't he, Judd?"

"Yes he does."

"So tell me what happened after that."

Judd did not find it easy to admit to how he had acted as a spy at Wickham Court on the orders of Kane Weston. Not for the first time he felt like a traitor. But as he told how he listened in to conversations, followed Haydn and Daisy after work and then fed back everything he learned to his gangster boss, a weight of burden seemed to lift from his young shoulders. He felt as though he was in the confession box with Andy as his priest.

For twenty minutes he poured out his heart about what he had done and his conversations with Weston. At last he fell silent, his soul emptied.

Andy sat back. "Thank you, Judd, for a full and detailed account. We just need you to sign a witness statement now."

Judd nodded sadly. "I wish I didn't have to do this. I wish none of it had ever happened."

"You're putting things right now."

At last it was time to leave. Judd was not sorry. His day of atonement had dragged on and become a serious test of character. He walked out of the station with Haydn.

"You did well," said the older man. "You should be proud of yourself."

"I just hope it's all worth it. My neck will be on the line if nothing happens. Do you think you will be able to put him away?"

"That's not for me to do any more. But I think your evidence will be enough to revoke Kane's licence and take him back into custody. Then the police can set about getting the proof to link him to the crimes."

Haydn thought for a moment. Then he said: "It would be nice if we had some corroboration to your story. Do you think Keeley would talk to us?"

"She might. She hates Kane enough. I'll ask her."

"Good. Let's get back to Wickham Court. There's work to be done."

Chapter Twenty-Nine

A few days later, Haydn was asked to attend a case conference at the Crown Prosecution Service office in Leeds. Also at the meeting were Andy Watson, Max Bannister, CPS case worker Jan Richmond, Regional Deputy Crown Prosecutor Michael O'Neill and probation officer David Parsons. Haydn knew that this was D-day. The summit would decide what to do about Kane Weston.

Jan Richmond began by outlining the inquiries that had been made and the evidence that had been gathered. Haydn already knew most of the detail. He had been present at Judd's interview, which was the key evidence, and he had been kept well informed about the investigation by Andy and Max. His fear was that the CPS would reject taking any action. He had no reason to think attitudes in the organisation had changed from his days as a detective, if the case wasn't nailed on they would find an excuse not to proceed with it. But to him, Judd's testimony was compelling.

Deputy Crown Prosecutor O'Neill seemed to agree. "I find his statement to be convincing. He speaks clearly from the heart and with the benefit of inside knowledge. There can be no doubting his word."

O'Neill pushed Judd's statement to one side. "However," he continued. "If I was Kane Weston's lawyer I would be treating it with a large degree of scepticism. After all, isn't Judd out to save his own skin? He has admitted to having sex with Weston's wife. He says he fears the consequences of that. If I was Weston's lawyer I would be arguing that Ward would make anything up about his client because that would ensure Weston was locked away for many years."

Andy Watson interjected. "If a jury was to accept that, it would also be accepting that Weston intended to take criminal action against Judd as punishment for what he had done."

"It might indeed embrace that possibility," said O'Neill. "But in doing so it might conclude that Judd Ward had every reason to make up allegations about him. It would inevitably put doubt in the mind of any right-thinking juror."

Now Haydn spoke up. "But on the balance of probability, surely a jury would be driven to accept Judd's story. Only a fool would make it up, and his statement makes it clear he is no fool. The devil is in the detail."

"And yet, at the end of the day it comes down to one man's word against another. Without corroboration, who do you believe? And who might you choose to believe if the man in the dock fixes you with a look that could kill?"

Haydn knew all about that steely stare across the courtroom. He had felt its intensity himself. But he also knew in his heart that Weston could back up that look with action. He was sure the gangster could kill if he felt driven to it. "We have to believe that a jury would not be intimidated and would come to the right conclusion," he said.

O'Neill sighed: "Belief is one thing, certainty is another. We have to be certain or we are creating false hope and wasting time and money. We cannot go ahead without corroboration."

So nothing changes, thought Haydn bitterly. The CPS still hasn't got the balls.

"Do we have enough to revoke his licence?" asked Andy.

"I doubt it, unless the probation officer can provide us with anything."

David Parsons shuffled in his seat. "I don't think I can. Mr

Weston remains a model prisoner on licence. He has attended all appointments and done everything asked of him."

O'Neill now moved the meeting to its end. "I'm afraid our hands are tied for the moment. If you can provide something, or someone, to support Judd Ward, then we can move things forward. Until then, we have to bide our time."

Haydn shoved his chair back and stood up. "And in the meantime, what do we do? Wait until Kane Weston comes and blows us away? Or take up arms against him?"

"We have to work together until we have what we need," said O'Neill.

Haydn marched to the door and wrenched it open. Pausing in the doorway he turned and focused on the prosecutor. "What we need is justice. Are you going to get that for me?"

There was no answer. Haydn slammed the door behind him.

"I don't know whether I can do it."

Keeley looked into Judd's frightened eyes, as he sat next to her on the sofa in her apartment, and pondered on what he had asked her to do. There was no easy answer. Could she really give a statement to the police? She repeated: "I don't know whether I can do it."

"I know it's a lot to ask. But I have already put myself in the firing line, if you know what I mean," he pleaded.

"Let's hope it doesn't come to that," she said. "You've been very brave and I know I encouraged you to do it. But the difference is my children. If I stand up against Kane, he might make sure I never see them again and I couldn't bear that."

"But if you don't back me up, everything is lost and I'll be dead."

"I'm not sure there's anything I can say that would convince them anyway," she said.

"They seem to think it would make a difference. Please, Keeley. I can't do this on my own."

"Let me think about it, Judd. I just need some time."

"All right. But we haven't got long. In five days I start work at the wine bar. If it's not sorted by then, I think I've had it."

He got up and walked to the door. "Let me know – soon."

She nodded.

Judd plodded down the flights of stairs from her apartment, deep in thought. It seemed he was getting deeper and deeper into a mire of shit and the way out was hidden from him. He had committed himself to helping Haydn Daniel and the police. He'd had no doubts that if he told them what he knew, Kane Weston would be imprisoned for so long it would not matter if and when he got out again.

The police interview and statement had been an ordeal, but he had gone through with it because of that belief that it would all be okay.

Now things were very different. The prosecution's failure to back the police had taken him completely by surprise. The risk he had taken now seemed huge. He was sure that Kane would somehow find out about what he had done. Someone would talk. They always did. And what would happen then? Would his life be forfeit? Or just his good looks?

He reached the bottom of the stairs and wandered towards the glass exit doors, his mind in turmoil. He pressed the button to leave. As the doors slid open he became aware of a man outside. Judd stood back to allow him to enter. But the man waited and said politely: "After you."

Judd walked forward and nodded his thanks to the stranger, whose features were partially hidden by a black woolly hat covering his ears and a thick overcoat with the collar pulled up round his face. The thought crossed his mind that he was a little over dressed for September. Then he noticed a black Range Rover parked near to the entrance. Its engine was running. Suddenly he had a feeling of foreboding. And then he felt something hard and cold digging into the small of his back. Hard and cold like a gun. A voice behind him said: "Don't turn round. Keep walking."

Judd took a couple of steps. He was close to the back of the Range Rover when its rear door swung open. He heard a familiar voice: "Get in, Judd."

The hard, cold object was still pushed into his back. He felt a firm shove from the man behind and he slid into the back seat of the car, next to Kane Weston. The door closed behind him. The driver put the car in gear and it set off.

Weston clamped his big hand on Judd's shoulder. "Thought we'd have a little ride, if that's all right with you."

Judd laughed nervously. "Yeah, great." His stomach was churning and he felt in the icy grip of fear.

Weston was jovial. "Funny, bumping into you like that, Judd. I was just going to visit my wife, I have some news for her about our children, when – would you believe it, who should walk out the door!" He chuckled.

Ignoring Judd's silence, Weston continued: "Now the odd thing is, I am sure I gave explicit instructions that she was not to see you again. But there you are, giving her a shag."

Judd found his voice. "No, it wasn't like that, Mr Weston. We were just talking, that's all."

The gangster guffawed. "Talking? My wife doesn't talk. She fucks. Especially good-looking boys like you."

"No, no, really, Mr Weston. We were just talking," the young man repeated.

Weston laughed again, but it was a cold and mirthless sound. He leaned towards Judd and spoke quietly but menacingly into his ear. "Now what on earth would the two of you have to talk about? You wouldn't be plotting against me, would you?"

Judd could feel the gangster's hot breath on his neck and the malevolence in his eyes, even though he was facing to the front and could not see them. He stuttered, his fear almost overwhelming him. "N, no, M, Mr Weston. Why, why would I do that?"

"Perhaps you've enjoyed yourself too much at those fancy stables, perhaps you've got too close to that old detective. Perhaps your loyalties have switched."

"No, no, never. I will always be loyal to you, Mr Weston," Judd lied, desperation shoving his fear to one side. "Always."

The gangster's voice became more soothing. "That's good to hear, Judd. Very good. You understand the question had to be asked. A man like me can't be too careful." And he patted Judd on the shoulder.

Judd stifled his gasp of relief, but he was not safe yet. Even if he could take Kane's words at face value, and he had his doubts about that, he was still trapped in the car. He noticed that the driver had taken them to a huge park and woods to the south of Leeds. They were now driving down a track between thick clumps of trees. No other vehicles were in sight. They passed a woman walking her dog and the car then turned on to a smaller track, where great trunks hemmed them in and thick leafy branches bent over and embraced them in a natural cocoon. The stony roadway came to a halt before a copse of trees, through which Judd could see a small clearing. They were alone.

"Let's take a stroll," said the gangster. Judd's passenger door was opened and a hand signalled him to get out. As he did so, he noticed a second car was parked behind them. Two men now emerged from it.

He heard Weston's voice. "Join me, Judd." The gangster

was stood on the opposite side of the car, his arm outstretched in what seemed a friendly invitation. Judd felt a prod in his back and did as he was bid.

Kane put his arm around Judd's shoulders in a fatherly fashion and they walked together towards the clearing.

Almost at the end of the belt of trees, Weston stopped and stepped back, observing the young man, assessing his level of fear and calculating what was going through his mind.

"I really don't know what to do about you, Judd," he began. "You claim to be loyal, and those whose opinions I respect believe in you. And yet you still indulge yourself with my wife. So how can I trust you? How do I know you are not planning to betray me in some other way?"

"I have been stupid, but that's all it is. I am not going to betray you, I promise." Judd knew he was now bartering for his life.

Kane could clearly see that the young man was trying to save himself. But he also detected that he was speaking the truth. It would be easy to lie in Judd's position, but Kane did not believe he was a liar. He meant what he said. "If you are not being honest with me, you know what I will do, don't you?"

Judd nodded furiously.

"I have no wish to continue with a criminal life – unless, of course, I am forced into it by treachery. I want to make my money legitimately. The wine bar in Bradford is crucial to that. Are you going to make that a profitable business for me?"

Judd nodded again. "Yes, I will. You won't regret giving me the chance."

"I don't have regrets, Judd. If something is wrong, I put it right, in whatever way is best. You should never have regrets, for anything or anyone. There is always somebody to take one's place, don't you think?"

"I do."

"So, nine o'clock, next Monday morning at the wine bar. I will join you at 6pm for the grand opening."

Weston turned to leave, then paused and faced Judd again. "Oh, and one more thing. You will never see Keeley again, ever. Do you understand?"

"Of course, I promise."

"I have asked Darren and Dwayne to make sure that the message is clear to you."

Judd saw that the two tough-looking and well-built men from the other car were now standing a couple of yards away.

"I'll leave you with them. I'm sure you can find your way home. Au revoir."

Judd watched Kane stride away. He looked into the cruel eyes of Darren and Dwayne and realised that payback time was upon him.

Chapter Thirty

Judd sat on a stool in front of the bathroom mirror and dabbed his face with a flannel. The beating could have been worse. He had grazes to his cheek and chin and his ribs and back ached from the bruising that was already starting to come out in blotches of deep purple. Darren and Dwayne had mostly avoided hitting his face, concentrating on thumps and kicks to his body. Weston had probably told them to leave his looks alone, so as not to frighten off customers at the wine bar. But Judd had got the intended message loud and clear. Stay away from Keeley. This time he could not ignore it. He would not get another warning.

But he had to let her know that he could not see her again. She deserved that. He knew he was abandoning her to her fate, but he had no alternative. After all, she had chosen to marry the bastard in the first place.

Judd opened a can of strong lager, picked up his mobile phone and began to write a text message.

"Keeley," it began. "I am sorry, but I can't see you anymore. Kane had me beaten up. I am okay but it's over. I am taking the job with him at the wine bar. Take care. Love Judd."

He felt guilty to end it with such a short and impersonal message, but there was really nothing more to say. He pressed the send button, then switched off the phone and flung it on the sofa. He grabbed his jacket, closed the front door of his flat behind him and went to the pub, determined to get drunk.

The next morning he woke with a headache. But his mind was clear. Today he would go to the stables. He would say his goodbyes to everybody, and the horses. He had loved being there, but it was now obvious to him that there was no escape from the dark world he had entered as an impressionable young man. Nobody was going to protect him from Kane Weston. The beating had told him that. He had to protect himself and the only way to do that was to carry on working for Weston and make sure he was in his good books.

Before leaving the flat he switched his phone back on and saw that he had three missed calls from Keeley and several text messages asking him to call her. He pocketed the phone. It was pointless contacting her. He had made his decision.

He arrived at Wickham Court and as he drove through the electronic gates he was hit by a wave of self-pity. Why did he have to turn his back on this wonderful place? But he knew that he must.

He parked up and headed to the office. He could see that both Haydn and Scott were there but as he entered, Scott rose to his feet. "I have to give a lesson. I'll leave you to it."

Judd watched Scott disappear. "He doesn't like me, does he?"

"I wouldn't say that, Judd. But you did nearly burn down the stables, he's bound to be a bit peeved."

Haydn had noted with concern the injuries to Judd's face. Now he asked: "What happened?"

"I tripped and fell into a wall."

"I see."

"There's nothing to worry about."

"Good."

Judd was hovering by the door. It was obvious to Haydn that the young man was lying about his injuries, and that something else was on his mind. He waited.

"I'm sorry, Mr Daniel. But I am going to have to leave," said Judd, at last.

"I see," Haydn repeated.

"And I'll have to withdraw my statement. I can't go through with it."

"So Kane Weston is responsible for your injuries."

"He's not responsible, Mr Daniel." Judd looked alarmed.

"But you didn't fall, did you?"

Judd was silent.

"Look, Judd. I told you the police would support you, every step of the way, and I meant that."

"But they didn't. They threw the case out."

"Not the police."

"It doesn't matter who it was. I just can't do it, and that's the end of it."

"What about Keeley?"

"What about her?"

"Won't she make a statement?"

"I don't think so. Anyway, I shan't be seeing her again."

"He's properly put the frighteners on you, hasn't he?"

"I just have to do the best thing for me and that means giving up my job here and going back to where I belong."

Haydn did not believe that sentiment for a moment. But he could see it was useless to argue. "Then I have to accept that, though it saddens me to do so."

"I wish it was different. Anyway, thanks for everything. I did love it here. Goodbye, Mr Daniel."

"Judd, you know where I am if you need me." Haydn held out his hand.

The young man shook it, turned, and left Wickham Court for the last time.

Haydn and Daisy relaxed together on the living room sofa, her arm draped around his waist and her head resting lightly on his shoulder. Two large glasses of red wine were before them on the coffee table. Timmy was stretched out luxuriously on the rug in front of the cheery blaze of the stove. It was a scene of domestic bliss.

Daisy uncoupled herself from him, leaned forward and sipped her wine. Then she said: "It's only three days to the event at Northallerton. Have you decided if you will come with me?"

Haydn dragged himself from his own thoughts and focused on her question. He had made up his mind days ago. "Of course I will. I'm not letting you out of my sight, and anyway you will need a good groom."

She smiled. "Well, I suppose I'll have to settle for you!"

They sat in silence. Haydn stared ahead blankly.

Daisy watched him for a few moments, then said: "What's wrong?"

He jerked back his attention to her and saw the concern in her eyes. He sighed. "Don't trouble yourself, Daisy. It's just that Judd isn't going ahead with the case. He's withdrawing his statement and he's left the yard."

"Oh no! I thought I hadn't seen him today. Does that mean the case won't happen?"

"I don't know what it means. But the CPS certainly won't prosecute without his evidence, so I guess that's that."

She bowed her head. "So there's nothing to stop Weston coming after us again?"

"We can't lock him up unless we can prove his involvement. But he's not a fool. Judd got beaten up. Weston must be behind that, which means he may suspect we are on to him. He's not going to risk trying anything else if he has that knowledge."

"But we can't be sure?"

He took her hand. "No, love. We can't be sure."

Haydn was up and about early the next day. He had slept badly, tossing and turning as his mind refused to switch off from the terrible dilemma he faced. How could he now keep Daisy and himself safe? Would Weston dare to try to harm them one more time? It seemed to him that the gangster could have a last card to play before feeling that his revenge was complete. But what would it be? And where and when would he show his hand?

Haydn had thought about discussing it with Andy. But this was his problem, and only he could solve it. By the morning, he had his answer.

Chapter Thirty-One

Sicily House could loosely be described as a fortress. The two-storey, modern stone building might not have had the appearance of a stronghold of the kings of old but it was equally impregnable.

Tucked away on a quiet country lane, and yet only a stone's throw from a sprawling, gangland estate on the outskirts of Bradford, it was almost invisible from the roadside. High, solid walls ran round the entire property, enclosing both house and garden. Huge, thick wooden gates, topped by a stone arch, at the front provided the only access, and gave no glimpse of what was beyond.

But while visitors had no clue of who, or what, was inside Sicily House, the occupants could see everything and everyone on the outside. CCTV cameras covered the entrance, while others were set up at strategic points around the perimeter. Jim Lee's office at the back of the house contained half a dozen TV screens, projecting the CCTV images at all times of day or night. The cameras were supported by a high-tech alarm system which would activate at any sign of an intruder. The entrance gates had a buzzer system for callers and could only be opened electronically from the office, if Kane Weston approved of the visit. A man of Weston's power and importance needed to have proper protection from the dangers of the outside world – and he had it. He knew he was safe at the heart of his lair.

Weston was reading the final draft of a letter from his solicitor to Keeley, which would prevent her from seeing the boys until further notice, and documenting photographic evidence of her affair, when there was a knock on the study door and his deputy walked into the room.

"There is a visitor for you, Boss," Lee said. "You might want to come and see who it is."

Kane glanced up at Lee but was met by his usual deadpan expression. Without a word, he stood up and strode to the office. He looked at the front gate monitor. Hardly comprehending what he was seeing he stared closer at the screen to be certain. Then he stepped back. "Okay. Open the gates. I'll be in the office."

Haydn knew the property well. He had examined every room when the search warrant had been executed following Weston's arrest. He had been struck by the expensive paintings on the walls and the vintage furniture around the rooms and recalled thinking to himself: "Crime does pay, after all."

Now, as he drove down the lane to Sicily House, he remembered the sophisticated security of the place and knew that his identity would be instantly known. He was heading to the dragon's den but the brooding host would be forewarned that he was there. Briefly, he questioned the wisdom of the course of action he had chosen. But he reassured himself with the thought that the dragon might huff and puff, but he could not risk breathing fire over him. The consequence would be life behind bars.

At the gates, Haydn got out of the car and pressed the communication buzzer. It was answered straight away by a metallic voice. "Please state your name and business."

"Haydn Daniel. I am here to see Kane Weston."

"Please wait while I check whether he is available."

There was a click and the voice disappeared. Haydn idly looked around him. Nothing moved. The occasional twitter of birds was the only sound to disturb the silence. Two minutes passed. Then there was a click from the buzzer and the metallic voice returned. "Enter and park in front of the house."

The gates swung silently open and Haydn drove in. They closed behind him with a firm and definite clunk. He was inside the fortress walls. One hundred yards ahead of him was the house. He steered his car round the circular drive, the gravel crunching gently beneath the tyres, between colourful flower borders and lawns to the porched entrance, guarded by stone pillars on either side of the thick, wooden door which stood open. He parked next to a black Range Rover and got out.

In the entrance, waiting for him, was a tall, fit-looking middle-aged man. He held out his hand. "Mr Daniel. I am Jim Lee, I manage Mr Weston's business affairs. Please come in."

Haydn followed him into the large entrance hall. It was as he remembered it, with its high ceiling, dangling chandeliers and black and white mezzanine floor. Solid wood doors led into rooms on either side and to the back of the hall. In the centre, a wide, balustraded staircase, encased in a luxurious, thick red carpet, wound its way upstairs.

"This way," said Lee, with a sweep of his arm, and he led Haydn to one of the doors, at the back and to the right of the hall.

Entering the study, he motioned to a comfortable chair, facing the garden, at the big oak table. "Take a seat."

Indicating a silver tray bearing a tall coffee pot, china cups and saucers and plates of what appeared to be home-baked biscuits, Lee added: "Help yourself. Mr Weston will join you shortly."

He left the room. Haydn looked around. The study was large but a log fire burned in a marble fireplace and the room was warm. Portraits and landscape paintings adorned the walls. Apart from the tray, the desk was empty. Haydn imagined anything of importance had been put away from prying eyes. He strolled beyond the desk to the wooden-framed windows and gazed into the back garden, which was home to a small orchard of fruit trees and a little pond. Beyond was the inevitable high wall.

After a few minutes, he heard a click behind him and turned to see a side door open. Lee emerged into the room, followed by a figure who Haydn knew well but had not seen for years. Kane Weston appeared to be more of a bull of a man than ever. His body was bulked up, not concealed by the loose-fitting suit he was wearing. His piggy little eyes peered out at him from his thin facial features. For a moment Haydn thought he caught them shining with malevolence, but Weston quickly cloaked the hatred in them.

"Mr Daniel. What a pleasant surprise. I see you are admiring my lovely little garden."

He smiled coldly and waved Haydn into the chair chosen for him, but did not proffer his hand in friendship, instead taking his seat opposite his enemy and placing his hands together and resting them on the desk.

Lee poured the coffees, placing one before Haydn and offering him biscuits, which he politely declined.

Weston sipped his coffee. "Perfect, Jim. You may leave us now."

Lee retreated out of the side door and closed it behind him.

The two men sat in silence and visually squared up to each other, trying to stare each other down, looking for any weakness and seeking out such fear as might be lurking beneath their determined exteriors. But there was none on either side.

At last Weston spoke. His voice was calm but his manner was curt. "So why are you here?"

"You don't have to ask the question. You know why I am here."

"To continue your persecution of an innocent man, as you have done for so long?"

"Innocent? You are a convicted drug smuggler."

"I was not guilty."

"The jury disagreed."

Weston leaned forward across the desk. His whole presence embodied menace. But Haydn ignored the implied threat.

"I am here to tell you that I am not afraid of you. That your campaign of hate will not succeed. And that I am going to bring you to justice – once more."

Again, the cold smile. "I don't know what you mean."

Haydn knew that Weston was lying. But he was not going to debate the point. He too leaned forward, so that their faces were just inches apart, their eyes boring into those of the other man. "You realise that when your licence is revoked and you are taken back to court and prosecuted for serious offences, on top of those you have already been convicted of, you will be an old man before they let you out again."

Now Kane thrust his chair angrily to one side and began to stalk around the room, his face black as thunder. He paced to the window and stood looking out, while cracking his knuckles in an exasperation of fury. Regaining control of himself he turned and sat back down.

He said: "What you fail to understand is that I am a legitimate businessman. Whatever wrong conclusion the courts came up with in the past I now make my money in the entertainment industry, running high quality wine bars and snooker centres for high quality clientele, many of whom are highly respected in the community and in authority. You would be making a big mistake if you tried to falsely connect me to any criminal acts."

"Is that a threat?"

"No, it is simply a statement of fact."

"So you are not going to send someone to shoot out the rest of my windows?"

"If I wanted to shoot out anybody's windows, I would do so myself. But, of course, that is purely theoretical, as I have no wish to cause damage or harm to anybody. And I am sure nobody would want to suggest that."

Haydn was about to say that that was only because they had been frightened out of it, but he stopped himself in time. Judd was in enough danger. Instead he said: "Well, we shall see what the evidence tells us."

Weston snorted. "You have no evidence – because there is no evidence."

As things stand, he's right, thought Haydn. But I have to put doubt in his mind, or the visit will have been wasted and he will never leave us alone. He stood up as if to go, but put his hands on the desk and leaned towards the gangster. "You may believe you are above the law. But never forget that I put you away once, and I am going to do it again. You will see the proof I have. Remember that."

He walked to the door and took hold of the handle. But before he could leave, Weston spoke again. "You're not a copper anymore. Remember that."

Weston watched his old enemy go and then thumped the desk hard with his fist and announced to anyone who cared to listen: "The bastard has to die."

Haydn walked into the hall. His heart was thumping with adrenaline, anger and fear – a fear that he had refused to admit to. Lee was waiting. "I'll walk to the gate and let you out. Have a safe journey."

Haydn got in his car and put the key in the ignition. For a moment he hesitated as the thought went through his head that the vehicle might have been tampered with. He dismissed the idea and turned the key. The engine burst into life and he drove to the gates. They were open and Lee waved him through.

Haydn accelerated away, relief sweeping through him as he took the road home.

Chapter Thirty-Two

"I can't believe you did that. Are you crazy, Haydn? He could have killed you." Daisy reached across the kitchen table, grasped the bottle of wine and poured herself a full glass. She drained half of it and then grasped Haydn's arm and demanded: "Why?"

"I had to give him back some of his own medicine. I hope threatening him with what he fears most – being sent back to prison – will make him think twice about doing anything else to us."

"It's a huge gamble, Haydn. It could just provoke him into doing something even worse."

"I know that's a possibility. But if I was a betting man my money would be on him seeing sense and forgetting about us. His vendetta would be worthless if it meant I did put him back where he belongs. And he prizes his freedom more than anything."

"I hope you're right, Haydn. I think he's terrifying. I'll never be able to sleep properly again if you don't put him away. But how are you going to do that without Judd's evidence?"

"Don't worry, Daisy. I'll find a way."

Keeley curled up on the sofa, buried her blonde head in a cushion and wept. Her world had fallen apart. First, Judd had ended their relationship. She accepted it was over. He had refused to answer her calls or reply to her messages. She understood why. Kane had had him beaten up. It would be asking for trouble to ignore that. But she could not help feeling a little disappointed that Judd had not stood his ground. She liked her men to be macho, after all she had married Kane. She knew it was unreasonable to expect Judd to take him on, but the thought still niggled at her.

And Keeley would miss him. She would miss his slim and toned body, his energetic lovemaking, and the way he doted on her like a wide-eyed puppy, her very own devoted and drooling toyboy who would do anything she asked of him to make her happy. She would miss all of that.

But, for once, there was more to it than just sex and good looks and having a slave to her desires. She would also miss the way Judd cared for and protected her, in a genuine way that no-one had done before. She realised that she had cared for him too. He had not simply been a young stud who satisfied her avaricious sexual needs. She now knew that she had actually loved him, still loved him. And so her sadness over the break up was that much greater.

As if that loss was not enough for her to bear, that morning she had received the letter from Kane's solicitor. Now she reached to the floor and picked it up from where she had let it fall. She blinked away the tears and focused again on its words.

"Dear Miss Calvert," it began, using her maiden name as if her marriage had never existed.

"Despite previous requests for you not to openly conduct a sexual relationship with Mr Judd Ward, you have continued to do so.

"This was done with complete disregard for the agreed terms of the divorce settlement, which made it clear that the generous access granted you to the children of the marriage, Al and John Weston, was subject to you ending the aforementioned relationship. This clause was to protect the moral well being of the two named children.

"Mr Ward has confessed to your continuing affair, and we further enclose photographic evidence supporting this.

"Our client has instructed us to inform you that, in light of these facts, your access to Al and John Weston is now denied until further notice, for the reasons stated."

Tears again streamed down Keeley's cheeks. Then she screwed up the letter and flung it away from her. "You bastard," she shouted.

She perched on the edge of the sofa and dabbed her eyes. Then she took a deep breath and announced to the empty room: "You will not win. I won't let you."

Keeley grabbed her phone and googled 'Wickham Court equestrian centre.'

It was midday. Haydn was in the office and was about to look for Daisy to suggest a pub lunch when a vehicle pulled up outside the car park. He saw that the Nissan car was a taxi. Haydn was immediately on his guard. It was highly unusual for anyone to come to the yard by taxi. Livery customers, staff and visitors had their own vehicles.

A chilling vision entered his head of a gunman emerging from the car and opening fire. But when the passenger got out he saw that it was a woman. The taxi turned and drove away, leaving the woman standing uncertainly on the yard. Clearly, she did not know where to go, so Haydn left the office and walked towards her. She saw him approaching and turned to face him.

Haydn could see that she was a blonde woman, in her early thirties, wearing tight white jeans, black ankle boots, and a zipped-up, short, black leather jacket.

As he got near, Haydn suddenly recognised the woman and stopped in his tracks. "Keeley Weston?"

She nodded.

"I'm Haydn Daniel."

"I know."

"You better come in."

She followed him across the yard and settled herself on the settee in the office.

"Please, make yourself comfortable. Would you like a coffee?" he said.

"Thanks," she said, unzipping her jacket and revealing a tight-fitting white top with a plunging V-neck, exposing an excessive amount of cleavage.

She doesn't change, thought Haydn. But Keeley obviously wasn't here simply to flaunt her charms.

"I didn't want to come here, but I had to," she began.

Haydn said nothing. Don't interrupt, just let her say what she's come to say, he thought.

"Judd said you wanted me to give a statement about my husband."

"Yes," Haydn encouraged.

"I wasn't sure about it, I was worried, because of my husband."

"I understand that."

"Anyway, I've decided to go ahead with it."

"That's good. What has made the difference?"

"Things have happened, that's all. I guess I've nothing to lose."

Keeley looked around furtively, as if she was expecting Kane to suddenly and inexplicably appear out of thin air. "Can we get it out of the way now?" she said.

Haydn smiled, and then saw that she was being serious. "Unfortunately, we can't. The fact is, I am no longer a police officer, so I cannot take your statement. It will have to be done by an officer at a police station."

Her face fell. But almost immediately it brightened again

and she said: "All right, when can we do it?"

She certainly had spirit and determination, Haydn thought. But it was not unexpected, considering she had shared her life with Kane Weston for more than fifteen years. He replied: "It won't be before next week now. But I'll contact the police and see if it can be arranged for then. Can you give me your contact number so I can confirm it with you."

She looked uncertain but said: "I suppose so. But don't tell HIM I gave it to you."

"Don't worry, I won't be doing that."

She scribbled down her mobile phone number and passed it to Haydn. Then she said: "You will have to persuade Judd to give evidence. There's no point me doing it if he won't."

"Can't you persuade him?"

"He won't talk to me. He's scared of Kane."

"I can understand that. Well, I will try to change Judd's mind. But he's had a beating and it will not be easy."

Keeley stared into space. Then she said: "Nothing's easy with Kane around. He's a horrible man. I hate him. I wish he was dead."

"The best we can do is lock him up for many years. But I need your help, and Judd's help, to do that."

"Yes."

Keeley stood up, flicked her hair over her shoulder and zipped up her jacket. "I have to go. Could you order me a taxi?"

"I can drop you back."

For the first time since she arrived, Keeley laughed. "I don't think that's a good idea. You don't want to be seen with me. I'll take the taxi."

She sat back on the sofa to wait for the cab. Five minutes later, it arrived.

Haydn proffered his hand. "I'll speak to you before next week. And thanks. I have to say I think you are being brave."

She briefly shook his hand. "Brave or stupid."

She looked him in the eyes. "It's you who needs to be brave. Nobody crosses Kane – but you have. Watch out – or he will kill you."

Chapter Thirty-Three

There was an autumnal chill in the air as Haydn walked Timmy through the woods. It was seven o'clock on Sunday morning and they were both wearing light coats. They were out early because it was Daisy's final equestrian event of the season and they would need to be at Wickham Court in plenty of time. Des would have to be brushed and have his plaits checked and his hooves oiled, while his tack and Daisy's riding clothes would need loading into the horse wagon.

The stroll through the woods, as always, gave Haydn the chance to reflect. Keeley's visit, and her decision to testify against her husband, had been as much a surprise as her clarity of thought and her refusal to be cowed by him. Her final words of warning had got him thinking. Although he knew that Weston was a dangerous and violent man, Haydn had never considered him to be a killer and did not believe that his vengeful path would take him in that direction. Now he was not so sure. His wife clearly thought Kane was capable of murder.

Haydn had considered contacting Andy Watson, or Max Bannister, about the developments, but decided it could wait until after the weekend.

He had, however, tried to get in touch with Judd. He was sufficiently concerned about Keeley's theory to redouble his efforts to get Judd back on board. Without him there was no chance of a prosecution.

But Judd's mobile had gone straight to answerphone.

Haydn had left a message, in which he pulled no punches. "Judd, it's Haydn. I need to see you. Keeley has come forward and is prepared to make a statement against Kane, as long as you go ahead with yours. It's really important that you talk to me about this. If we all pull together we can put him away for good. Daisy and I are going to a competition at Northallerton Equestrian Centre on Sunday, I could see you there if you wanted to talk on neutral ground. Anyway, give me a ring."

Haydn had left the message on Friday evening but he had heard nothing from Judd. He resigned himself to the possibility that the young man simply would not call, that it was just too much to ask of him to stick his neck on the line against the biggest gangster he would probably ever know.

But if that was the case, where did it leave Haydn? How could he possibly succeed in his quest to bring Weston to justice? And would the gangster really try to kill him to prevent him from doing so? If the beast felt cornered he might take desperate measures.

Haydn and Timmy were now heading down the track, just a few yards from home. The dog was trotting ahead but Haydn called him back and fastened his lead to his collar. He glanced around to see if anyone was about, but there was no-one. "You silly old fool, nothing's going to happen on your own doorstep," he thought. But Keeley's words repeated themselves in his head, and he hurried inside.

That morning Judd was also awake early. He had slept badly. He'd had a lot to think about in the last couple of days and his mind refused to relax.

He had gone out and got drunk on Friday night, trying to forget about his new role at the wine bar which he would start on Monday. He was terrified that he would not be able to do the job to the standard that would please Kane and feared the consequences if that happened. More than that, the last thing he really wanted to do was work for Kane Weston. He did not want anything to do with him, but he felt trapped. His foolishness in messing about with Weston's wife had left him permanently vulnerable, forever at risk. And the only way to keep the animal at bay was to work hard for him and to somehow try to win his respect and maybe then his forgiveness. It seemed a tall order and Judd felt that he was all the time walking on egg shells.

He had woken on Saturday with a thumping headache. As he tried to clear his head with a strong coffee he checked his phone, and discovered the message from Haydn. Judd was horrified. Keeley's decision to back up his story was completely unexpected. But beneath her flighty exterior, he knew that there was a strong and determined woman.

Now what was he to do? He had made his statement to the police because he had been promised their support. But he had been let down, so he had felt driven back into Weston's criminal arms. Now Haydn Daniel was trying to tempt him back – and just two days before he started his new job with Kane.

As he grappled with this seemingly impossible puzzle, his phone rang. It was Jim Lee with another summons to Sicily House.

"Mr Weston wants to discuss a few details about the wine bar."

Judd shoved the phone in the pocket of his jeans and pushed all other thoughts out of his head.

The meeting with Weston had been surprisingly amicable. The gangster had seemed in a good mood and excited about his new project. He appeared to have no doubts that Judd was up to the task and the young man did nothing to dissuade him, some of his old swagger suddenly returning alongside Weston's confidence in him. No mention was made of Keeley – though

Weston would have known that Judd had not seen her – and Judd left the house with a warm handshake and a cheery 'good luck on Monday' from the crime boss.

It was only when he got home that Judd realised his phone was missing. He searched every pocket but it was not there.

His heart beat furiously. What if it had fallen out of his pocket at Sicily House? If Kane examined it and heard the message from Daniel, he would know everything about Judd's treachery. Then what?

He did not have a landline so he could not call his mobile, but even if he had, what would he have done if Kane had answered it? He spent the evening hiding in his flat with the lights out. He went to bed early but lay there for hours listening for any sound that might indicate an intruder. He drifted off to sleep for a couple of hours but when he woke in the morning he was shattered.

He stumbled into the kitchen, made another strong coffee, lit up a cigarette and sat at the table, wondering what on earth he was going to do. But he had no answers.

He swilled his face, trying to revive himself and get his brain working, put on a shirt and jeans and sat smoking in the lounge. He stubbed out his sixth cigarette and laid his head back on the settee, trying to think his way out of the mess he was in. But still there was no solution.

He must have dozed off because he suddenly became aware of a loud banging at the door, jerking him awake. He shook his head, not certain of what had woken him. Then the noise came again – bang, bang, bang, BANG! And a loud voice: "Open up!"

Judd was afraid of what he would find, the caller was clearly unfriendly. But he knew he had to open the door – before it was stoved in.

"Hold on, I'm coming," he shouted.

He grabbed his keys from the kitchen table and cast around

for something to protect himself with. His eyes fell on a small cutting knife with a serrated edge and he snatched it up, holding it behind his back.

The voice called out again: "Open up."

"I'm here now," said Judd. He unlocked the door, replacing the keys in his pocket, then slid off the chain and bolt and immediately took two strides back from the door. At the same moment it was flung wide open.

Framed in the doorway were the familiar bulky figures of Darren and Dwayne, Weston's henchmen who had administered Judd's beating just a few days ago.

Judd took another step back and looked at the men fearfully. He clutched the handle of the knife tighter. "What do you want?"

Dwayne grinned menacingly. "Seems like you forgot something yesterday." He dangled Judd's phone in front of him. "Mr Weston thought you might be missing it. He said you have some important messages."

So the game was up. Judd tried to stay calm. "I've been looking for that. Thanks for bringing it." He reached out for the phone but Dwayne closed his hand around it.

"Mr Weston says we are to take you to see him, so he can have a little chat," said the big man.

"Yes, of course. I'll just get my jacket."

Judd backed away down the hallway, keeping the knife out of view. He stopped just before the bedroom door. "I better put the phone on charge before we go."

Dwayne looked at him suspiciously, then casually tossed the phone across the hall. Judd snatched it out of the air with one hand and dived into the bedroom.

"Don't be long," snarled Dwayne.

"Wait there, I'll just be a minute."

Judd thrust the phone deep into his pocket and dropped

the knife on the bed. He grabbed his wallet and jacket and went to the window. His mind was clear. If he did not escape now, he was a dead man walking. Then the thought struck him that he ought to arm himself. He glanced at the knife on the bed and then, as another idea entered his head, he walked to the bedside table. Opening the bottom drawer he drew aside a heavy piece of old cloth and, smiling at the irony, picked up the revolver Kane had given him and stuffed it into the inside pocket of his jacket.

He dashed back to the window, opened it and looked down on the communal back garden. His flat was on the first floor and it was a good twelve feet to the ground. But below was a grassed area and it had been raining, so it would be a soft landing. He threw his jacket and wallet on to the grass and clambered out of the window, twisting round to face the building. Holding on to the ledge with both hands he lowered himself as far as he could, then let go. He bent his knees as he landed, cushioning the fall, his body rolling over in the momentum. He was unhurt but the impact momentarily knocked the wind out of him and he lay with his face in the grass, getting his breath back.

After a couple of seconds he felt able to get to his feet. He knew he had to get away quickly before his escape was discovered. Darren and Dwayne would not allow him long before they searched for him. He glanced up at the window. No-one was there. Snatching up his jacket and wallet he sprinted to the side of the building and hurried round to the front where his car was parked. He peered anxiously round the wall. The coast was clear. His car was fifty yards away. He reckoned it would take him no more than thirty seconds to run over to it, unlock the door, start the engine and drive off. Just long enough.

Bracing himself, he took a last look and then set off. He was at the car door in just a few seconds. As he opened it he heard a shout. Looking up he saw that Darren and Dwayne had emerged from his front door and were looking over the maisonettes' communal balcony. As he watched, they dashed to the stairs. Judd dived in and turned the keys in the ignition. The engine burst into life and he thrust the car into first gear. The men now appeared at the bottom of the stairs, fifty yards ahead of him and to the left. They began to run towards him. Judd put his foot to the floor. The tyres span and screeched in protest, then the car leaped forward. The men reached out, but he was gone. He swerved between two cars on to the Leeds Ring Road and, accelerating through the gears, he disappeared out of sight.

Haydn swung Daisy's horsebox into a handy parking space at the end of a row of wagons and switched off the engine. In the back, Des let out a big neigh announcing their arrival at Northallerton Equestrian Centre.

Daisy jumped out of the cab, opened the side doors of the vehicle and patted her horse. She had put her fears and anxieties about Kane Weston temporarily out of her mind. Nothing mattered now except her horse and the event they were about to compete in. She was totally focused on that.

"Good boy," she said, patting Des again.

Haydn appeared at her side. "Do you want me to walk him round while you get yourself sorted?"

"Thanks." She smiled at him. He knew the ropes now.

Soon she was ready to get on her horse and they headed out to the warm-up field to prepare for the dressage. Haydn walked with them. He noted Daisy's look of determination and her air of confidence. He said nothing, not wanting to disturb her concentration.

As they walked, Haydn found himself checking out every

person that they passed, imagining they were gun-toting criminals setting their sights on them. But all he saw were smartly-dressed riders and their beautifully turned-out horses. He tried to relax and tell himself that this was a horse competition at a pretty rural location. Evil did not visit places like this. Then he remembered how Daisy's tyres had been slashed at a similar venue, and he redoubled his vigilance.

But there was nothing for Haydn to worry about, no sign of any suspicious characters, and he was able to enjoy an excellent performance in the dressage which put Daisy and Des in third place. A lovely clear round in the showjumping ensured they would be near the top of the leaderboard with just the cross-country to go.

But now Daisy faced a long wait. There were thirty competitors in her class and she was one of the first to go. It would be nearly an hour before the showjumping phase was completed and she could start out on her crucial cross-country round. She tied up Des in the horsebox and went inside the main building with Haydn for a coffee.

When they came back out, Daisy stopped and grabbed Haydn's arm. She pointed. "There's someone lurking by the horsebox."

Haydn looked across and saw a young man in jeans and a leather jacket loitering suspiciously at the side of their wagon. He had his back to them and his head was inclined towards the ground. As Haydn stared over, the figure slowly turned and looked in their direction. Haydn instantly recognised him. "It's Judd," he said.

He raised his arm in a welcoming wave and strode up. Judd responded with a nod and a hesitant smile.

"Hello Judd. I didn't expect you to come."

"Nor did I. But something has happened and I didn't know where else to go."

Haydn saw that the young man was glancing nervously around him, as if expecting someone to pounce on him. He looked scared. Whatever had happened must have been serious. But he would have to wait to find out what it was. Right now, Haydn needed to help Daisy prepare for her cross-country round. He knew that if she jumped round clear she could win the competition.

"Don't worry, we can talk about it in a while," said Haydn. "I'm glad you're here. I could do with a hand to get Des ready for the cross-country. It will take your mind off things."

Judd was immediately interested in the event. "How are you doing in the competition, Daisy?" he asked.

"We were third after the dressage and then went clear in the showjumping."

"Oh wow! That's ace!" said Judd enthusiastically.

"I think the showjumping has just finished. I'll go and find out what position we are in," said Daisy.

She returned a couple of minutes later with a big smile on her face. "We're in second," she said.

Judd's face lit up. "It would be really cool if you won!"

The men worked together to change the horse's saddlecloth, alter the bridle and tighten the girth, and when Daisy emerged in her cross-country colours, Des was ready for action. They watched the pair soar over the practice jumps and then stood nervously to one side as Des and Daisy walked into the start box and waited to set off. When the call came the horse sprang forward and cantered off to the first fence.

"Go for it, Daisy," yelled Judd, suddenly immersed in the competition, his troubles briefly unimportant.

Daisy and Des flew over the first few obstacles, before disappearing from sight into the countryside. Haydn and Judd listened intently to the commentary as it broadcast the pair's journey around the course. At last they came back into view and galloped towards the finish. As they crossed the line the commentator announced: "And Daisy Langridge and Secret Desire have jumped a clear round within the time, so they have no penalties to add."

"What does that mean?" asked Judd.

"It means the worst they can finish is second," replied Haydn. "Well done, Daisy," he called as she jumped off her horse.

She beamed at him. "He's an absolute star, a machine."

She led Des back to the wagon park, while Haydn carried the saddle and Judd brought the bridle.

"You were ace," said the young man excitedly. "When will you know if you have won?"

"We've a long wait, I'm afraid. The leader is the last to go, so it will be at least an hour."

The three of them spent twenty minutes showering the sweat from Des, drying him off and walking him round so his legs did not get stiff from his exertions, and then loaded him into the wagon. He began tucking into his haynet.

"I'm going to stay with him for a little while, just to make sure he is okay," said Daisy. "You two go and enjoy the action and I'll join you in a few minutes."

Haydn looked dubious. "I'm not sure about leaving you on your own."

"I'll be fine. Look, Haydn, there are no dodgy characters here. We're perfectly safe. I'll be with you in plenty of time to see my rival go round."

Haydn was still uncertain. But Daisy was surely right. And it would give him the chance to talk to Judd. "All right. But don't be long."

The two men walked to the cross-country course and found a vantage point on a little hillock which gave them good views of the start and finish of the circuit. They stood together, watching the horses and riders go round.

Then Haydn said: "Do you want to tell me what happened?"

"They came for me. I had to escape out of a window."

"Who came for you?"

"Kane's henchmen. They turned up at my flat this morning. They had my phone with them. I'd been at Sicily House yesterday. It must have fallen out of my pocket."

"Why would they bring it round?" Haydn had not made the link.

"They were going to take me to Kane. He heard your message. He knows everything."

Haydn sighed. "I see."

"What do I do now?"

"Trust me. Stick to your statement. Tomorrow morning I'll talk to the police. Come with me to see Keeley and we'll take her to the police station so she can give her evidence. I'll make sure the prosecution goes ahead and we will nail him – I promise."

Judd looked at the older man. "I'm frightened, Mr Daniel."

"I know. We are all frightened. But together we will come through it."

Judd wanted to believe him, and he almost did. If anyone could save him, it was Haydn Daniel. But he could not go back to his flat.

Haydn read his thoughts. "You can stay with us tonight. I have a spare room. You'll be safe. Tomorrow, we'll sort everything out."

"Thanks, Mr Daniel."

"Haydn."

"Thanks, Haydn."

Haydn looked over to the warm up area. There was just one horse and rider exercising there, it must be Daisy's rival. Daisy would have to hurry or she would miss her. He strained his eyes back towards the wagon park but he could not see her.

"Come on, Judd. Let's head back and fetch Daisy."

They strode past the start box and along a grassy walkway until they reached the wagon park. Their feet crunched on the stony surface as they made their way towards the horsebox. As they walked, a black Range Rover swept by. Judd nervously glanced at the vehicle, which seemed somehow familiar. He glimpsed two figures in the back. Then the car turned to head down the drive. As it did so, the driver came briefly into view. Judd saw him for only a couple of seconds, but it was enough for him to recognise the man. It was Dwayne.

Chapter Thirty-Four

Haydn heard Judd's cry of alarm and saw the rear of a dark 4 X 4 vanish down the road. "What is it?"

"It's Kane. He was here."

Haydn looked at him in disbelief. Then he said: "Daisy."

They ran to the horsebox. Des peered round nonchalantly at them, then carried on tugging at his haynet. He was alone. There was no sign of Daisy. Haydn flung open the drivers door and put his head inside the cab. She was not there. He raced to the back of the horsebox and checked the little living quarters. Still nothing.

He stared desperately at Judd. "Where is she?" The young man did not reply. He did not want to voice what he feared was the awful truth. But Haydn had already come to the same terrifying conclusion.

"He's got her, hasn't he?"

For a moment Haydn wondered if this had been a set up and Judd had been a part of it. But the young man's fear when he arrived had been obvious and now there was a look of horror in his eyes which was plainly genuine.

"Quick," he said. "Run inside and check that she's not in the cafe. I'll call the police."

He pulled out his phone as Judd turned to go. "Do you know the registration of the car?"

"No." Judd hesitated.

"Never mind. Go on inside, hurry up."

Haydn was about to ring 999, but he paused. Perhaps we

should wait until we know for sure that she is missing, he thought. But by then it could be too late. He made up his mind. He must call now, but he would ring Andy Watson. He had the inside track and would be able to set the right wheels in motion, just as quickly as the emergency call operators.

He got up his list of contacts and pressed the green phone icon to call his friend and prayed that he would answer. As he did so, Judd reappeared. He shook his head. At the same time, Andy spoke. "All right, Haydn?"

"Andy, Daisy has been kidnapped. I think Weston has got her."

"Okay. Tell me everything."

Haydn related where they were and what they had seen.

"Are you certain she has been kidnapped?"

"She's not here, Andy. And Judd saw Weston's muscle man. He recognised the car he was driving and saw two figures in the back. I'm sure it was Daisy and Weston."

"All right. I'll get some traffic cars mobilised and see if we can spot it. I'll have some checks done to see if such a vehicle is registered to Weston and get a plate number to look for. And I'll put armed response on stand by."

"Andy, I don't want a shoot out."

"Don't worry, it won't come to that. I'll be in touch."

"Okay. And Andy, please get her back."

He ended the call and turned to Judd. "There's nothing more we can do here. Let's get Des home. Daisy will be glad to see him when she gets back."

He deliberately used the word 'when' and not 'if.'

They were well on their way when Haydn's phone rang. He was driving the horse wagon, so Judd answered it.

Haydn listened intently to the one-way conversation, trying to work out what was being said.

"It's Judd. Haydn's driving."

"Okay. Where was that? "

"Right, where are they?"

"So what happens now?"

"I see. Yes, I'll tell him."

Judd ended the call. Haydn was unable to contain himself. "Well, what did he say? Have they found her?"

"Not yet. They're still looking for the car. They stopped a black Range Rover not far from here, but it wasn't them. He says they are struggling without the registration number, but they are sending out as many patrol cars as they can between Northallerton and Bradford, and armed officers are waiting at Harrogate nick. He says he will ring in an hour unless he has news before then, and you mustn't worry."

Haydn was near to exploding. "Mustn't worry? He's got to be kidding."

A sudden thought struck Haydn. "Judd, you better ring Scott. We should tell him what has happened."

Half an hour later they arrived back at Wickham Court. Scott was there to meet them. "I'll put the horse in his stable and park up the wagon. Both of you go up to the bungalow. I'll be there shortly."

He joined them ten minutes later. He could see the pain of worry etched on both their faces. "I think large whiskies all round are in order," he said.

Haydn smiled thinly. "Just a small one for me, with hot water please. I'll save the rest to celebrate when we get her back."

Scott prepared the hot toddy and handed it over. "So how much do we know?"

"Not a lot," said Haydn. "Judd saw the car and recognised the driver as one of Weston's men, otherwise we would not have known so quickly. It's a black Range Rover, but that's it."

"Haven't you heard anything from Weston?"

Haydn looked surprised. "Would you expect me to?"

"All along, he has been trying to get revenge on you. This is his ultimate act of vengeance. He'll want you to know that he is responsible."

"He really must be mad if he thinks like that."

"Anyone who kidnaps young women or shoots at people's homes has to be mad, or bad, or both."

Judd interrupted. "Don't you think there's something else? Don't you think he might want something in return?"

Scott pondered this. "You mean give him something in exchange for Daisy's safe return? A ransom, or some kind of blackmail? Yes, that's possible."

Haydn interjected. "I guess he's greedy enough to try, but does he really think he's clever enough to pull it off? Either way, you could be right, he might make contact."

Just then, Haydn's phone rang. He jumped at the sound, but it was Andy's name on the console. Jabbing the answer button, Haydn exclaimed: "Andy, have you any news?"

"I'm afraid not, Haydn. We're still looking for the car. Have you heard anything?"

"No."

"I'm coming over to Wickham Court. We need to discuss what to do next, and whether to put out an appeal on the media. I'm going to bring a trained negotiator with me. Somehow we'll have to make contact with Weston and see what he wants. I'll be there in half an hour."

Haydn flung his phone to one side. "I don't like this. Weston is holding all the cards. He doesn't have to contact us. He can just do what he likes with Daisy and leave me to worry about it."

"The police know what they're doing, Haydn," said Scott. "They'll find her."

"Not unless we find her first," grunted Haydn.

Scott looked concerned. "What do you mean?"

"The police haven't a clue where to look. But maybe we know someone who does."

Haydn turned to Judd. "Keeley was with him for long enough. Could she suggest somewhere he might take Daisy, a special place to him?"

"I don't know."

Haydn spoke urgently. "Find out, Judd. Call her."

Keeley answered straight away. "Judd, babes! It's so good to hear from you. Where are you? Can you come and see me?"

"Not right now. But I need your help, Keeley. Has Kane been in contact with you?"

"No, just that awful solicitor's letter, the bastard. Why?"

"He has kidnapped Daisy. We are trying to find them."

"Oh shit. That's awful. But you mustn't go looking for him. That would be suicide."

"We have to find them, Keeley. Is there anywhere he might have taken her?"

She hesitated. "There is a place, an old farm he bought in the middle of nowhere, where he used to take me for weekends before we were married. I think he still has it."

"Where is it?"

"It's off a country lane between some little villages above Otley. But promise me you are not going to go there. I won't let you put yourself in danger."

"It's not up to me. Just a sec, Keeley."

Haydn was getting impatient. "What has she got?"

"A farm somewhere."

"Give me the phone, Judd." He handed it over. "Keeley, this is Haydn. What was the farm called?"

"I think it was Sycamore Farm."

"Are you sure?"

"Yes, I think so."

"And where was it?"

"It was on the hills between Otley and Harrogate, you went through a village and it was set back from a narrow, winding road, not far from a reservoir. You mustn't..."

Haydn interrupted. "Thanks, Keeley. This is really important."

He ended the call and went straight on to Google Maps. After a few seconds he jabbed the phone. "Got it," he said triumphantly. "Sycamore Farm, just past the village of Farnley."

He stood up and put on his jacket.

"Hey, just a minute, where are you going?" said Scott.

"Sycamore Farm."

"No, you're not. Wait for the police, let them go."

But Haydn's mind was made up. "I can't wait, Scott. Every minute that passes could be costly. I need to know that Daisy is alive."

"At risk of your own life?"

"If necessary."

"Then, at least ring them and meet them there. Don't go in on your own. And take Judd with you." The young man had also risen to his feet.

"I should go alone."

"Please let me come," said Judd. "I would like to be there at the end. And you'll need someone to navigate." He reached inside his jacket pocket and was reassured to feel the cold steel of the gun.

Haydn considered Judd's earnest expression. It would be a comfort to have a companion. And Haydn had always felt that his destiny was linked to the young man. Perhaps this was the moment. He nodded. "Okay. You can ring Andy Watson on the way." They headed for the door.

"I'll hold the fort here," said Scott. "For God's sake, Haydn, don't do anything stupid."

Haydn turned to his friend. "I am going to bring Daisy home – whatever it takes."

Chapter Thirty-Five

Haydn sat brooding behind the wheel of his Land Rover. Beside him, Judd entertained himself by flicking through the BBC football website on his phone. They were waiting impatiently.

The journey from Wickham Court had taken only twenty minutes. As they climbed out of Otley on a quiet B-road Judd followed Google Maps, passing on directions to Haydn as he drove them to their destination.

They reached the village of Farnley and passing through it began to ascend the road to the isolated hillsides. Great hedges crowded in on either side of the road, which was empty of traffic. After a couple of minutes Judd said: "It should be coming up on the left."

Haydn slowed down and soon a large driveway appeared set back from the road on their nearside. He stopped the car outside the entrance and they stared in. The gates were wide open and one hundred yards down the rutted drive they could see an old stone farmhouse. Next to it was a shed and beyond that a barn, which looked disused. A sign on a wooden post in the gateway announced 'Sycamore Farm.' There was no obvious sign of life on the premises.

Haydn unbuckled his seat belt. "Let's go in."

He was about to open his door when Judd said: "No, no. Please wait for the police."

Now he was here Haydn wanted to burst into the farmhouse and rescue Daisy, like a brave medieval knight. But, frustrating though it was, he knew that Judd was right. It was folly for them to charge in suicidally. Their destinies may be linked, but perhaps not on that path. And he could hear the fear in Judd's voice. He had a responsibility to take the young man's welfare into account.

"Damn it," he said, refastening his seat belt. He drove on and found a gateway to a field where he was able to turn the car round and head back. Again, he brought the vehicle to a halt as they passed the farm entrance. But there was still nothing to be seen.

"We'll go back to Farnley and wait for the cavalry," said Haydn. "But if they're not here in twenty minutes, I'm going in."

Ten minutes had already passed. They were parked on the edge of the village, facing the hill to the farmhouse. Nothing moved on the road.

Judd opened the passenger door. "I need a smoke," he said.

Haydn drummed his fingers on the steering wheel. "Don't go far. And make sure you put the fag out properly. We don't want any more fires."

As Judd took a drag from his cigarette he heard the noisy roar of an agricultural engine. A tractor drove past and immediately turned right and trundled off down a track. Moments later he heard what was unmistakably a car engine.

Haydn heard it too and stared into his wing mirror, hoping to see a police vehicle at last. But instead a silver saloon car appeared. As it went by, Haydn noticed a taxi company livery on the side and back of the vehicle. He sighed in frustration and got out of the car to stretch his legs.

"If they're not here by the time you've finished your cigarette, that's it. But whatever happens, when we go back to the farmhouse you must stay in the car. I can't let you put yourself at risk."

Then he said: "Ah! Who's this?"

They could hear another car approaching. They stood on either side of his Land Rover and waited. A vehicle came into view. As it got nearer Haydn could see it was not a police car. It was black, without markings. "Bugger it!" he exclaimed, his patience rapidly running out. Then he looked again. The vehicle was almost upon them. Now he could see that it was a Range Rover, a black Range Rover. As it swept by Haydn tried to peer inside. He caught sight of a lone man behind the wheel. His face was turned towards him. Haydn could not quite make out his features from the fleeting glimpse. But it surely had to be Kane Weston. It was the right car in the right place.

There was only one thought in Haydn's head. He jumped into his car, started the engine and set off in pursuit. Judd was about to grasp the passenger door handle when the Land Rover surged forward. He hurriedly stepped back and watched the two cars disappear up the hill. Then, as there seemed nothing else to do, he ran after them.

Haydn had pushed the accelerator almost to the floor and within moments he had closed to within one hundred yards of the Range Rover.

He sped along until only fifty yards separated the vehicles. The entrance to the farmhouse was now in sight.

"Now I've got you," he shouted. Then he saw the brake lights of the Range Rover come on.

There was a horrible squealing, like a small animal in terror, as the tyres of the big black car gripped the road.

Haydn slammed his brake pedal to the floor and wrenched the steering wheel sideways to avoid the screeching vehicle in front of him. His car lurched to the left and skidded to a stop, its bonnet buried in the hedge running alongside the quiet country lane.

He clung to the wheel and stared in disbelief at the black car which had stopped ten yards ahead, its engine idling in a strangely menacing manner.

"What the hell was he playing at?" he muttered.

Nothing moved. The seconds ticked by. Then the driver's door of the black car flew open. A man emerged and turned to face him.

Haydn immediately saw two things, and they sent a chill through his whole body.

The man's face was covered by a black balaclava, with slits for eyeholes. And in his right hand he was holding a weapon. A lethal weapon. Haydn did not need his twenty-odd years as a policeman to tell him it was a sawn-off shotgun.

Slowly and deliberately, the man raised the gun and pointed it at Haydn, frozen in fear behind the wheel. He motioned with his free hand, indicating he was to get out of the car.

Haydn remained where he was. His heart was thumping in sheer terror. He was unable to move. And then it dawned on him that this was the nightmare he had endured for all those months. But now it was really happening. And the reality was even more terrifying than the nightmare – because he knew what was going to take place.

His body was numb, but slowly the fog that shrouded his brain started to lift. He began to think. Maybe he could restart the car and reverse away from the danger?

Freeing his body from its paralysis, he frantically turned the key in the ignition. Nothing. He tried again, yanking desperately at the key and pumping the accelerator furiously. Still nothing. But he knew there would be nothing.

He raised his head and looked at the masked man. He was still pointing the gun at him. Then he took a pace forward and gesticulated angrily with his left hand. For the first time he spoke. One word.

"Out!"

The voice was familiar.

Fearing to alarm him by any sudden movement, Haydn reached for the handle and gently pushed open the driver's door. The gunman's eyes narrowed, but his weapon arm remained rock steady.

Haydn slid out of his seat. Slowly, he raised himself to his full six-foot height and stepped away from the car. He kept his hands clear of his body, the palms outstretched – like a Wild West gunfighter preparing to draw. But he was unarmed, and he wanted the gunman to see that.

"Stop!" the gunman ordered.

Haydn stood silently and waited. He gazed at the barrel of the shotgun, barely ten feet away and aimed at his chest. Without moving his head, he raised his eyes and met those behind the mask, narrow slits peering out from the eyeholes.

He knew who they belonged to. And he knew he was about to die, just as the dream had predicted. A certainty about the end of his own mortality, right here and now, hit him – as surely as the vicious pellets of the shotgun would at any moment. And he was afraid. Terribly and painfully afraid.

The gunman saw his fear, felt it, breathed it, like a lion with his doomed prey in front of him the moment before he pounces.

His eyes glinted and from within the mask came a laugh – long, deep and grating. And mirthless.

Haydn knew, because he had dreamed it time and time again, that the gunman would now reveal his identity to him. He watched Kane Weston raise his left hand and, in one swift, deft movement, whip the balaclava from his head.

He laughed again. Gloating. Then he stopped and smiled. A cold smile. The smirk of an executioner.

He spoke for the last time. "So, Haydn Daniel. Prepare to die."

He saw the gunman's hand grip the gun tighter, his finger on the trigger. A scream of sheer terror rose in his throat. The nightmare was about to come to its much rehearsed conclusion.

But the ending suddenly altered. Haydn's death was put on hold. He became aware of footsteps running up behind him. And then a voice shouted breathlessly: "No, don't do it, don't do it. I won't let you."

He did not turn round but he recognised the voice. It was Judd. So this was how their destinies were linked.

Haydn kept his eyes fixed on Kane. He watched the gangster glance towards the advancing Judd, and saw his lip curl in a sneer of contempt. "And how are you going to stop me?" Weston swivelled the shotgun towards Judd.

Then the cold, piggy eyes switched back to Haydn and he again pointed the gun at his chest. Haydn saw Weston's finger twitch almost imperceptibly on the trigger and heard again the mirthless laugh. He prepared himself once more to die.

Then a shot rang out and he fell to the floor.

Chapter Thirty-Six

The echo of the gunshot faded and was followed by an eerie silence. Nothing moved. No-one spoke.

Haydn had thrown himself forward in a desperate bid to avoid the lethal pellets of the shotgun. Now his prostate body lay face down with his knees bent and his arms stretched out above his head. His eyes were closed. He could not see or hear anything. But his mind was working and the thought struck him that the fact that he was blind and deaf must mean that he was dead. So this was what it was like to exist as a spirit and not a physical entity. But where was he and how did he move around in this ethereal world? He wondered whether anyone would welcome him and, if so, who would it be? Would it be God? And how would he recognise Him?

As if in answer, Haydn heard a voice. It was speaking his name. "Are you God?" Haydn asked.

"It's Judd," came the reply, and then he felt the unmistakable touch of a hand on his shoulder. "Are you all right?"

"I think I'm dead."

"No, you're not. You're alive."

Haydn opened his eyes and saw the daylight, and the surface of the road in front of his face.

He shuffled round until he could see Judd staring down at him. The young man's eyes were wide with terror and disbelief. Haydn looked into them, seeking answers. "How? How am I alive? He shot me."

"No, look." He nodded towards the entrance to the drive.

Haydn got to his knees and gazed at the place where Kane Weston had stood pointing a gun at him. The gangster was in the same spot. But now he was sprawled face up on the ground. The gun was still clutched in his right hand, but the right side of his head had exploded and a great river of blood flowed from it into the road. His left eye, the only one that remained, stared unseeing at the sky.

"Help me up."

Judd grasped Haydn's outstretched hand and hauled him to his feet. The pair stood together, looking down at the grisly corpse. The last of their energy and resolve was spent, they did not have the strength left to feel satisfied or rejoice that they were finally safe.

"The world's a better place without him," said Haydn. "But I can't believe he took his own life. Did he really shoot himself and not me?"

"No, he didn't," Judd replied. "Oh my God," and with shaking hand he pointed at a figure he had just noticed in the shady entrance to the driveway.

Haydn looked up. Clinging to the gate, her blonde hair in a ponytail, was Keeley. Her face was white and she swayed like a drunk. In her hand was a small silver pistol.

Judd ran across to her. "Keeley!" As he did so, she let go of the gate and tried to meet him. Her legs buckled and she fell faint into his arms, the pistol clattering to the ground.

"Put her in the back of the car and stay with her, Judd. Don't touch the gun. Help will be on hand soon. I'm going to find Daisy."

Haydn ran up the drive to the farmhouse. He tried the front door but it was locked. He hammered on the wooden door but there was no response. He looked through the windows at the front but could see no-one inside, then raced round to the back.

Another solid wooden door barred his entrance and the windows again disclosed no secrets. He returned to the front and considered his options. She must be here somewhere, I have to get in. He looked around for a rock to smash one of the windows and saw a pile of stones near to the shed. He ran over and was about to pick one up when his eyes were drawn to the big old barn next to it.

"That would be the perfect place to hide someone," he thought.

He plunged inside. The gloomy, solid building was in semi-darkness. Haydn could make out old bales of straw piled high at the back and a rusting tractor abandoned in a corner. Against the far wall he could see a row of metal pens, which had probably been used in the past to keep sheep in. As he approached, he detected a muffled cry. "Daisy!" he called. Again he heard a faint sound. He ran the last few yards and peered into one of the pens. On a thin bed of straw, and covered by an old blanket, was Daisy. Her hair was loose, her eyes were wide with fear and across her mouth had been stuck a piece of thick, black tape.

Haydn leaped over the metal rail and dropped to her side. She sat up and he pulled the blanket from her. He saw that she was still wearing her cross-country riding clothes but her arms were tied behind her back and her ankles were tightly bound with the tape.

He put his hands on her shoulders and looked in her eyes. "I'm going to get this stuff off you, but it might hurt a bit, love." She nodded.

Her arms and legs were soon free, but he knew removing the tape from her mouth would be the worst bit. He squeezed her hand. "Purse your lips," he said, and then, as gently and slowly as he could, he drew back the tape. But even so, she yelped with pain as the adhesive took some of the skin from her lips with it and blood began to drip from them. He dabbed them with a tissue and then held her close to him as she wept uncontrollably, the fear and pain and relief combining to overwhelm her.

"It's all right. You're safe now," he soothed. Her sobs subsided but still she clung to him. Then she said: "Where is he, Haydn? He could come back at any time."

"He won't be coming back, Daisy. Not ever."

Then he looked at her closely. She seemed physically unharmed. But you cannot always see the hurt, he thought. She was a woman, at the mercy of a ruthless man. "Are you all right?" he said. "Has he hurt you, physically, or in any other way?"

She squeezed his arm and shook her head. "Not in any way. He just scared me. He said you would come for me and then he would kill you. How do you know he won't be back?"

"He's dead, Daisy. It really is over."

A paramedic emerged from the back of the ambulance and helped Keeley down the steps. He turned to Haydn. "She'll be fine now. She was just suffering from shock. I've given her something to calm her, but don't overdo the questioning for a while."

Haydn waited as Judd hugged her tightly, then said: "You'll have to be interviewed formally by the police in due course, Keeley, but they've allowed me to have a few minutes with you first. Is that all right?"

She clutched Judd's hand. "As long as he is with me."

"Of course. We'll sit in the car."

While Haydn was with Daisy in the barn he had heard the cacophony of sirens as the emergency services arrived. He helped her to her feet and walked her slowly down the drive as Andy Watson and Max Bannister came running.

"Thank God you're all right," said Andy.

"Unlike Kane Weston." Haydn pointed to the silver pistol in the gateway. "You'll need to bag the murder weapon."

Now he said to Keeley: "Why did you shoot him?"

"I just hated him so much. And I thought he was going to shoot Judd. I saw Kane pointing the gun and I heard Judd shouting. I was sure he was going to kill him. I couldn't let him do it."

"But what were you doing there? And why did you have the gun with you?"

"I knew you were both going to the farmhouse. And I knew Kane would probably kill you both. When I found out he had kidnapped the girl I knew he must have lost all control, and then he is capable of anything. I thought that maybe there was something I could do to stop him, so I got in a taxi and told the driver to put his foot down."

"And the gun?"

"I just put the bullet in it and stuffed it in my pocket. I suppose I had some daft idea about waving it about and frightening him. I never thought I'd be able to use it, or would want to. But it was easy. Funny, really, that I should kill him with the gun he gave me."

She paused. "What will happen to me? Will I get life?"

"Life doesn't mean life when it comes to sentencing at court. But you have to expect to spend a lot of years in prison, Keeley."

"I know. Will you wait for me, Judd?"

"Of course I will."

"Even if I'm old and grey?"

"Yes."

Andy Watson tapped on the driver's window. Haydn turned to the young woman with regret. "It's time for you to go."

Haydn and Daisy were curled up together on the sofa. A bottle of Famous Grouse whisky was on the coffee table. The long, lean shape of Timmy was stretched out on the rug in front of the merrily blazing stove.

The couple clinked their glasses together. "To us," said Haydn. "It's nice to be home."

"Yes, I feel safe at last."

Daisy sipped her drink. "What will happen to Keeley? Does it have to be murder?"

"I don't see how it could be anything else. She shot her husband dead because she thought he was going to kill her lover. And she took the weapon to the scene."

"But couldn't she argue justification?"

"Is anyone justified in taking the life of another, even if that person is evil and is about to kill someone? I doubt it. But she has some very powerful mitigation if she pleads guilty, and a good solicitor will make sure that she does. I can see her getting away with not much more than the minimum sentence of fifteen years."

"It all seems such a shame, especially for Judd. He seems to really care for her."

"Yes, but not enough to wait around that long, I think!"

He leaned forward to pour more whisky but was stopped in his tracks by a loud knocking on the door.

Daisy looked at him with big eyes. Her fears remained unspoken.

Haydn stood up. "I'll get it. Don't worry, it can't be what you think it is."

"Please be careful."

She watched him disappear to the door, heard him unlock it and then the sound of voices, Haydn's and that of another man. Then she heard footsteps approaching. She turned to face them, the terror sweeping over her. The living room door creaked open – and in walked Scott, followed by Haydn.

"Oh God, it's you!" she squeaked.

"Yes, and look what he's brought you."

Scott held out a sparkling red rosette. "What's that?" she said.

"Well, as you were kind of busy elsewhere, I thought I'd nip up to Northallerton to see if they had anything for you, and this was it."

Daisy jumped up, all smiles. "I won, I won the event. How can I thank you for fetching it?"

Scott eyed the bottle of whisky. "A tot of that will do!"

Haydn filled three glasses and they raised them aloft. "To friends," he said. "And no more nightmares."

Printed in Great Britain
by Amazon